Erica Wooff is 35 and comes from Newport. *Mud Puppy*, her first novel, recently won an Arts Council of Wales writer's bursary.

Erica Wooff

Mud Puppy

First published by The Women's Press Ltd, 2002
A member of the Namara Group
34 Great Sutton Street, London EC1V 0LQ
www.the-womens-press.com

British Library Cataloguing-in-Publication Data
A catalogue record for this book is available from the British Library.

ISBN 0 7043 4739 3

Typeset by FiSH Books, London
Printed and bound in Great Britain by CPD (Wales) Ltd, Ebbw Vale

to M & D and to Giles,
who believe truth is in the story

Acknowledgements

Thank you to Linda Leatherbarrow, Alison Burns and everyone in the Towards Publication writers' group for guiding and believing in this novel from its earliest conception. Thank you also to Derek Stears, Tina Edwards and the staff and pupils of West Monmouthshire Comprehensive for answering my endless questions on the Welsh education system and to Maureen Butterworth and the stage management team at the Dolman Theatre, Newport, for filling in the theatrical blanks.

Especially large thank yous to Giles Goddard and Sophie Wolf for their enthusiastic support throughout and all the reading time they gave in the final painful stages. More of the same to Elsbeth Lindner for her wise words and editing and, of course, to my family for their love and forbearance.

Finally, a huge thank you to the Arts Council of Wales for the generous gift of time and space to make it all possible.

ELEMENT I

Vicar discovers American newt in Newport

A Newport vicar made a miraculous discovery yesterday when he found a large American salamander in the River Usk, near the Glebelands recreation ground, three thousand miles from its native habitat.

The Rev. Rhodri Jenkins, vicar of St Matthew's, Allt-yr-yn and vice-president of the Newport Wildlife Association, was on a nature ramble with children from his Sunday school when he came across the astonishing creature, known as a mud puppy after the unproven belief that it barks like a dog.

'I knew right away that it wasn't a normal newt,' said Rev. Jenkins. 'It was much too big.' The mud puppy, at over 35 cm in length, is three times the size of any of Britain's three native species of newt. It has a stout body speckled with blue-grey spots, a flattened tail, four weak legs and a complete set of lungs that it does not use. Instead it breathes underwater through three pairs of bushy red gills.

Local experts are mystified as to how the mud puppy came to be so far away from home. 'Mud puppies are bottom dwellers that spend their entire lives in fresh water,' said Michael Llewellyn-Jones, senior lecturer in biology at Allt-yr-yn College, University of Wales. 'They are found in the lakes, rivers and streams of the eastern United States and Canada, but never in salt water. And, like many amphibians, they are quite sluggish. So it is inconceivable that this one could have swum all the way across the Atlantic.'

The mud puppy, christened Idris by the children of St Matthew's, after the famous Welsh dragon, is currently being cared for by the Biology Department of Allt-yr-yn College.

South Wales Argus
Monday 1 March

Chapter One

I come from a long line of mud. Over seventeen miles of it. For nine years now I've tried to shake it off. This year I thought I'd finally succeeded. But not quite. Mud sticks after all.

My name's Daryl. Funny name for a girl, I know. At least in London it is. Not so much in Wales, though. There are a lot of funny names in Wales. Being Welsh has become my special feature. My trademark. Being Welsh is very sexy at the moment. At least a certain type of Welsh is sexy. You know what I mean. Wacky, eccentric, slightly-exotic-in-an-arty-type-of-way sexy. I've milked being sexy Welsh for all it's worth. Well, you have to in London. You have to find something to make you stand out. So I've played on the funny name and kept my accent lilting higher than the Brecon Beacons. Higher than it ever was when I lived in Wales. I am now Welsh with a capital W. Picture postcard Welsh. Dragons, daffodils and mountains. Nothing to do with coal mines. Or mud.

Which is a bit rich seeing as I come from Newport.

Newport lies at the mouth of the River Usk, twelve miles east of Cardiff. Just fifteen miles over the Severn Bridge into Wales. Newport has its own special feature. The rise and fall of the tides at the river mouth reach over fifty feet, the second highest tidal range in the world. Newport's special feature is caused by the sudden constriction of the water in the narrow funnelling of the Bristol Channel. This squeezing and squishing of the sea between England and Wales forces the water up and up. Right up the mouth of the Usk, through Newport and up again for another seventeen miles. Then the tide turns and it all goes down again.

In the process, the side-effect if you like, vast quantities of mud are deposited around the mouth of the river, around Newport and up the seventeen tidal miles of the Usk. Fine grey-green-brown mud. Mud of the highest quality. It is the first thing you see when the train crosses over the railway bridge and draws you into Newport station. You look down, your eyes searching for the water. But all you ever see is mud. Mud is all there ever is.

Fifty feet. The second highest tidal range in the world. Second only to the Bay of Fundy, Nova Scotia, where at times the water rises and falls by as much as sixty feet.

At times.

Second.

Not all the time.

The Old World versus the New. Why does everything always have to be so much more over there? Sometimes it must be less. And then at those times, on our side, there'll be more. So much more. Stands to reason. Sometimes Newport must come first. After all, second is only one away from first. And what's ten feet between friends?

Everything.

Fifty feet. Up and down. Up and down. Twice a day. Over seventeen miles of it. For nine years now I've tried to shake it off.

Funny thing is it never used to bother me. Mud used to make me feel right at home. I can't tell you how much I pined for it the first year I moved to London. You don't get much mud in London. Not even on the banks of the Thames. All you ever see is concrete. Concrete is all there ever is. Even the river banks in London are made of concrete.

Oh, I know the Thames used to have loads of mud. Down the East End, maybe a hundred, a hundred and fifty years ago. Mud crawling with destitute children searching the river bed for objects of value then hopping off to Windsor to shake old Victoria out of her slumbers. They even made a film about it. But that's London for you. You'd never catch anyone from Newport making a film about mud.

And now the Thames is all developed. There's still a little bit of mud, when the tide's out. But not enough. And even that little bit is controlled like you wouldn't believe. The average tidal rise of the Thames is twenty-three feet. Pathetic. Yet the powers that be have spent millions of taxpayers' money building and maintaining a massive movable barrier to protect the capital from flooding. They call it the eighth wonder of the world. No, I'm serious, they really do. Just go and have a look in the visitor centre at Woolwich. It's written there for the whole world to see. The Thames Flood Barrier – the Eighth Wonder of the World. Without even the slightest trace of irony. But that's London for you.

That first year I would come home to Newport for the weekend, and from the moment the train came out of the Severn Tunnel, from the second we entered Wales, I would be up out of my seat, at the door, waiting. I was that homesick for the mud. I'd stand at the door window for ten minutes watching the fields and hedgerows change into the furnaces and smoke of the steelworks, into the golf course, into rows and rows of washing lines and kitchen windows.

When the train finally pulled across the bridge I would pull and press down the door-window catch and hang my head out to feel the wind pinching my cheeks. I would close my eyes against the skewering rain and breathe in great big gasps of mud. The sweet-salt-sulphur stink of it.

Glorious.

I would pull and press down the door-window catch and lean my head out so I could see clearly all the way down, over the bridge's rusted railings, down and down. All the way down to the Sainsbury's beacon sending its orange glow shooting out towards the opposite bank but only making it halfway before being pulled and pressed down, away into the mud.

I would jump onto the platform – always number two – when the train was still moving! so I could be the first off the train. The first to come home. The first to spin my tales of life in the big city, away from mud.

But I haven't been home for a while. Nine years, in fact. Been too busy. You know how it is. And I had to get rid of the mud. You don't stand a chance of making it in London if you're covered in mud. And now the train has been modernised and the door window sealed.

There's no pull and press down window catch, no salt-mud fresh air. No horizontal rain. Just a yellow warning light and air conditioning.

For the comfort and safety of all our customers this door has been locked automatically and will not be opened until the train has come to a complete and final stop at the station.

Now I can only press my head against the door window. Now I can see the mud but not taste it, smell it, be a part of it. Be apart from it. I've wanted this kind of detachment for years. So why do I feel like my right arm is missing?

*

Dad's car in the taxi rank, parked illegally, engine idling for a quick getaway. The latest in a long line of beat-up Fords. This one's white. I haven't seen it before. But I know it's Dad's. The green and white JESUS SAVES sticker across the windscreen is unmistakeable. The driver door swings open and a boot appears underneath. Large, brown and absolutely certain of its position. It's not the sort of boot to be phased by a bit of mud. I stop and sink slowly into the ground and watch as the boot is joined by its twin and then a head and two shoulders unfold themselves over the top of the door and Dad is standing square over me. I bend my neck and look up into his face.

Dad looks exactly the same. A little older maybe, a few more lines. Same sharp grey eyes. Same white, white skin. Same beaky nose. The clothes are the same too. Black corduroys, blue and grey jumper, dog collar gleaming against Adam's apple. Bristling grey beard, clipped close to match his bristling grey hair.

I stand completely still except for my right hand, which I flex and unflex and shake about, acting like I'm just resting it a little from dragging my suitcase, but I'm not really. I'm working out whether if I turn and run now I can make it back onto the train before the guard blows his whistle. Then Dad picks up my suitcase and the guard blows his whistle.

Dad and I stand there in front of the car looking at each other for a long time until I finally get my mouth to move. And after nine years I say,

'Hello Dad.'

'Hello love,' Dad says and lifts my other bag off my shoulder.

We stand and look at each other some more; his grey beard, his grey eyes, his gleaming dog collar. I don't know what else to do so I step up to him and wrap my arms around his waist and squeeze. Hugging Dad is like hiding from the rain in an open bus shelter. The wind still blows but it's dry and your legs don't have to hold you up any more, you can just lean. And something else – I'd forgotten with the effort of shaking off the mud – but burying my head in his blue and grey jumper reminds me what it is.

After nine years, Dad smells exactly the same. Being an artist, you'd think that it would be my eyes and maybe my hands that would be most sensitive, not my nose. But the smell of the paint, the clay, is as much a part of the creation process as the look, the touch. The smell and the change of smell are just as important.

Dad smells of Persil Automatic and Heinz Tomato Soup. Dog hair, and the inside of a bag of compost when you first cut it open. Sunny August days blackberry picking down the nature reserve. Boiled eggs and Marmite soldiers in front of the fire, Wednesday evenings, after Bible study.

I lean hard into Dad again, smell and squeeze a second time and this time am rewarded by three stiff pats on the back. Then Dad shifts one step backwards and wriggles his hip, pulls back his shoulders. I manage to unlock my arms from around his waist and shove my hands into the pockets of my coat, where I stand, trying not to sway too much in the wind, watching Dad stow my bags in the boot of the car until the rain has washed away my tears.

We drive out of the station, swing left onto the dual carriageway and let the rush-hour traffic sweep us down towards the Castle, the river. At the bottom of the hill I wind down the window and hang my head out to feel the wind and rain slapping my face. I crane my neck all the way out to breathe in the mud.

The sweet-salt-sulphur stink of it.

Chapter Two

My name's Ani. I fucking hate my job.

Sunday morning. I'm on pumps. Kat's crouching under the counter at my feet, hiding from the customers and crumbling dope for a spliff. Halfway through me serving some old bloke twenty B and H, Kat's hand shoots up between my legs. Her fingers snap open and shut against her thumb like the beak of a baby bird. Only this bird is hungry for baccy, not worms. I check my bag. Empty. So when the coast is clear I get Kat to dust the shelves next to the security camera while I lift a pouch of Golden Virginia off the display.

Kat mugs at the camera. 'Don't forget the Rizlas,' she says.

This is what I sell in two hours:

Forty-six litres of petrol.
A hundred cigarettes.
Four tubes of Rennies – one spearmint, three regular.
One can of tuna and mackerel cat food.
Eight *News of the World*s.

I fucking hate this place.

'What do you mean?' Kat says, coming up behind me and tickling my ear with the duster.

I practically jump out my skin. Always sneaking up on me, she is.

'Nothing,' I say, flick her off. 'Just that I'm fed up with this dump. It's so boring.'

I slip the baccy in my overall pocket. The pockets are the only good thing about these overalls. Plenty of room, all within grabbing distance.

'It's not that bad,' Kat says. 'We had fun last night, didn't we?'

'Yeah, but that was last night. Not this dump. I fucking hate this dump.'

Kat gives me her Cheshire Cat grin. Kat isn't wearing her overall. Kat almost never wears her overall. Kat hates her overall the way I hate my job. Kat only ever wears her overall when Ron is on the prowl, doing his rounds.

'And which particular dump might that be, then?'

'You know. All of them. This shop, Bettws, Newport. They're all as bad as each other. Boring. Boring. Boring.'

No, Kat isn't wearing her overall. Kat is wearing her leather coat. I love Kat in that leather coat. It's long and black and makes a swishing sound when she walks. She's got matching boots too, with spiky heels and a zip that goes right the way up. Kat was wearing her leather coat and those spiky zipped boots the day I asked her out. She was wearing her coat and her boots and her hair was falling across her face in a long silky wave.

I love Kat's coat and boots. I love them so much that I want her to wear them every day.

Kat loves them too. Kat says she's saving up to buy another set. In blue.

I grab hold of Kat's black sleeve, shake her arm. 'Why don't we just go? Why don't we just grab what's in the till and piss off to London or somewhere?'

As I say it, a picture flashes across my brain. Me and Kat living in some posh place in London, going to clubs, meeting loads of people. Maybe even some famous ones. It'd be great. Really great.

I say again, 'Why don't we just go?'

But Kat only looks at me the way Mam does when she thinks I'm wasting her time with my stories.

'What would we do when we got to London?' she says. 'We don't know anyone there. Besides, there's not enough money in that till at the moment to get us to Chepstow, let alone London.'

Kat's always doing this. Pointing out the problems before we even get to have the fun. But this time I'm ready for her.

'I've got a bit put by,' I say. 'And I could sell my car. We'd be all right.' I put on my best grovel voice. Puppy dog eyes. 'Oh go on, Kat. Please. Let's just go. Right now. Why don't we just go?'

Kat just shakes her head. 'Ani,' she says, 'how many times are we going to have this conversation? I keep telling you. Your car money wouldn't last us more than a couple of weeks in London. Maybe a month. Then what would we do? We'd be stuck with no money, no mates. We wouldn't even be able to get shit jobs like this one. We'd be out on the streets in no time.' She flicks the duster across the counter, down the side. 'Just forget about it, will you?' she says.

I can't look at her. Just keep my head stuck down on my chest and scuff the toe of my trainer along the floor. Sniff up a big ball of snot.

Meanwhile Kat finishes her dusting and pats the top of my head like I'm a bloody dog or something, then walks off for her smoke like nothing's happened. I stand stock still shooting daggers at her. Then all of a sudden I've got to be moving, got to be doing something. So I stomp across to the magazine rack to straighten out the papers.

I had them all in neat piles an hour ago but they're in a right mess now. People round here can't keep anything nice. *Sunday People* mixed up with the *Mirror*, pages of the *Sport* – all boobs and bums – scattered everywhere. And some idiot's gone and trodden on the one copy of the *Observer* so that the front page is all ripped. No one'll buy it now. Not that anyone would've anyway. Ron only orders it for show. Doesn't hurt to show a bit of class, he says. Yeah, except he's never read it in his life either. Ron takes the *News of the World* and the *Sun* like everybody else round here. I fucking hate this place.

I take the fashion section behind the counter. A bit muddy round the edges but still legible. Rip open a Snickers. It's against the rules of the management to eat in front of the customers. But then the management have never had to work the early bird shift without breakfast. I've settled down to a good read when Kat starts yelling for a light. So I go through all my pockets again for matches but only find this piece of pink paper folded into a square from last night.

We'd been able to drive into Cardiff for the first time in weeks. Keith finally fixed up my car like he's been saying he would, so we didn't have to take the train. Could go where we wanted. Stay out all night without having to fork out for the cab fare home. Kat was up for us hanging out over the Students' Union like always, but I wanted to try out that new bar down the Hayes. The one opposite Toys R Us. The one with the giant rainbow flag above the door.

We didn't leave the bar till late. There was this cabaret on – Sing-along-a-*Sound-of-Music*. Thought it was going to be really naff at first, just a bunch of queens dressed up like nuns doing karaoke. But it was miles better than that. We didn't stop laughing all night. Ended up with a lock-in till gone two. After working all day I was shagged out, so I didn't even notice the patrol car until it was right up my ass, siren screaming.

It was a bad situation. Both me and Kat had done some E. I'd only had the one. But Kat had had so many tabs she was rattling. The cops only had to take one look at her to see she was on something. Her eyes were bloodshot, her lips were all puffed up like she'd been stung by ten wasps and all she could do was shake and cry and mutter under her breath about how much trouble she'd be in if her dad found out. Kat's dad's really strict. If Kat's dad knew Kat did drugs – even dope, even E – he'd skin her alive.

14

One of us had to stay calm. Do all the talking. And anyway, I was the one driving. So I did what Keith does when he gets nervous before a show. I imagined waves of icy water were rolling slowly though my body, down my legs and out the end of my feet. In the mirror I could see the cop who was driving say something to his partner and climb out of the patrol car. But I kept breathing slowly in time with the waves until I was cool.

Not as cool as that cop, though. He strolled towards us like he was walking his girl down Penarth Pier. All the time in the world. Tight blue pants, sharp jacket. Cap pulled down low over his eyes. If it had been daylight, he would have been wearing mirrored sunglasses.

I watched him approach in the side mirror until he disappeared into the blind spot, then I rolled down the window and handed him my licence with a great big smile.

'Evening, officer. Is there a problem?'

'Nice car,' he said. 'Would look even prettier with the lights on.'

I could hardly believe it when I heard him. This guy was straight out of some movie. He even had an American accent. America by way of Pontypridd probably, but it still sounded good on him. I mean the guy was a complete poser, right? There we were in the centre of Cardiff at two-thirty in the morning and he's acting like he's in an episode of *NYPD Blue*. You had to laugh. But at the same time you couldn't help admiring him. I mean he did it so well. He was . . . he was a dude. There's no other word for it. This guy was a real dude.

But the main thing on my mind was not getting a ticket. There was no way I could afford a fine. So I smiled at him again.

'Sorry, officer,' I said, 'must have forgotten to switch them on. Stupid of me, I know.'

Like butter wouldn't melt, I was. Didn't do much good, though. This cop was the ice man coming.

'Step out of the vehicle please,' he said.

I tried to reason with him. Told him we'd only just moved off. But it was a big lie and we both knew it. I mean this cop had chased me from the Hayes halfway up Park Place before I'd even registered he was there. But in for a penny...

'The street is so well lit, see? I would've noticed as soon as we rounded the corner.'

Captain America just stood there and stared straight ahead like I hadn't spoken at all.

'Step out of the vehicle please.'

I gave in and got out. He was even more arrogant up close, bristling like a cat at an intruder. Good-looking, though, you'd have to give him that. Dark like an Italian. But not as stocky. I wasn't the only one giving the once-over. His eyes trailed up and down my body, clocking my biker jacket and Doc Martens. Then he laughed right out loud and curled up his top lip and nose like he was smelling a big bag of shit.

'My,' he said. 'Look what we have here. A baby butch.'

I wanted to smash his face in then, I can tell you. But remembering the E, I just shoved my hands deep down my jeans pockets, thought icy waves and gave him my best fuck off and die stare instead. That usually softens even the hardest prick, but this one just handed me a black box topped with a white plastic spout.

'Blow,' he said.

I told him I hadn't been drinking. It was true. I never drink and drive. You can kill someone doing shit like that.

'Just blow,' he said.

I blew hard into the breathalyser then gave it back to him. Nothing registered on the scale, I could tell from the way his forehead creased up. But he wouldn't believe it of course. 'Again,' he said. 'Harder.'

So this time I blew into the bloody thing until the insides of my lungs peeled off and lodged in the back of my throat. The cop peered at the reading again.

'Told you,' I said.

That got him really mad. He took a step forward and for a moment I thought he might be going to hit me but he just put his hand on my shoulder and shoved me a little bit.

'Turn around,' he said. 'Spread 'em.'

Like he was Arnold bloody Schwarzenegger!

What is it about cops? Always trying to scare you, make you feel guilty.

But I wasn't having any of it, knew I hadn't done anything, see.

I was just about to tell him what I thought of him when out of the corner of my eye I saw Kat in the passenger seat, practically wetting herself. The dope in her bag glowing bright red.

So I rolled the icy waves down my body one more time and placed my hands palm-flat on the car bonnet. Opened my legs six inches.

The cop frisked me for drugs. For cheek. He lingered for hours between my legs, his peak cap grazing my back. Came away empty handed, though.

Ani, Warrior Princess: two.

Forces of Darkness: nil.

But time to quit while I was still ahead.

'Look,' I said, 'I'm sorry, all right? I forgot the lights. I'm tired and I forgot to switch them on. But I haven't been drinking and I don't do drugs. So just give me my ticket and we'll call it a night, all right? You've got better things to do, I'm sure.'

The cop didn't speak. He opened up the flap of his notebook – black leather, gold trim – wrote something and ripped off a pink paper ticket. He handed me the ticket, winked at me, then turned and started to walk away. After about five yards he looked round and winked at me again, then walked the rest of the way to his car, backside swaying.

Inside the car Kat was crying snot into her sleeve. I switched on the lights full beam and waited for the cop to drive away and my hands to stop shaking before looking down at the ticket.

King Carlos' Packing Workshops
For all you girls who want to
'Walk like a man, talk like a man...'
4 week course: £60

At the bottom, under the phone number was scrawled:

Just for you,
50% off
Call me! C.

Kat wanders back up to the counter looking for matches, sees me reading the cop's note.

'What you got there, then?' she says and tries to snatch the paper out of my hand.

But I pull away before she can reach, fold the note back up into a square again.

'Nothing,' I say.

It's no good telling Kat about this yet. Not till I'm sure. She probably wouldn't believe me anyway. She'd probably say it was just another one of my stupid stories.

So I say nothing and push the note deeper down inside my back pocket.

Chapter Three

Mud is a long-term preservative. Down there, down on the flatlands, the marshes with their high acidity, low temperatures and absence of oxygen have become repositories of past life over thousands of years. Bodies, clothing, tools, even pollen grains preserved in bogs can reveal to us now something of human life over two thousand years ago.

But even up here on the hills, where the drainage is good and the air free flowing, life can be preserved for a decade or more.

The room is small and square, tucked in at the back, below the eaves where the house-martins nest. It, like the rest of the Vicarage, is exactly the same as it was nine years ago. My bed is still opposite the window, the desk and chair still block off the fireplace and the two bookcases are still crowded with my old books: Agatha Christie, James Herriot and Elinor M Brent-Dyer.

Everything exactly the same.

I move away from the window, snuggle down under the duvet again and lie still, listening to the birds singing their songs, telling each other their stories.

This is my story.

This is my song.

When I was a child my mother would tuck me up in bed and ask me what story I wanted to hear. My answer was always the same – the Dream Box. The Dream Box was a sealed-up shoe box covered in coloured wrapping paper with a hole cut out of one end just big enough for a child's fist to pass through. Magic streamers of crêpe paper and silver foil fringed the hole. My mother would pick up the Dream Box and shake it so the contents rattled and the streamers flew around my head. Then she would say the magic words and I would reach into the Dream Box and pull out whatever lay inside. A spoon maybe or a cotton reel. From this everyday object, my mother would then weave me a story. Each story was different. Each story told of a great adventure. When she had finished my mother would tuck the Dream Box up in bed with me so I could travel with the story to Dreamland.

After nine years the Dream Box has finally led me back home. For weeks now I have had this recurring dream where I put my hand inside the Box but I cannot reach whatever lies inside. I try to pull my hand away but it becomes wrapped up in the streamers and I cannot break free. I turn to my mother for help but she has vanished. In her place is my father. He tries to free me but he too becomes entangled.

Downstairs I can hear Dad in the kitchen talking to the dog just like he always does, following the same early morning ritual he always has:

Click, the kettle switching itself off.

Rattle, the cups on the tray.

Creak, the tread on the stairs under Dad's feet.

I count him up... twelve, thirteen fourteen... Dad walks past the bathroom, knocks at the bedroom door and before I can say come in, he's in the room. The alarm clock shows 7:35 am and it's Sunday, but Dad is already showered and dressed, hair combed carefully into a side parting. He sets my cup of tea down on the bedside table, then moves to the window and flings open the curtains, arms stretched wide. The energy he puts into this deserves in return a raft of blazing sunlight and a chorus of angels singing the *Gloria*. But all he gets are two starlings arguing half-heartedly with a sparrow. Rain-spattered window.

'Da-ryl. Wakey, wakey. Rise and shine. The sun is scorching your eyeballs.'

This is what Dad always says first thing in the morning.

I groan and pull the duvet over my head. But Dad yanks it back and digs his fingers hard into my left shoulder, shaking me.

'You're missing the best part of the day,' he says.

This is what Dad always says right after the sun is scorching your eyeballs.

I know he won't leave me in peace until I give in, and the next step would be for him to pull the duvet right off the bed and tickle my feet. But I haven't let him get to the next step since I was thirteen. So I sit up in bed, feign a yawn and pick up the teacup. Satisfied, Dad moves back towards the door, then turns.

'Breakfast in ten minutes,' he says.

*

Breakfast is at the kitchen table. The dining room is only ever used at Christmas and Easter. I walk downstairs and into the kitchen to find Dad already sitting in his place, the same place. The place which always used to be facing Mum when she was alive, but now it's just the garage door. I can't bring myself to look at the empty chair so I concentrate on the table. It's the same table, dominated by the same white Tupperware boxes. Three tall ships of cereal surrounded by tugs of jam and rowing boats of crockery. An armada of order laid out in formation every evening ready for the morning battle against tardiness.

My mother died when I was thirteen. My father told me she died in a car accident. Truth is, she killed herself. My mother killed herself when I was thirteen. Carbon monoxide poisoning: car exhaust, hose pipe, suicide note. The whole nine yards. I found out by accident nine years ago. I found the note.

Dad chops up a banana, sliding the pieces along his knife with his thumb before dropping them into his cereal, the same cereal. Long white fingers, reddened knuckles. Two spoonfuls of muesli, two of Rice Krispies and one of bran flakes. He looks up at me, squinting at my jeans, my jumper. Sharp grey eyes.

'I take it you're not coming to church, then?' he says.

I edge past him to the sink and place my cup on the drainer.

'No,' I say. 'I thought I might go for a walk. Take Blackie up over Ridgeway.'

From the top of the Ridgeway you're on the top of the world. You can see clearly all the way across town, all the way down to the estuary. You can see as far as the eye can see. And all you can see is the mud. Mud is all there ever is. Ten million tons of it, suspended, swirling around in the clouds.

'It's going to rain,' Dad says.

'Doesn't matter,' I say. 'A little rain won't kill us, will it, Blackie? Will it, boy? We don't mind a bit of rain, do we?'

Blackie struggles up out of his basket and wags his hind-quarters at me arthritically. Dad picks up the juice carton and rocks it back and forth with slow twists of the wrist. Waves of orange lava roll up and down the length of the box.

My mother killed herself when I was thirteen. My father hid the note, hid the truth from me for over six years. For nine years afterwards I thought it was because he was a coward. Truth is, it was my mother who was afraid. She put her hand in the Dream Box, but she didn't have the courage to follow what she pulled out.

'Have you got any coffee?' I say.

Dad points at the cabinet above my head. Inside the cabinet is a brown smoked-glass jar with the word BISCUITS etched in orange. A matching white and blue jar proclaims the existence of teabags.

'Top shelf,' Dad says.

I look up and spot a half-empty jar of instant on the top shelf. Decaffeinated.

'I can't drink this,' I say. 'Haven't you got any proper coffee?'

'That's all there is,' says Dad. 'Aren't you going to eat anything?'

'I'm not hungry,' I say.

'You should eat something. Some toast. Have some toast.'

The toast is on a plate in the middle of the table. Four pieces stacked up on top of each other, all the same size, the same shape. I sit down at the table, take a piece of toast off the pile.

Dad begins to shovel his cereal into his mouth.

'How long are you planning on staying?' he says between mouthfuls of banana.

'I hadn't really thought about it.'

I don't want to decide yet. I just want to sit here and be quiet. I don't want to make any plans.

I don't say this out loud.

I say, 'Why? Do you want me to leave?'

'Of course not,' Dad says. 'It's just about planning the meals. I need to go to Sainsbury's today, so I need to know how much food to buy for the week.'

I begin to butter the toast.

I wish he'd look at me. I wish he'd stop eating his cereal and look at me.

But Dad's eyes stayed rooted to his bowl.

'I'm not sure,' I say. 'There's nothing pressing for me to get back to in London. I'm thinking about a new exhibition. I thought I might get some ideas staying here.'

Liar. Liar. Pants on fire.

I stare at the empty chair. The garage door. Drip a dollop of marmalade over my toast.

'I thought I might stay a little while,' I say. 'A few weeks. Maybe longer. If it's OK with you.'

Dad sips at his juice. 'It's fine,' he says.

I spread the marmalade around my toast, right out to the edges, mixing it in well with the butter.

'I mean, I know it's been a while since I came down for a visit. I don't want to get in the way.'

Dad reaches for some toast. Stumpy dark hairs poking out below his knuckles.

'You can stay as long as you want,' he says.

'This is your home,' he says.

I pick out the bits of orange peel from the marmalade and lay them down next to each other on the side of my plate. There are seven pieces. Thick cut. Dad used to give me ten pence for every chunk I could eat. We'd sing the rhyme together: tinker, tailor, soldier, sailor. One day I ate as far as the rich man, then refused to eat any more, saying I didn't want to be poor. Dad had roared with laughter and doubled my money.

'Yeah, I know,' I say. 'But after everything I think we need to talk.'

'What about?'

'About Mum, about what happened.'

Dad stands up, scraping his chair on the tiled floor. 'That's all over now,' he says.

I just eat my toast.

Dad picks up his cereal bowl and spoon, drops them into the sink, then gulps down the rest of his juice standing up and puts his glass down in the sink too, inside his bowl. A flake of bran has lodged in his beard.

His grey beard.

'There's no rush,' I say. 'You've got plenty of time.'

'No,' he says, 'today's the third Sunday in the month.'

'So?'

'The third Sunday in the month is Fellowship Sunday. Where all four sister churches get together to celebrate the Eucharist. This month it's over at Bettws. I have to leave before nine.'

'Oh,' I say.

'Tell you what,' Dad says.

'What?' I say.

'You can go to Sainsbury's for me,' he says, 'while I'm at church. You can go to Sainsbury's for me. You can give me a lift to church and then go on from there. That way you can get whatever type of coffee you like.'

'OK,' I say.

'You'd be doing me a favour,' he says. 'There's a nature walk this afternoon for the Sunday school. I said I'd get some stuff for the picnic.'

'OK,' I say.

Dad moves back over to the table, picks up two of the cereal boxes and opens the cabinet door to his right. The bottom two shelves of the cabinet are stacked up with tins. Big tins, small tins, all lined up, all different colours.

'I said I'd meet Louise at Sainsbury's and get the food,' he says. 'Not much. Just sandwiches and crisps. Some lemonade.'

I say, 'Louise?'

'You remember Louise?' he says, sliding the cereal boxes onto the top shelf of the cabinet.

'No.'

'Yes you do,' he says. 'Louise. You were at school together. Her parents live over at Malpas. The Phillips. Louise Phillips.'

A face flits across my mind. Earnest-looking, glasses. Greasy hair.

'Oh that Louise,' I say.

'Of course she's married now,' Dad says. 'Teaches over at Rhiwderin. Comes to St Matthew's, though. Helps out with Sunday school too.'

'Right,' I say.

'You'll be able to catch up with each other. It's not much. The list is up on the noticeboard, next to the phone. I'll give you the money.'

'OK,' I say.

On the windowsill above the sink is a plant, an African violet with purple flowers in a terracotta pot. The edges of the pot are painted in purple swirls to match the petals.

Dad turns and walks out of the kitchen, goes upstairs to put on his cassock. I scrape the marmalade peel off my plate into the waste disposal unit.

Chapter Four

Kat calls me back in early off my break. Number Four's display is stuck on zero, its little red light flashing and beeping fit to bust. So's Kat. Even though this computer panel is simple. Even though she's been on the training course twice. She hates it when anything beeps at her. Won't even use an alarm clock, just the radio or her mum.

I tell Kat to press clear. She wants to know what the hell I think she's been doing.

Across the forecourt a woman has Number Four's nozzle rammed down the tank of her white Escort. The woman's neck is twisted back over her shoulder towards the pump and she's shaking the nozzle like a lunatic. I lean across Kat and press the clear button. Twice. But the little red light keeps beeping, keeps flashing. The panel display keeps stuck on zero. So I drag the mike out from behind the extra strong mints, switch it on. Tannoy dust splutters and hisses.

'Hello,' I say into the mike but all that comes out is squealing feedback, rupturing my eardrums.

Kat spits a laugh into her hand. I slap her arm and twiddle the volume knob.

I'd like to see her do any better with this piece of junk.

'Hello. Hello.'

This time there's just my voice bouncing off the concrete, knocking at the windows of the pub opposite. The woman stops shaking the nozzle and looks towards the shop window. I wave at her.

'Sorry,' I say. 'Got a problem with the system. Can you replace the hose, please? Just for a minute, please.'

The woman nods and sticks the nozzle back in the head. I turn the panel key to off, count to ten, then flip the key back on. But the pump's still stuck. So I wave at the woman again, talk into the mike again.

'No, sorry. Pump's definitely broken. Use Number Two, please.'

The woman gets back in her car, reverses it down to Number Two and pulls out the pump handle. I press clear. Me and Kat hold our breath and stare at the display screen.

One Mississippi. Two Mississippi...

Number Two's display flicks to a row of eights, back to zero, then starts climbing. The woman waves and gives the thumbs-up. Kat and me breathe out again.

'Are you going to shut down Number Four?' Kat says.

'Give me a minute,' I say. 'I'm still on my break, remember? Haven't even drunk my coffee yet.'

Kat nudges my cup towards me.

Stone cold.

Kat laughs. 'You could ride a bicycle round your bottom lip,' she says, stretching across the countertop.

Flecks of mascara and glitter speckle her cheeks and when she reaches her arm up to brush her fingers through my fringe I can see the entry stamp from the bar last night half rubbed out on the back of her hand. Dirty cow didn't even wash this morning. I wriggle my fingers up the sleeve of her overall, stroke the hairs on her arm and then we're chewing each other's faces off.

While we're at it the woman from the pumps comes in and stands behind me. But I'm so wrapped up in what Kat's tongue is doing in my mouth that I don't notice her until I take a step back to get my body in a better position and stand right on the woman's foot. Twist round so sharp in

28

surprise I lose my balance and fall against her. Nearly knock her over. The woman stumbles and her hand grabs at my chest. Digs her nails in really hard, right on my tit! When it works out exactly what it's got hold of, the woman's hand jerks away like it's touching hot metal.

'Sorry,' the woman says.

'Sorry,' I say, exactly the same time.

My voice sounds like I'm still speaking through the tannoy, all squeaky and distant. My tit's all throbbing and sore. The woman and I stand in front of each other, up close. Neither one of us knowing where to put our eyes. Mine lock onto her left ear. Dangly silver earrings cut into the shape of feathers. Curly brown hair. Her arms folded tight across her stomach. My brain screaming for my feet to move but my eyes telling them to stay there, telling me how pretty the woman is.

'Pump Number Two? Ten pounds please,' Kat says, cool as anything.

A smile stops halfway across my face because the woman is now staring at me like I'm a Martian or something, like she's trying not to be sick.

The woman reaches her arm round me, careful not to let even her coat sleeve brush against me and lays some money on the counter.

'The other pump,' she tells Kat. 'The one that's broken?' Even though she's speaking really quietly, I can tell her voice is dead posh.

'I think there's something stuck up the nozzle,' she says. 'I could hear it rattling inside.' Then she walks straight out the door, almost breaking into a trot in her hurry to get away.

My eyes follow her scuttle all the way to her car. Watch her get in and drive off. As she turns round and heads back up the road I can see she's got some Jesus freak sticker on her windscreen.

I walk to the end of the storefront and watch her drive away down the road.

She can't wait to get out of here. Kat and me, what we are, always makes Jesus freaks sick to their stomachs.

Not that it bothers me. I mean, who cares what Jesus freaks think? Bloody weirdos.

Funny, though, she didn't look like a Jesus freak. Not with those clothes. Too trendy.

But then Kat's banging on the window at me, pointing out towards Number Four again.

I turn and look and sure enough there's some bloke trying to squeeze some juice out of the lemon. It's that Gareth Matthews from over the chippy.

'Gareth,' I yell, cupping my fingers round my mouth, 'it's broken. Use Number Two, will you?'

But the wind whips my voice away. And I'm not going to make a tit of myself using that tannoy thing again, so I start to walk slowly up to the pumps. And that's when I see the cigarette in his hand, its end glowing bright and round above the holding tanks, fresh-filled with gas just yesterday.

Next thing I know I'm racing across the forecourt, overall flapping. My chest feels like I'm having a heart attack. The wind blowing grit in my face, wrapping lead weights around my ankles, and the whole time Gareth the Moron is poking his finger and something else up the spout of the nozzle, cigarette hanging just out of reach.

I finally make it, swallow down cold air as fast as I can and slap the cigarette down onto the ground. Grind it flat like it's Gareth's head.

Gareth's moon-face shining down on me.

'What d'you do that for?' he wails.

Point over at the sign above the pump, my stomach doing flip-flops. 'Can't you read? You could've blown us all to smithereens.'

Gareth shrugs. 'Sorry,' he says. 'Forgot, didn't I?'

My head doesn't even reach up to his shoulders. My eyes are only level with his chest. But I can see now what he's poking down the nozzle's end. It's a biro. A bloody biro!

'Quit fooling around with that, will you?' I say and try to wrestle the handle from him but he's got a grip like cement. 'The pump's blocked up.'

'I know,' he says. 'A stone or something. See?'

'Don't point that thing in my face.'

'Kids I bet,' he says. 'Messing.'

'Give it to me,' I yell and grab the nozzle again, this time with both hands. 'Let go,' I tell him.

But he still won't. So we dance round in a circle; me swinging from his arms, swearing, and Gareth pulling the nozzle higher and higher out of my reach, still fishing down the head with his pen.

'I can see it,' he says. 'If I can just reach it. If I...There...'

Petrol pumps out over my boots and splashes up my jeans. Soaks right through, blistering my skin.

'Oh shit,' he says. 'Sorry.'

I am so mad I want to grab my penknife out my pocket and plunge it into his fat belly until his guts spill out onto the concrete.

But instead I just say, 'You stupid asshole. Now look what you've gone and done.'

Heave the greasy nozzle out of his fingers.

'I've got to stay like this all shift now. I'm freezing and I stink.'

'I'm really sorry, Ani,' he says.

'Sorry's not much use, is it? How much did you want anyway?'

'Three quids' worth,' he says.

'All this for three quid? You must be joking.'

'S'all I can spare, isn't it?' Gareth says.

'Well you've thrown twenty-seven pence of it over me already. Don't think you're getting that for nothing.'

I push him out the way and slip the nozzle down the hole. Caress the trigger until the tension is right. The pump display ticks forward slowly. I relax my grip. Two seventy-five, two

31

eighty... Easy girl. Easy now. Ninety-eight, ninety-nine...

Bingo. You'll never catch me going over by a penny. I'm a professional.

'That'll be three quid, then,' I say.

Gareth drops a tenner into my open palm. 'And a packet of Marlboro Lights,' he says.

I really, really, really hate this place.

Trudging back to the store, I try plucking at the thighs of my jeans to dry them off a bit, but they just bounce right back, stick to my skin like cling film. From the moment I step back inside the store the central heating warms up the petrol and wafts the fumes up around me until my stomach heaves again. I look around me at the rows of shelves with the novelty toys, look at the chocolate biscuits advert – *buy two get one free* – look at Kat's face

and then I'm grizzling like a fucking two-year-old.

Kat leads me out to the storeroom and sits me down on a stack of upturned crates between the sink and the back door. Then she's fetching me a spliff, telling me to smoke some of it.

I go to light it.

'Oh gross,' I say. 'You haven't even put a roach in it.'

Kat rolls her eyes, but tears a strip off her Rizla packet and fixes up the roach, lights the spliff up for me, then sits there rubbing my back while I have a good cry.

Eventually the well dries up and I blow my nose in a tissue. Stink of petrol still making my head spin. 'Sorry. Don't know where that came from,' I say. 'Guess I'm just tired.'

'I think you should go home,' Kat says.

'Can't,' I say. 'There's still four hours to go and anyway I need the money.'

I give up with the tissue and wipe my face with a dish-cloth from off the drainer. It's caked with coffee granules and God knows what else but at least it doesn't make me high.

'Just go,' says Kat. 'Have a bath. Get some sleep. I'll cover for you.'

'But what about the shift change?' I say. 'You'll be the only one here. We'll get caught and then we'll both get fired.'

'We won't,' Kat says. 'Joan's doing the afternoon shift. Joan won't split, she's a mate.'

I blow my nose again. A picture flashes in front of my eyes. Till, shopfront, forecourt. Till, shopfront...

Shit.

Ron never checks the security tapes normally. But, knowing my luck, today will be the day when there's a major drive-off. And he'll want to see if we caught the guy's licence-plate on tape. And then he'll see I'm not there.

Shit, he'll see me and Kat snogging, frightening off the customers. He'll love that. Have a real perv over that, Ron will.

'We'll just have to wipe it,' Kat says.

'Won't he be able to tell?'

'Nah,' she says. 'Watch this.'

Pushing me out the way, Kat takes one of the crates, turns it on its side and stands on it on tiptoe. Stretching up, she rewinds the tape, then reaches round the back of the VCR and pulls out a cable. The TV screen flickers, then goes snowy. Kat checks the tape has wound all the way back, then slots it back in the recorder and presses record.

'Now Ron'll think the wire got knocked out some time last night,' she says, 'probably when the door slammed or something. There's a loose connection. Happens all the time.' She gets down off the crate, gives me a wink.

Devious cow. I'd never have thought of that. Grabbing my coat off the hook, I'm just about to walk out the door when the bell at the front of the shop rings and a voice calls out.

'Ani? Are you there? Ani? Hello.'

Gareth! Forgot all about him. Left him standing out there

in the cold waiting for his change and cigarettes. Kat looks at me, I look at Kat and then we're laughing and laughing. We're laughing our fucking heads off.

Chapter Five

My hand is only on her breast for a second. Two at the most. But long enough for her nipple to get button-hard, triggering my whole body to grow. First my arms, then my legs, head, they all stretch and swell. My arteries bulge with blood. My nerves open and spread like a flower in the sun. Bigger and bigger until I am towering over her, over everything in the store.

As I surge upwards, the objects around me, around us – cigarette display, shelving units, the other girl serving – they peel back from their edges, fold into themselves, then dissolve in a hiss of vapour, like someone has just covered them in acid. Definition fades into shadow, then darkness, oblivion, until not even memory remains.

When someone speaks, someone moves – I don't know who – the world rushes back into focus. Expanding to its previous limits, then racing on past until colours and edges fuse and explode. And this is when my body starts getting small again, shrinking down and down until all there is left is a single point of light.

Then half a point.

A quarter.

Just before I disappear altogether, I grip onto myself for balance, root myself down between the cracks of the linoleum floor, pattern long since flayed off by feet and buggy wheels.

I have to get out of here.

*

I know what you're thinking – I'm running away.

And you're right. I am running away. Truth is, running away is what I always do. Truth is, running away is what I do best. Away from danger, away from change.

I just never seem to get very far.

*

Traces of her return to me on the drive back to town. Blue-rimmed eyes, pupils as black as cave water, are superimposed on the traffic lights at the top of Bettws Lane. Flashes of orange hair mix in with the white lines of the Malpas Road. At the Harlequin roundabout her whole face appears so suddenly that I miss the exit sign and have to swing back across two lanes, dodging a blue Fiesta. Flare of angry car horn.

I don't know how I do but somehow I make it to Sainsbury's. As I turn into the driveway, the world is still shaking. But gently now, a mere trembling around the axis. I don't yet trust myself negotiating tight corners so I drive right down the far end to where the car park balloons with open spaces. Only when the car nose is pressed right up against the steel safety barrier in front of the wire fence, only then do I pull up the handbrake, turn off the engine and face the river.

The tide is in, the water brown and fast-flowing. I can feel the water calling to me. It wants me with it. It wants me to be part of it. When I open the car door the force of this truth threatens to pull me through the wire mesh, push me down into the depths. Looping my fingers through the fence, I close my eyes and breathe in great big gasps of mud. The sweet-salt-sulphur stink of it.

And when I open my eyes again the world has righted itself. Everything is back to normal. Everything is as it should be. There is even a trolley waiting for me in the trolley park. I rest my stomach against the trolley's orange bar and push myself forward up the slope towards the glow of the supermarket.

Louise stands in front of the café, her eyes scanning back and forth across the car park.

Louise looks exactly the same as I remember her, but at the same time she looks completely different. I stop a short way off and take advantage of the few seconds I have before she spots me to try and work out what has changed.

At first all I can see is the same. Same shape, same size, even the same style of clothes, for heaven's sake. Then I work it out. The woman by the café, the Louise of now, stands bold and self-assured. Her shadow has only crisp edges.

The Louise of nine years ago was frail and smudgy. The Louise of nine years ago would tremble when anybody talked to her, looked her directly in the eyes.

She was bullied right through school. Nothing too serious, of course. Stealing her clothes from her locker when she was in the shower, that sort of thing. But her reaction, the way she cried and begged the bullies to stop, just urged them on. She got the reputation for being an easy target. So the pranks lasted. Right through to Sixth Form.

The Louise of now strides to the other end of the store, arms swinging, and looks round the corner towards the exit ramp. Pale blue jeans, lilac jumper. Her hair, which she still wears in the same French plait, a dark arrow pointing down the middle of her back.

I clearly remember the last bullying incident. Isn't it weird how these things come flooding back? You don't see someone for years, you don't even think about them, then you meet them again briefly and wham – off down memory lane you go.

It was summer, just before A Levels, and the whole of the Upper Sixth was bristling with pre-exam tension. Nick Morris, self-styled leader of the In Crowd, decided to relieve some of his by dumping Louise in one of the giant wheelie bins behind the Common Room.

Just for a laugh, you understand.

Except the walls of the bin were stainless steel and six foot high.

Except she was stuck in there for nearly three hours before someone heard her shouting and fetched a stepladder.

Except they also fetched half the Sixth Form to witness her humiliation.

Just for a laugh, you understand.

Of course, the Louise of nine years ago wouldn't do anything about it, wouldn't tell any of the teachers. So when I found out I decided to teach Nick a lesson myself. I stuck a stamp on the Common Room wall and next to it a poster signed by five of his friends, including his girlfriend Deborah, testifying that the stamp was the same size as Morris's penis. Everyone thought it was a great laugh. In fact, my poster was such a success I used it as a base for my final Art exam project.

Changing the names, of course.

You could say that Nick Morris gave me my first critical success.

The Louise of now walks back up towards the café, looks right in my direction. My stomach jolts in shock. The light coming out of her eyes is as clear-cut as a laser.

I need more time.

I spin around until my back is to her and poke my hand down in my rucksack, rummaging around like I'm looking for my keys. But it's too late. She is already calling my name. So I turn back, fix a smile on my face. A look of happy surprise. We hug and Louise kisses me on the cheek.

'Daryl! It's so good to see you,' she says, laying her hand on my arm. 'I couldn't believe it when your dad told me you

38

were back. How are you?'

'Not too bad,' I say and wrap my coat across my chest, fold my arms. 'How are you?'

'Oh fine, fine. God, I can't believe it. How long has it been?'

'Not since school,' I say. 'How are things? Dad tells me you're teaching now?'

Louise smiles. 'Over at Rhiwderin. I'm Head of English, for my sins. Been there about three years now.'

'Sounds like you're doing well,' I say.

'Not as well as you, though. I've seen photos of your work. Your dad showed me.'

'He did?'

'Of course he did,' she says. 'Your dad's really proud of you. Always telling people at church what you're up to. Hey, listen, I really wanted to get down to London to see your latest exhibition. But I was all tied up with exam work.'

'You didn't miss much,' I say.

Nothing much at all.

I turn and look over my shoulder towards the river. But from back here all you can see is the wire fence and the warehouses of Rodney Parade on the opposite bank, hunkering down against decay.

'Shall we go in?' I say, pointing towards the café doorway.

Louise pushes open the door. I follow behind, wedging the door open with the trolley while she weaves through the tables towards the food counter.

Danish pastries. Plastic triangles of sandwiches. Mineral water. The hot-plate section: five breakfast items plus free toast and coffee just £1.99. The coffee area. They serve proper coffee here. In those individual cafetières.

I stop pushing the trolley. Louise is now walking into the supermarket proper. I call her back. 'Do you fancy a coffee first?' I say.

Louise looks at the cafetières, then at her watch. 'Better not,' she says. 'I told your dad we'd be back before Sunday school starts. Anyway, there's usually coffee available after the service. We can get some then.' And she heads on through to the fruit and veg.

Steering the trolley past the checkout till, I give one last look to the cafetières. Just big enough for one good cup. But Louise is already bagging up a dozen Golden Delicious. The apples are so highly polished they reflect the neon light hanging from the ceiling, giving Louise's face a brackish tinge. She moves over to the tangerines. I push the trolley on through.

The supermarket aisles clash lights and colour. Fresh-baked bread wafting through children's screams. After the cathedral gloom of the car park it all makes my head spin. But I don't know why I'm so surprised.

After all, the surface of a mud bank is practically barren. No plant life, just a few wading birds. And yet if you peel back the top layer, inside it's a different story. One acre of estuarine mud is more productive than an acre of the finest agricultural land. A rich harvest of tiny mud-dwelling animals specifically adapted to thrive in the local conditions. Strange creatures who, lacking any firm ground on which to leave their offspring, carry them around with them wherever they go, on their shells, or better still on a relative's. Creatures who stay buried in the mud but extend long syphonlike arms to suck in nourishment from their surroundings. Creatures who, as studies have shown, grow faster on the Welsh side of the estuary.

You see, at times, on our side there is more. So much more. At times Newport does come first.

I steer the trolley up and down the aisles, just watching people go about their business. Louise chooses this packet of honey-roast ham, discards that packet of Cheddar, all the time chatting, filling me in on the lives of people from school. After throwing some real coffee and filter papers in the bottom of the trolley, I ask her about Nick Morris. Turns out he's an electronic engineer with one of those big computer companies out at the Coldra. Works with her Greg. He's married, of course, with two kids. Louise says she sees quite a lot of him.

Half an hour later, I drive us out and up past the castle. As we circle the Old Green roundabout, Louise's purse, which she tossed casually down on the shelf of the dashboard, slides across towards me. Single key hanging off the key ring, blue plastic tab.

The dual carriageway has been widened and there's a new flyover connecting straight to the motorway, bypassing the Malpas Road bottleneck. But the banks of the carriageway are still covered in daffodils. Great big waves of yellow.

Louise and I joined the school orchestra together. We were the first violins, elevated by the music teacher because we were the only two in the entire string section who could read music. The orchestra's anthem was the theme from *The Dam Busters*. We always used to play it at the school Eisteddfod. Louise and I took it in turns to be leader. We wore daffodils in our lapels.

Louise and I used to play the the theme from *The Dam Busters* at the school Eisteddfod concert wearing daffodils in our lapels every year. For seven years.

The Malpas Road is empty of cars. Dark and shuttered shop windows, nobody out walking. Just me and Louise, alone in Dad's car. I'm tempted to put my foot down but there are speed cameras everywhere these days. So I keep the needle wavering around forty-two.

'Hey, Lou,' I say. 'Remember *Dam Busters*?'

Louise screws up her nose, covers her eyes with her hand, bends forward and shakes her head so her plait bounces up between her shoulder blades. 'Oh my God, yes,' she says. 'We were terrible.'

'We certainly knocked the stuffing out of those dams. Those Germans never stood a chance with us in charge,' I say.

'Except for that bloody last one,' she says. 'We never did manage to hit that last one.'

I drive parallel to the new bypass, past a blue motorway sign. London 132 miles.

'Seven years,' I say. 'And every one of them my dad and your parents sitting in the front row, trying not to wince and looking proud anyway.'

'Don't know why, what with you messing up the ending every time.'

'Me? What about you? At least I used to try to play all the tune, you just used to give up and pluck open string.'

'Only because it gave me a one in five chance of hitting the right note.'

We are both laughing now. Emerging from under the motorway, I move across to the far lane for the Bettws turn-off. Louise's purse slides back down along the dashboard. She picks it up, holds it in her lap.

'You know they've made Upper School into an adult education centre?' she says.

'I heard,' I say.

'And they've turned Lower School into a block of luxury apartments.'

'Really? That kind of thing's all the rage in London at the moment. Didn't know it was popular back here.'

'Oh sure,' she says. 'There's lots of things like that going on here. Newport's changed a lot.'

'So I've noticed. What are they like, then? These new luxury apartments? Have you been inside?'

'Better than that,' she says. 'Greg and I have one! It's fantastic. Really easy to keep clean.'

Louise's face is flushed and she's grinning like she's really proud of herself. But I can't get my head round this. First she's a teacher and now she's living in our old school. What is she, a glutton for punishment?

'Top floor, South staircase. We've got half the art room and a bit of the biology lab. Been there about a year now. It was really weird at first. I mean, teaching all day and then coming home to school. Talk about a glutton for punishment. But

Greg and I love the place now. It's so modern and there's loads of light. You should come over some time.'

'I'd like that,' I say.

Five-a-side rugby in Crindau Park. Scrape of wiper blades across the windscreen.

'Hey, Lou,' I say, 'I've got an idea. Let's meet up in the week.'

'Sounds good,' Louise says.

'Yeah, we could go to that diner we used to go to after orchestra practice, what was it called?'

'Scarlett's?'

'That's the one. Is it still there?'

'Sure. But what do you want to go there for? There are much better places we can go. We could go into Cardiff, or there's a really good French restaurant on the road to Usk. It's Egon Ronay recommended.'

'I know,' I say. 'And we can go. But just this once let's go to Scarlett's again. Have cheeseburgers and Coke floats like we used to.'

'Oh, Daryl, I can't go there,' she says. 'It'll be full of teenagers. Probably half the kids I teach. It'd be horrendous. Come to my place. Come and meet Greg. He'd love to meet you.'

We're now at the top of Bettws Lane. From the brow of the hill you can see, jutting out behind the playing field, the flat roof of the petrol station.

Everything exactly the same.

Blue-rimmed eyes.

Shaking the streamers around my head.

Pupils as black as cave water.

Saying the magic words.

'I guess you're right,' I say.

At the bottom of the hill now, where the speed bumps are, passing Bettws High School, the flat-faced caretaker's house.

We all have to stop running at some point.

I press down the indicator stick, turn right onto Monnow Way.

43

Louise sits up straight in her seat. 'Wouldn't it be quicker going straight on?' she says.

'I just need to call into the garage,' I say. 'Forgot something. I won't be long.'

Chapter Six

I'm dying. Fucking dying, I am. My head's all woozy and my arms and legs all pins and needles from where the blood's run out of them.

I know it's down to the blood because when I look in the mirror, instead of my face there's just this great big monster face looking back at me. It's a hand mirror, the one that's part of the set my Nana gave me for my birthday. It's horrible. Ruched white satin back with a gold trim. Wouldn't be caught dead using it normally, but today I can't bring myself to stand up and look in the wall mirror. Today I hardly have the strength to hold my head up off the pillow. So I'm just lying here with my Nana's hand mirror, staring at the monster face hanging in the air above me.

Not even my room is making me feel better. And my room always makes me feel better. I nicked this posh magazine out the shop with this whole section on loft-style living. You know, everything in one big room, no walls. Ripped the picture out and copied it, made my room into a loft. Took me ages and I had to spend nearly all my birthday money on it. But it's practically perfect now.

I've even got an uplighter. The magazine said no loft is complete without an uplighter. I had to go all the way over to Bristol to get mine. It's black and chrome to match the rest of the room. 'Course it lights the place up like an operating theatre, so I don't switch it on much. But at least I've got one.

The only thing I haven't got is one of those tube chairs with leather strips, but they were too expensive and anyway there's not enough room because of the fitted wardrobes. But if I did have one it would go over there, underneath the window.

Ow, it hurts when I turn my head. Bet I've got one of those diseases. One of those blood disorder thingies so rare no one will spot it till the very last minute. Till there's no hope. They'll get loads of different doctors in, specialists and that. But none of them will have a clue. I'll just be lying here getting weaker and weaker and no one will have a fucking clue what's wrong with me. And Mam will go on telly to start this fund for me to go to America, to get this revolutionary new treatment. Only it will be too late. I'll grow worse and worse until one day, with everyone looking down at me helpless and Mam crying, I'll just die.

Wonder what my last words will be?

They'll take my body away to some science lab and do loads of tests that they couldn't do when I was alive because it would have been too dangerous and that's when they'll find out how rare the disease is. But they'll be able to use my body to find a cure and I'll be the last person in Europe, probably the whole world, to die of the disease. So they'll name the cure in my honour. My funeral will be televised and Keith will sing 'The Wonder of You', wearing his '68 Comeback Black Leather.

What time is it? I'm starving. But Mam said she'd only just put the potatoes on to boil. Dinner'll be at least another twenty minutes, she said. I'd better go and see if there are any crisps.

But when I get downstairs, who's sprawled across the sofa eating the last bag? You guessed it, my kid sister Lisa. Well, she's my half-sister really. Keith is her dad, not mine. When Keith first came to live with me and Mam, I think Mam wanted me to call Keith Dad. But, I mean, I might not see anything of him any more and he might be a two-timing shit like Mam says, but your dad's still your dad, right? Keith thinks so anyway. Keith says he'd rather be Keith than Dad any time. Dad makes him feel too old, he reckons. Even Lisa calls him Keith.

Mam and Keith are the bane of my life. Oh, don't get me wrong, I love them and everything, but they just don't understand the concept less is more.

Take this room. The magazine said living rooms should be plain, accented with just one or two blocks of colour. But there must be five different patterns in here at least. And it's pink. Pink flowery sofa. Pink plastic electric guitar on the wall above the fireplace. Even the cat's scratching post is trimmed with pink fake fur.

Now, is that sad or what?

Keith comes in from the kitchen and hangs his Aloha Eagle jumpsuit on the back of the door. The front's all ripped. I can see that from here. Down the eagle's left wing a few of the stones are hanging loose and some are completely gone.

'What happened to that?' I say. 'Looks like a dog chewed it.'

Keith heaves a big sigh, runs his hand down the torn bit like he's trying to stroke it better. From the back, Keith is the spitting image of Elvis. Tall and broad-shouldered. Duck-tail hair. He looks quite like Elvis from the front, too. Apart from the broken nose. Older Elvis, of course. Seventies Elvis. Hamburger and donuts Elvis. Hungover Elvis.

'Caught it on a hook last night when I was changing in that prison cell of a dressing room,' he says.

But when I walk over to get a better look I can see the rip's not that bad. Definitely needs patching but nothing that can't be covered over with a couple of Hawaiian garlands. The eagle might end up with one wing bigger than the other, but it will still be able to fly.

I know better than offer to fix it, mind. Keith won't let

anyone but his official dressmaker Joyce go anywhere near his jumpsuits, and even then he hovers over her, watching her every move. Keith makes more fuss over his Elvis gear than he does over his cars. But a new jumpsuit can cost him more than three hundred pounds. And that's not counting the matching boots and belts. I can't believe how much money Keith will pay to get his look right. He does all the leather and studwork himself, too.

Keith pulls his cigarettes out of his jeans pocket, plucks one out the box with his teeth and lights it. 'That was the suit I was planning on for my finale next month,' he says, puffing on his fag, scratches his chin. Five o'clock shadow Elvis.

'Going to pull out all the stops, I was. And now Joyce will have the devil's own job getting it fixed in time.'

I don't know what to say. He's right. This could ruin everything. Next month is the regional finals of the Elvisly Yours competition. Keith's big chance. If he makes it into the top three then he'll go on to the nationals in June. Maybe make some real money. Maybe even get on *Stars in their Eyes*. So everything's got to be perfect. Keith's been practising his routine for weeks. We've all been roped in. Mam and Lisa are going to wear matching red, white and blue poodle skirts and dance in the background and I'm supposed to hand out red, white and blue free gift scarves to all the screaming fans.

I'm not wearing a poxy poodle skirt, though. No way.

'Joyce will sort it for you,' I say. 'And if she can't you can wear one of your other suits. The Spanish Flower, maybe. Or the Peacock.'

'Maybe,' Keith says.

But I can tell he's not convinced by the way he slumps down on the sofa and shoves Lisa's legs out his way. Lisa whines at him but then sticks her legs straight back up over Keith's lap and goes on watching telly like nothing's happened.

The Waltons is on. John Boy is standing at the college

gate, all dressed up in a bow tie and woolly tank top, looking nervous. It's his first day.

Keith takes a swig out the can on the coffee table.

'Hey, that's mine,' Lisa says.

Lisa's still in her Graceland nightie. All messy blonde hair and jam stains round her mouth. She must have got straight out of bed, had her breakfast in front of the telly and stayed there. All right for some. Keith's hair is combed but the pompadour is loose and flopped over on one side like a balloon with a hole in it. Roots showing through.

I wish he wouldn't let himself go so much. He should have more respect, even just sitting round the house. Keith's always telling me how much the King deserves respect. If it were me, I wouldn't let myself go. I'd be Jailhouse Elvis, Hound Dog Elvis, 24/7.

'Are there any female Elvis impersonators?' I say.

I have to ask Keith this twice before I get his attention. He is too busy tapping two fingers on Lisa's right shin in time with the music coming out of the telly. The music is fast and loud because John Boy is upset that his car is old and worn out compared to the rich boys' wheels.

'A few,' he says eventually. 'Mostly in the States, but I heard there's one in Bury St Edmunds.'

'Do you think that's wrong?'

'Not as long as it's done with respect. Anyone can pay tribute to the King as long as they do it with respect,' Keith says.

Lisa drops her empty crisp packet down on the carpet. John Boy walks slowly up the steps towards the main entrance to the college. He looks like he's going to be sick.

Keith heaves himself up off the sofa and looks over at me. 'You've got the figure for it. Early fifties Elvis, Hound Dog Elvis maybe,' he says, then goes out to the kitchen for more Cokes.

As soon as he's out the door Lisa starts up, bleating 'Ani wants to be Elvis' over and over again like a scratched record. She won't shut up till I pin her down by the arms, straddle her knees with my legs, then lean over her, the tips of our noses touching.

'I'll tell Mam,' she says. Cheese and onion breath.

'Yeah? Then I'll really give you something to cry about,' I say.

But right then Mam and Keith come in through the kitchen door, so I climb off Lisa before Mam can give me an earful. Lisa's her baby.

'Ani was saying she'd like to do Elvis, early fifties,' Keith says, chucks some knives and forks onto the table.

Mam comes over and tugs at my hair with her fingers, hoping I will magically turn into one of those dolls whose hair comes out the top of her head when you pull it. She hates my hair this short.

'You'd have to dye it. No one will believe an Elvis with ginger hair,' she says.

'Ginger pubes! Ginger pubes!'

God, I really hate my sister when she's in one of her moods. Throw a cushion at her.

'Ow, that hurt.'

'Serves you right.'

'Mam! Tell her.'

'Shut up, you little brat.'

'Shut up yourself, carrot face.'

'Shit head.'

'Dog breath.'

'Ani. Lisa. That's enough, the pair of you.'

I can tell from Mam's face that she means it, that I'm this close to a hiding. Meanwhile, Keith, who has been doing his usual trick of keeping his head down, starts jiggling his neck from side to side because I'm in his way of the telly. So I kick the soles of his slippers, tell him he's supposed to be on my side. Keith stops jiggling, holds his arms out to the three of us and next thing I know he's on his feet, singing at the top of his voice with Lisa and Mam belting out the chorus.

'"Suspicious Minds"'

My family think they're the funniest thing on the whole fucking planet.

Lisa's got all the moves. She's much more Elvisy than Mam. Almost as Elvisy as Keith.

John Boy has met a girl. It's love at first sight. But he's troubled about his country-boy ways and because he doesn't have any money or a fancy car like the other boys. He asks the girl out but all the time he's with her he's embarrassed and desperate to leave. Then he goes home and he sees how poor his family is and he's even more embarrassed.

The adverts come on and the phone rings. Mam goes out into the hall to answer it.

'Hello, Katrina love. Yes hang on, I'll just get her for you.' She kicks open the door with her foot. 'Ani!'

The phone's on the table next to the pink crystal wine goblets from Las Vegas. I pull the extension lead as far as it will go, till everything goes black.

— Kat?

— Hiya. Feeling better now?

— A bit. Don't stink any more, anyway. Going to have my dinner and then get some kip.

— You sure you're all right? Your voice sounds weird.

— I'm in the cupboard under the stairs. It's the only way to get any privacy round here. This place is a total zoo. Did Ron say anything about me dogging off?

— No way. He didn't even show. Told you it would be OK.

— Great. Listen Kat, I'm sorry if I was off with you before.

— S'OK. You had a bad day, that's all.

— Yeah, well after this morning I've decided.

— You're leaving?

— As soon as I collect my wages.

— Ani, you can't do that!

— Watch me.

—Well, what are you going to do instead?

— Dunno. Work in a bar. Anything except go near that poxy garage again.

Through the cupboard door I can hear Mam calling out for me to fetch the Sunday plates out of the sideboard.

— I've got to go, Kat. My dinner's nearly ready.

— Hang on. I haven't told you yet. You know that woman? The one from this morning. From when the pump was broken?

— The Jesus freak?

— Yeah, except she's not. Not a Jesus freak I mean. She's an artist, a real one. Her name's Daryl. Daryl Jenkins.

— Never heard of her.

— No, me neither. But my mum has. My mum says she's famous, she's had exhibitions and everything. In London. Anyway she came back into the shop after you'd gone and she was really nice. Dead chatty. Wanted to know where was good to hang out, you know, in Cardiff and that. So I told her about that bar last night. And, guess what? She only wants to meet us there next weekend!

I take the plates through to the kitchen. Mam's thickening up the gravy with her back to me. Blonde hair tied up with Lisa's silver scrunchie. From behind she looks just like Lisa.

Barbie.

I can't believe Kat told that Jesus freak we'd go out with her on Saturday. Even if she is dead famous. I mean, walking into the garage and asking Kat out like that, bold as brass. Who does she think she is? She better not fancy Kat. She better not let me catch her fancying Kat. She'll be sorry if she does, I can tell you.

It might be OK, though. She might just want us to be mates. It might be really great. Having an artist as a mate, I mean. She can introduce us to all the famous people she knows. In London. We can go to their parties. And then, after we've got to know a few, we can move down there. To London. Live in a loft. A proper one, just like in my magazine, with wooden floors and great big windows overlooking the Houses of Parliament.

Mam hands me a saucepan full of peas. 'Here, drain these, will you?' she says.

And that's where we'll have our parties. In the loft. Parties like they had in that artist's flat in New York. What was it called? That place where the walls were all covered in silver foil? Anyway, at one of these parties I'll get my big break. Meet someone who owns an art gallery. I'll show him my stuff and he'll love it, insist on giving me my own show. I'll be an overnight success. In the papers and everything.

'Ani! Watch what you're doing!'

Steam billows up around me. Mam crouches down with a tea cloth, soaks up the mess on the floor. All the time going on at me for not paying enough attention.

'Honestly, I don't know what's wrong with you these days,' she says. 'Half the time you're in your own little world.'

I spoon the rest of the peas onto the plates. 'Sorry,' I say. 'I was just thinking how great it's going to be having a famous artist as a mate. You know, all the parties we'll be able to have in London. All the famous people.'

But Mam just grunts and throws the dirty cloth inside the washing machine. 'Why would a famous artist want to know a silly little girl like you?' she says. 'You and your wild imagination! It'll be the death of me one day. Now take your head out of the clouds and take those plates through, will you? *EastEnders* will be on in a minute.'

I pick two plates up off the drainer. 'Mam?' I say.

'Yes love?'

'Can I have loads of gravy on mine?'

Chapter Seven

All cultures have a creation story. All cultures believe in an ultimate reality, from which and to which everything else flows. A time and space beyond time and space where there are no borders, no limits. An infinite, ceaseless maturation and exploration.

How you choose to name this reality, how you choose to tell the story, is not a question of fact but a question of belief.

The fact is it exists.

It is what drives and lifts our spirits: how we can think and act and be beyond and above. Our spirits, if not our imaginations, have the capacity to be infinite, are able to create and become all intelligible things. Our spirits, our souls, are not limited to time and space. The innermost coil of our being is a wellspring throwing us forward into...

Into what?

You know what I'm talking about here.

The age-old quest for perfection.

Just occasionally you think you've got it. Just for a second there's a glimpse of something timeless, ceaseless. A molten stream of energy. Pulsating luminescence. Eternity interpreted through constant transformation, limitless possibilities.

And then it's gone again. Until the next time.

At first I thought I could achieve it with glass. Molten glass: chaotic, liquid, random. Boundary-less. But it always cooled. Became too static, too fragile. Then I decided the material wasn't important. What was important was the story the material told.

I realised I wasn't really after a physical representation of perfection. That would be impossible. What I really wanted was a physical representation of the quest.

We all have to try.

I have spent the past nine years trying.

I tried too hard.

It took over my entire life. All my time, space. I locked myself into my studio, my dark and dingy basement studio, and worked and worked. As time went on I became more and more absorbed. I ignored the phone, the post. The only time I went out was when I had to earn enough money to pay the mortgage or buy food. I barely acknowledged my friends.

At first they didn't mind too much. That sort of behaviour is expected of artists, isn't it? And there are a lot of artists in Hackney. But when eccentricity and reclusiveness go on month after month...

Well, there are limits, even in Hackney.

Gradually the phone calls and the friends began to tail off.

I didn't notice. And then when I thought I was finally getting somewhere, at the end of last year, having jacked in my day job, lived off my savings, bought myself time and space...

I should have known.

You mustn't try too hard.

You mustn't get so engrossed in the minutiae of what you are trying to achieve that you fail to notice your horizon growing flat. Flatter and flatter. Until it becomes your prison, a prison of time and space.

Nothing but time and space where your soul should be.

But that's all over now. All left behind me, in London. I don't have to think about it any more. I can make a fresh start.

It's why I came back home. To make a fresh start.

No, that's not true. You know that's just not true, don't you? And you, you deserve the truth.

Truth is, I ran away.

Away from failure. Away from change.

Before that, I ran out of money.

After nine years I thought I had enough to show and anyway, as I said, I was running out of money. So I scraped together what was left, called in every last favour I was owed and put on an exhibition.

My magnum opus, so to speak.

Called it 'Quest'.

The idea was to stimulate discussion.

The idea was to raise publicity, raise more money to continue my work.

Oh, let's be honest here. For once.

The idea was fame and fortune.

Except that the sophisticated London critics, the sophisticated London public weren't interested in what I had to say.

The sophisticated London audience doesn't want abstract concepts. It wants *questions exploring the inherent values of contemporary culture.* It wants *strategies to appropriate popular culture's language and imagery in order to undermine it.*

It wants installations.

Simplicity,

purity,

truth.

These are all passé, outré.

Dead.

So I've left London and come back home. Back to the land of my fathers. Back to a land where they understand about roots, about story. Back to where people live a simpler life.

A fresh start.

*

After lunch we get ready for the nature ramble.

Dad is at the heart of things. The wind whipping the hood of his cagoule up the back of his head, he hands each child a blue plastic folder and a newly sharpened pencil. The process is solemn, ritualistic. Dad takes these rambles very seriously. Dad is Vice-President of the Newport Wildlife Association.

The ramble is down the Glebelands. I haven't been here for years. Not since school. They used to bus us down once a week to do cross-country running. But mostly we'd skive off behind the trees and smoke or, if there were boys around, practise getting to third base. Everything is as I remember it. Same big trees, open park. Grass full of dandelions. The park entrance is through a damp concrete tunnel right under the motorway.

We are down the far end of the park where the gravel path bends round, tracing the line of the river. Either side of the path is a line of plane trees. The trees follow the path the way the path follows the river. Halfway. Back to the tunnel, then ending abruptly, leaving the path naked in the sunshine, the gravel glittering like broken glass.

I group the kids into teams of three, ready to begin, but Dad pulls me up short.

'They'll be fine in one big group, Daryl,' he says. 'Help Louise with the picnic.'

I open my mouth to contradict him, throw out my arm to indicate the many places where children can disappear from under the gaze of responsible adults. Dad takes no notice, marching the kids through the trees and over to the bramble hedge which separates the park from the river. It would take a normal human being twenty minutes of shouting and cajoling, eyes in the back of her head, to keep nine seven- and eight-year-olds in line. But Dad merely barks out a couple of orders and off they all trot. I turn to Louise for support but she just rolls her eyes, then scurries after them, her arms full of food and equipment. I have no choice but to pick up what's left and follow.

At first all I can see is a thick blanket of brambles hanging off a precipice. The sound of water flowing far below. This is no good. What is Dad thinking of? From up here you can't even make out the water's edge, let alone spot three types of native wading birds. But twenty yards down, Dad, Louise and all the kids suddenly plunge into the undergrowth. I quicken my pace to catch up with them. And when I reach the place where they disappeared I can see that someone has sliced open the brambles and a narrow but definite track winds back along the bank. A terrace of roots eases my progress down until I emerge into a secret meadow.

Well, all right, not a meadow. More a clearing, really. But meadow sounds more romantic, more in spirit with the occasion. Anyway, I'm an artist. I almost always exaggerate the aesthetics of any given situation.

The meadow forms a plateau three-quarters of the way above the water. It is framed on one side by the bank of brambles and on the other by tall marsh reeds vibrating with the calls of finches and sparrows. Early buttercups speckle the grass. At one end of the meadow is a group of trees, saplings really. And down the other end, at the exact point where the river bends round towards Caerleon, there is a mud bridge, about six feet wide, sloping down from a grass verge and continuing out into the centre of the river before petering away, disappearing under the surface. Gulls, dunlins and plovers wade in the calm brown water lapping at its sides.

While I stand turning circles of disbelief, Louise stretches a car blanket out under a young oak tree.

'All those times coming down here for Double Games and I never knew about this place,' I say.

Louise flashes me a grin. 'The Wildlife Association doesn't want it all ruined by courting teenagers,' she says. 'Before he let them come, your dad swore all the kids to secrecy. He even made them sign a pact.' She laughs. 'They loved it. Kids that age really go for all that cloak and dagger stuff.'

'Kids any age,' I say, looking at Dad who, having settled the kids down to read through their folders, marches over to the bramble hedge and cuts out two long sticks, then slides down onto the bridge and starts banging the sticks into the mud halfway along. I ask Louise what he thinks he's doing.

'Marking the boundary point,' she says. 'The kids know they're not allowed to go out past those sticks.'

'Isn't it dangerous? What about the current?'

'Not along the sides,' she says. 'The mud bank forms a natural break. As long as the kids stay this side of the boundary there won't be a problem.' Louise turns and looks up at me. 'Your dad always keeps a close eye on them,' she says. 'Don't worry.'

Who's worrying? Since we arrived, Dad has had all the kids hanging off his every word. Their acquiescence is scary. Mum always reckoned Dad was a warlock in another life, the way he could cast a spell on people, get them to do his bidding with just a few quiet words. Never raising his voice. Never asking twice. Sometimes he just willed something to be done and it was.

Two of the boys are released from the magic circle and sidle up to Louise, completely ignoring me. The older one, who's wearing a blue baseball cap, asks Louise if they can please have the fishing net and bucket we've brought, that Reverend Jenkins said it would be OK.

'What do you want them for?' Louise says.

'Newting,' the boy in the cap says.

'OK, but stay this side of the boundary. And remember...'

'Yeah, yeah we know. Chuck 'em back in after.'

Louise hands over the net and the boys race each other back to the river, back to Dad.

I sit down on the edge of the car blanket, look out over the water. To the north you can see as far as Twmbarlwm. The sun pours down behind me, across the river and on up

59

the mountain's side. On each bank, trees stick their bare arms out of the ground, stretching fingertips up, trying to touch the light. The air smells damp and despite the drone of the motorway traffic the atmosphere is peaceful.

'Bet you don't go on many nature rambles in London,' Louise says, offering me a sandwich.

I shake my head.

'No. Much more interesting things to do on a Sunday afternoon in London,' she says.

'Different things, anyway,' I say. I lie down on my back and peer up through the oak tree to the sky, a mottled mauve and yellow cloudbank with wisps of grey chased by the wind.

'All those art galleries,' Louise says. 'Do you get chance to visit them much?'

'All the time,' I say. 'Dozens of them.'

'Right, of course. Dozens,' she says. Something about the way her voice falls away makes me prop myself up on my elbows and look at her properly. Louise sits hunched forward, her head drooping between her knees, tearing and shredding grass with her fingers.

The sharp tang of sap rises between us.

'Newport's getting a new Arts Centre,' she says. 'Of course it's nothing like the ones in London, but it'll be something.'

'I didn't mean to sound superior, it's just my job,' I say. 'Going to art galleries keeps me informed of trends and new ideas. Things I'd have to know wherever I was living,'

'Still, it's better in London, isn't it?' Louise says with a grimace. 'More choice. More cosmopolitan. Not like Newport, however hard we might try to pretend otherwise.'

'At least here in Newport you feel you're part of something,' I say. 'In London you've no idea how you fit into the machine.' I pull my coat up round my neck. It's really too cold to sit around outside like this. Actually it's Dad's coat. His spare Barbour. The coat I brought back with me is much too long for crawling through brambles.

'Or whether you fit in at all for that matter,' I say. 'Most of us are just tiny specks of dust floating down through the cracks of the factory floor. Not even big enough to get swept away.' I look down at my feet. Dad's boots too. Luckily for me, my father has very small feet for his height.

Louise gives me a hard look. 'Is that why you came back?' she says. 'To be Newport's famous local artist?'

Her shrewdness catches me by surprise. I look away at the river, my face burning, then decide to front it out.

'Well, yes, eventually. Why not?' I say. 'I know it'll take a while. I'll have to do something else in the meantime to make some money. Supply teaching, probably.'

Without warning Louise is bearing down on me like an eagle diving on its prey. 'Teaching isn't an easy option, you know. It's bloody hard work,' she says.

'I know,' I say. 'I've been teaching for the past five years, on and off. OK, more off this last year but that was because I was working on a show. I just meant I might have to do some supply work temporarily while I look for something more permanent.'

'Oh,' says Louise, digging her hands deep into the pockets of her coat, staring at her feet. 'Well, maybe I was being oversensitive,' she says.

'Yes,' I say. 'You were. I like teaching. Most of the time anyway. Sure, it can be frustrating sometimes. Like when I can't face my own stuff because I'm too brain dead from yelling at eleven-year-olds all day. But you know what that's like.'

'Yes,' she says and takes a deep breath, like she's about to jump under water. 'Sorry,' she says.

I pour out two cups of coffee from the flask, then fish around in the drinks cooler for the half-bottle of brandy I snuck in earlier.

'For medicinal purposes,' I say.

Over to our right, a yellow-legged bird – a blackbird,

must be – lifts its wings and hurls itself out of the brambles and up into the air, screeching at us. The blackbird flies high above the meadow in a circle, then drops back down again further along the bank and disappears beyond the river bend.

Dad walks up to us, clapping his hands together to keep warm. 'Hello there, girls. Any more of that coffee going?' he says.

'Help yourself,' I say.

My heart is calling out to him, like the blackbird, begging him to notice me. I want to tell him why I've come home. I want to talk to him about Mum. But not just now. Later. When we're on our own. When we've got used to each other again. When I've decided how long I'm staying. If I'm staying.

We drink our coffee in silence.

Down by the river four of the girls have broken out of their Stepford trance and are practising cartwheels and back-flips up and down the grass. I watch them in admiration. I've always been hopeless at games. I've never been able to turn a cartwheel. I've never seen the world upside down.

To the east the clouds are beginning to hang heavy and full in the sky, so ripe they look like they will burst any minute. 'Maybe we should start getting the kids back,' I say, standing up.

Most are still playing on the grass verge but two of the boys, the ones with the fishing net, are down on the mud bank, way past the boundary sticks, peering at something in the water. They're way out on the edge, near the end where the current forces the water round the bend and away down to the sea. If one of them were to fall in ...

'Hey,' I yell. 'Come away from there.'

The boy in the baseball cap turns his head to look at me but neither of them makes a move.

Then in the same split second Dad, Louise and I start to

run towards the mud and the two boys come charging back up onto the meadow.

'A dragon,' the boy in the baseball cap yells. 'We've found a dragon.'

'A baby one,' yells the other.

Then all the kids run up to us, surround us, shouting about a dragon. A baby dragon.

'Don't be silly,' Louise says. 'There's no such thing as dragons.'

'No,' says Dad. 'No such thing as dragons.'

But the boys won't stop leaping and tugging and going on until Dad relents and says we'll come and look. So one by one we slide down onto the mud bridge and walk with wet bums over to the place where the boys say they've found this so-called dragon.

And there it is, about a foot out from the edge of the water, fully submerged, half-buried in the mud, but in plain view. A creature of fables and legends. A dragon. And from its size, a baby one. It's about fifteen inches long, plump and with a long fat tail. Its skin is more green than brown, and blue spots light up its back. Two red crests stick out from the sides of its head.

The responsible adults stand and stare in shock. I look away downstream, directly into the sunlight and blink twice. It couldn't be a dragon, could it? Not really. It must be the brandy. But I only had a drop. A teaspoon at the most. But when I look down again the thing's still there and it certainly looks like a dragon.

'What are we going to do?' Louise says.

'I don't know,' says Dad.

'I think we should catch it,' I say.

'How?' says Dad.

I bend down and undo the laces of my boots, Dad's boots, kick them off and before my common sense can get the better of me I slide my feet into the water, which immediately soaks through my socks. As I press down mud and slime oozes up over my feet, around my ankles. The water is so cold my toes go numb in seconds. But I keep on wading slowly towards the dragon until I can feel the current swirling around my shins, trying to coax me further out.

Then I crouch down. Nobody moves, nobody breathes. As slowly as I can I position the bucket just in front of the dragon's nose, then nudge its behind with the tip of the fishing net.

Obligingly the dragon does as it's told and when its head and front two legs are inside the bucket, I scoop it up out the water and onto the bank before it can change its mind.

'Oh well done, love,' says Dad as I slide the bucket over to him.

Everyone peers down at the catch curled up at the bottom of the bucket under several inches of water.

'Well, whatever it is, it's certainly a very strange-looking thing,' says Louise.

'What do you think, Dad?' I say. 'Is it a newt?'

'No,' he says. 'It's way too big for that.' He puts his hand down into the water, gently stroking the dragon's back. The creature's tail flickers against the side of the bucket.

'You know, boys,' he says, 'I think you might have really found something here. But we need to get it into something larger or it will die.'

The kids all erupt. One of the girls is so excited she spins cartwheel after cartwheel all along the bridge, careless of the mud splattering her arms and clothes.

'What about the drinks cooler?' I say.

'Good idea,' says Dad and he jogs off up the meadow to fetch it.

I pad back over to the grass verge, sit down and peel off my ruined socks. Louise puts the cartwheel girl in charge of the bucket and then gets the other kids to go round the meadow picking up all the litter while she packs the picnic away. Dragon or no dragon, once a girl guide, always a girl guide.

Dad comes back with the drinks cooler and makes the

dragon more comfortable. 'I think the best thing for us to do is get this whatever it is back home, then show it to someone who can help us identify it,' he says. 'I know someone up at the university who might be able to help.'

He picks up the cooler and, trailed by the still-shouting children, takes the dragon back up to the car park. I try to scrape the mud out from between my toes with a dock leaf but all I really manage to do is spread it more evenly around my foot.

'Come on,' Louise grins down at me. 'There's some dry towels and socks in the minibus. I keep them there especially for rescuing baby dragons and other such emergencies.'

And the two of us trudge back up through the brambles, my bare feet rubbing against the insides of my boots, coating them in a thin layer of mud.

ELEMENT II

Newport witnesses evolution in action

Scientific history was made today when the mud puppy discovered in Newport last month emerged from its freshwater tank and started breathing air for the first time.

The dragonlike creature, which was found in the River Usk by local vicar, Rhodri Jenkins, has spent the past three weeks under the safe-keeping of Allt-yr-yn College. But when Michael Llewellyn-Jones, senior lecturer in biology, went to check on the mud puppy this morning, he found it crouching down on the floor, six feet away from its tank. 'I thought it was dead,' said Dr Llewellyn-Jones. 'Mud puppies have never been known to survive for long out of water. But this one was still alive, and breathing air.'

'It is truly a miracle,' said Rev. Jenkins. His daughter, celebrated local artist Daryl Jenkins, 29, described her own encounter with the mud puppy as 'inspirational'.

Mud puppies are a species of salamander found only in the United States and Canada. They begin life in water, breathing through gills. Like most amphibians, they go on to develop four legs and a complete set of lungs. But, up till now, there have been no recorded findings of mud puppies ever using these lungs or living on dry land. They normally retain their gills and live their entire lives under water. 'It is as if they are stuck halfway,' said Dr Llewellyn-Jones. 'We are seeing this vital evolutionary leap for the first time. This is a momentous occasion for the people of Newport.'

The mud puppy, which is fast becoming a national curiosity, and attracting scientific interest across the world, is being kept under close guard at a secret location within the University of Wales. One mystery local experts hope to clear up is how it came to be found over three thousand miles away from its native habitat.

South Wales Argus
Monday 22 March

Chapter Eight

There was a time when the women of Wales wore wings. Sounds bizarre, I know, like some fairy tale souped up to comply with a feminist agenda. But there was no political separatism involved, the skies were open to everyone. It was just that the majority of men weren't interested in flying. They were way too busy, off fighting the marauding English.

But if you want to know the story you have to reach into the Dream Box, say the magic words.

The whole thing happened long ago, when dragons lived at the foot of almost every mountain in Wales. One summer's morning, a dragon nipped out of its cave to say hello to a woman strolling in the woods near by. When the dragon opened its mouth the gust of hot air that came out blew the woman right off her feet. Naturally, she was terrified. But the dragon explained about thermals and gave the woman a ride on its back to say sorry for scaring her. The woman was so excited by her first flying experience that she built her own set of wings out of balsa wood and old petticoats, and was soon showing them off to all her friends.

'Da-ryl. Da-ryl.'

My father's voice floats up the stairs, through the air vent and breaks my peace and quiet right open.

'Not now, Dad,' I yell, sitting upright, my skin prickling with heat. 'I'm in the bath. I won't be long.'

71

Silence. Slowly I dip down under again, close my eyes and try breathing through water, try to know how that feels, then come back up. Just a bit, just so my nose and mouth are bobbing on the surface. A soap bubble bursts on my chin and the sweet scent of apricot combines with fragrant lavender to infuse the air with the peace of a summer afternoon. Or at least that's what it says it does on the box, but it could just be the manufacturer telling stories.

Talking of stories, where was I? Oh yes.

The months passed and the flying fad spread like dragonfire. Pretty soon, women across the country were travelling the world, heading for far-flung places way beyond anywhere anybody had ever been before, aided by the prevailing westerlies and a little training and technical assistance from the dragons.

There are even reports of women hitching lifts on the jet stream and reaching speeds of over three hundred miles an hour. But these cannot be substantiated.

And the men? Like I said, the men were given every opportunity to join in. But most of them refused and, before long, had forgotten they had ever been invited. Night after night the men returned home to find no supper on the table and their wives and daughters chattering about sunsets over the Masai Mara. The men became jealous and bored and sought revenge. They banded together and slew the dragons. Every single one of them.

Without the dragons' breath the thermals died away. Rain fell almost every day and . . .

The bathroom door bangs open and Dad's clipped grey head peers round the side.

'Daryl? Hello? Are you in there?'

I just have time to pull the shower curtain across, shrink down behind it before Dad is over the other side of the room, opening the window.

'Blimey, it's hot in here,' he says. 'I don't know how you stand it.'

He turns round, takes a step towards me. I tuck the folds of plastic tighter under my chin.

'Dad!'

'What?'

'I haven't got any clothes on!'

'Oh, for heaven's sake,' he says. 'You've got nothing I haven't seen before. I used to change your nappies.' But his neck flushes red all the same and his eyes slide left, scrutinise the wall opposite.

'A thousand years ago maybe. But I've changed quite a bit since then.'

'Yes, all right, love. Sorry. But I needed to ask you something. Something important.'

The shower curtain is fighting to be set free. The bottom of the curtain is cracked and stiff with dirt like it hasn't been cleaned in years. In the struggle a line of mildew brushes across my lip.

'Well, what is it?' I say.

Eyes firmly averted, Dad stretches both arms sideways right and drops a tie down from each hand, dangling their ends six inches from my nose.

'Which one?' he says. 'The blue or the red? I was going with the red but then I remembered TV cameras can't cope with busy patterns. That's right, love, isn't it? You know about these things.'

'Why aren't you wearing your dog collar?' I ask, but I already know the answer.

My father doesn't believe in miracles. The Virgin Birth, turning water into wine, he sees them only in terms of metaphor. Even the Resurrection – that most central of tenets – even on that he's only really prepared to go as far as spiritual ascendance, not physical. He used to preach it, too, until my mother begged him not to. The bishop took her aside one day, told her that rational disbelief was dangerous in a parish priest, and that she should get Dad to consider his position carefully. So from then on Dad kept his mouth shut, toed the party line, even after Mum died. The same way he's kept the tangerine tiles she put up on the bathroom wall even though they clash horribly with the avocado suite.

'I don't want to be cast as the religious clown in a three-ring circus,' Dad says. 'I just want people to concentrate on the facts.'

'But the fact is,' I say, 'if you don't wear your collar, everyone will think you have something to hide. Just look at what the headlines are saying already. The media will use the Church angle whatever you do, so you might as well acknowledge the connection first. At least then you can control it.'

Dad sees the sense of this and consoles himself by pinning his scientific credentials to his lapel with his Wildlife Association Vice-Presidential medal. I guess I should be grateful he's not President. That role comes with a full chain of office.

Dad turns to walk out the door, but hangs back halfway. 'It is a good story, though,' he says. 'The bit about the dragon? I do like it. And your mother would have loved it. She was always making up stories like that for you. Remember?'

'I remember,' I say, smiling at him. I want to say more, I want to tell him how sorry I am, to explain. But nine years of silence stretch themselves out over the bathroom carpet between us. So I just ask him what Mum would have made of us going on TV, whether she'd have been pleased.

'Are you kidding?' Dad says. 'She'd have been in her element.' He smiles back at me, a little bit shy, a bit sheepish. 'Well, anyway, I'll leave you to it,' he says. 'Don't be long now, will you?'

'Five more minutes,' I say. 'I just need to rinse my hair.'

I told Ani the story of the women with wings last night and she loved it. The whole dragon-air thing blew her mind, she

74

said. We were sitting in the living room on the sofa. We were sitting close with our arms and legs just touching. We were sitting there, in the dark, thigh rubbing against thigh, watching the local news. This time tomorrow you'll be on that, she said. You'll be famous and I'll know you. I'll know someone who's been on the telly.

We were supposed to be watching an old Cary Grant movie. The one with Irene Dunne, where she's an explorer who returns home after being shipwrecked for seven years to find her husband has just married another woman. In the video store Ani said it was one of her favourites. But when we took it back to the Vicarage and started watching, it was obvious she'd never seen it before. She was just trying to impress me with how much we had in common.

I didn't mind her lying, though. In fact I quite liked it. And, for once, there was no sign of Kat. I've been trying to get Ani on her own since we first met and last night was my big chance. Thursday night – Dad's Open House night and Kat's regular midweek shift at the garage. In the end we switched off the movie, poured out some more wine and I told Ani the story about the women with wings. Then I told her another. Ani said my stories were miles better than anything out on video. I said we should make it a regular occasion.

Thursday night is story night.

Did you know it was a dragon right away? she said. Did you see it start to breathe? She was squirming on the sofa right up next to me. Was there a moment? she said. There had to be a moment.

That's what I love about her, her ability to get swept away. It's hard to believe that I've known Ani for less than a month. It's hard to believe that there was ever a time when I couldn't close my eyes and picture her face. Her beautiful face.

The first time I saw her, in that petrol station, in that awful nylon overall, I thought she was something out of a dream. I thought I'd closed my eyes and wished for a magic sprite, a celestial being, then opened them again and, flying out of the darkness, I'd seen bright copper hair framing a puckish face. Blue-rimmed eyes, pale cheeks. And, underneath, a mouth as wide as the river.

But her looks are not what's kept me coming back for more, not what's got me so bowled over I can hardly breathe.

We Welsh have a word which doesn't exist in English. *Hwyl*: the mood, the spirit. It can be good or bad. Both pain and pleasure. It's a yearning, a longing for something. That feeling you get in the pit of your stomach when you want something so badly it hurts. Winds of emotion churning around inside you, pushing against the walls of your chest, squeezing up and up, rasping across the back of the throat, then rushing out between gritted teeth in a sickly wail.

I could see it in Ani's eyes, in her whole body last night when she was looking through my portfolio, examining all the photos of my work. I've got pictures of almost everything I've made in that portfolio, from stuff I did in college right up to the present day. Well, almost everything. Everything except the last show. The less said about that the better.

Bending down, leaning in close over every page, Ani glowed with longing. Inside her clothing her skin became transparent, radiated light. Not the constant light of a lamp, but a pulsating luminescence. A stream of molten energy.

She lingered over the piece I'm best known for, the one that first got me noticed by the critics, the one that's part of the contemporary collection at the National Museum of Wales.

Her eyes hovered over the strata of clay, she ran her fingers across the cracked and bleeding face. It must be amazing to have made something that everybody knows, she said. That sculpture will last for ever. Even after you're dead, people will remember you, remember you created something beautiful for them. That's what art's all about, isn't it? she said.

Sometimes, I said. But other times it's more ephemeral than that. The art is in the memory, but it's the memory of a single moment that can never be recaptured: Creation – Emotion – Death. Everything in the same split second. And then it's gone.

That can be art too, I said.

If that's true, she said, then I want both. I want them both, together, at the same time.

You see, Ani understands. She understands everything.

Of course, she's too young for me, I know that. She's what, nineteen? Twenty at the most. God, what am I doing? I'm ten years older than her. But age doesn't matter, does it? Not really. Not when you care for someone. Anyway, I can't help myself. I can't eat, can't sleep. All I can think about is Ani.

I fill up the jug with hot clean water and pour it over my head. Shampoo suds sluice down between my breasts, over my stomach, then bleed cloudy-white into the water.

Can you see them? I said. Can you see the atoms dancing?

Yes, said Ani. I can see them.

We were up on the Ridgeway, giving the dog his last walk of the day. It was very late and, when you turned to face the mountain, very black. Black like you only get on a moonless night in the country. Black that makes no difference whether your eyes are open or shut, it presses into your skull, implodes your brain. But as we walked this solid absence of light became shot through with silver chains, leaving trails of red and blue as they flashed past our eyes.

As they grew, some of the chains began to wrap themselves around my wrists. I struggled but this only made them lock tighter. Then two large chains hung down and looped around my arms, crossed over behind my shoulders, pulling tight. I felt my feet lift up behind me. Instinctively, I held my arms out, rolled and tipped my body to keep my balance, the silver chains preventing me from falling flat on my face. I was terrified that the chains would break if I moved too quickly, but after a couple of minutes I found I could wobble a few feet over the edge of the slope without wanting to throw up.

Ani showed none of my timidity. Arms flapping wildly, she zoomed back and forth across the valley, screaming with laughter. Heart in mouth, I watched her catapult fifty feet up in the air, loop the loop, then nose-dive back down to earth again, just skimming the grass.

You'll kill yourself, I yelled.

Then I'll die happy, she shouted back.

Reality has stolen the heat from the water so I clamber out, wrap myself up in towels like Cleopatra and pad into the bedroom to prepare for my TV debut. My clothes are all laid out on the bed, pressed and ready. The look I'm going for is glamorous and, above all, expensive. No one takes starving artists seriously these days.

When the HTV Wales researcher rang up for background information on Dad, he insisted on telling her about me instead. He rammed down her throat how talented I was. Mind you, he did it in exactly the same way he used to boast about my violin playing when I was ten. Forcing friends and relatives to listen to me scratching and scraping for half an hour while he and Mum beamed out their pride. But it worked well enough for the researcher to go and check her archives. Two hours later she rang back, asking me to bring along my portfolio to see if there was any 'local colour' in it they could use.

Across the landing, Dad is in his study, collating his notes. Making sure he has all the information at his fingertips, ready for all the interviewer's questions. I leave my bedroom door half-open as I get dressed because all the time he's doing this he's talking to me, telling me about Marjorie down the road, Marjorie who lives in the bungalow overlooking the Lane, the one with that huge rhododendron bush out front? Her son David, the one who won a scholarship to Atlantic College, he's some sort of lecturer up at Oxford now, knows all about dragons. Marjorie said David gave her all kinds of interesting facts to pass on to you, love. Like, well, like all that apocalyptic stuff in Revelations. But did you know, Daryl, that the ancient Greeks believed dragons had the ability to convey the secrets of the universe? Yes, I thought you'd find that bit interesting. And apparently, love, even today Chinese people regard the dragon as a symbol of fortune and change.

Chapter Nine

I don't know why Kat's so pissed off with me. I mean, she started it. She's the one who invited Daryl to come out with us in the first place.

'Four weeks ago,' Kat says, her voice all shrill and tight. 'I didn't mean for Billy-no-mates over there to tag along every time we come out.'

'Oh, come on. We haven't had to put our hands in our pockets all night. And it's supposed to be a celebration, isn't it?'

'I thought it was. But you're more interested in sucking up to the rich and famous,' Kat says.

Saturday night. The pub's packed out, but we got here early, grabbed the best table. The one near the porch door where you can be private if you want to, but still get a good view of the stage. Daryl's up at the bar buying more cocktails. Being televised across Wales and the West deserves cocktails, she says. She's taking ages because people keep recognising her. She looks really great tonight. Tall and sexy in black velvet jeans, new haircut off her shoulders. Dead confident, too. Look at her, chatting away to a woman in a denim shirt, then laughing at a joke the bar manager makes. She doesn't know them, she's just being friendly. The whole time she's talking, her fingers are fiddling with the cross round her neck. She always wears it, she says. Her mam gave it to her.

Kat's convinced there's something going on between Daryl and me – ever since she found out about me going over to Daryl's on my own the other night. I've told her I don't think of Daryl like that, but the silly cow's winding herself up about it anyway. Every time Daryl opens her mouth, Kat's in there, sniping. Like when Daryl was describing the look on her dad's face when the TV make-up lady told him he had lovely skin? Straight away Kat starts telling some stupid vicar joke she's heard from Ron down the garage. Talk about embarrassing! She's going to ruin everything if she's not careful.

Kat lights up another cigarette, breathes smoke string out through her nose. 'You know she fancies you, don't you?' she says for the zillionth time.

I pretend I haven't heard her, just keep fiddling with the beer mats, humming along to the music. The stage curtain's covered with silver moons and stars. They weren't there last week. Must be something to do with tonight's act.

Kat whacks the top of my arm. 'Did you hear me? I said Miss TV Personality over there fancies you.'

'Ow. Stop battering me, will you?' I say, rubbing at the sore bit. 'I heard. But Daryl likes both of us, I told you.'

Kat just laughs.

'She does,' I say. 'She told me. She said you were really nice.'

Kat shakes her head and the ends of her hair tickle the back of my hand. 'She might "like" me. But she can't take her eyes off you. See? She keeps turning round to check you're still there,' she says.

We both look over at the bar and right on cue Daryl looks back over her shoulder, gives this cheesy little wave, like the Queen. I don't know what to do so I just wave back. Kat whacks me on the arm again, then yells 'Bitch!' at Daryl just as she turns to pay for the drinks.

'Shut up, she'll hear you,' I say.

'Good,' says Kat.

The two guys holding hands at the table opposite are staring. They're both slapheads, look like twins. I smile at them, shrug my shoulders. The one on the left winks back at me. He's got a biker jacket just like mine, only with buckles round the bottom.

Kat takes no notice, pokes her tongue way down inside her glass, licks out the last of the coconut. Then reaches over and sticks her tongue down my ear.

Warm, wet and wriggly.

I push her away. 'You've got a tongue like a fucking lizard,' I say.

But she knows I like it really. And then she's licking and sucking the back of my neck until I'm warm, wet and wriggly too. I put my arms round her shoulders, thread my fingers through her hair. I love Kat's hair. It's long and shiny and baby soft when you touch it. I keep telling her she should get a job on one of those shampoo ads. Kat's hair is as good as any of those models.

Right then Daryl comes back from the bar, so I brace myself for more aggro. But Kat just says thank you, takes her drink. Daryl sits down and I tell her about my new job.

It's in that swanky new café upstairs in the Waterstone's opposite St David's Hall. The pay's nearly twice as much as the garage. I'll be minting it. Kat's going to apply there too. As soon as Ron has trained up a replacement. I think she should apply now. The café's such a cool place there's bound to be loads of people wanting Saturday jobs. But Kat says she can't leave Ron in the lurch, especially after I walked out on him.

Daryl raises her glass. 'Congratulations,' she says. 'Actually, I've got a new job too. So we've got even more to celebrate.'

'Where's that, then?' Kat asks.

'Supply teaching,' says Daryl. 'I've had my name on the list for weeks now. A job's come up at the school where a friend of mine teaches. She put in a good word for me.'

The room starts spinning around me. 'Which school?' I say.

'Rhiwderin.'

Rhiwderin. Thank God for that! Rhiwderin's miles away.

'Rhiwderin's where all the posh kids go, isn't it?' Kat says.

'It sounds quite ordinary from what Louise tells me,' Daryl says, sips her drink. 'And what about you, Kat?' she says. 'Are you a student, like Ani? Or do you just work in that petrol station?'

'Kat's at college like me,' I say. 'Aren't you, Kat?'

Kat just looks at me.

'What are you studying?'

'Chemistry,' Kat says and squirts pina colada down my mouth with her straw.

I ask Daryl to tell us again about being on telly, about what it was like.

'Kat thought it was great what your dad was saying about the mud puppy, didn't you, Kat?' I say.

'Yeah, I love lizards, me,' Kat says, waggles her tongue at me again, making me snort pina colada out through my nose and all down my shirt.

'Mud puppies are amphibians. I would've thought you'd know that, Kat, being a scientist,' Daryl says.

Kat flicks her hair off her shoulder. 'Whatever,' she says. 'I've got to go to the loo.'

She can be such a cow sometimes.

I watch her walk off, then turn back to Daryl. 'Sorry about that. It's not you she's mad at. It's me,' I say.

'Maybe she just can't stand the competition,' Daryl says.

'What do you mean?' I say.

But from the way Daryl's eyes are laughing and her lips moving I can tell she knows I know exactly what she means. I look down at the table, count the empty glasses. Three pina coladas, one gin and tonic and, in front of those, six beer mats, all stacked from where I was trying to flip them before. I pick the top one up,

Never forget your Welsh

then look up at Daryl again.

It's no good. I'm going to have to tell her.

'Look, I wasn't going to tell you this but tonight's our five-month anniversary. Kat wanted it to be just the two of us,' I say. 'But I went and said you should come too, seeing as you've been on telly and everything. But it's still supposed to be our special night. So stop winding her up, will you?'

That works. Daryl's face droops down in the middle like one of Nana's skirts. 'You should have said something. We could have easily made it another night,' she says.

'Yeah, maybe. But I really didn't think she'd kick off like this. I mean, it's not like it's a year or anything.'

'Do you want me to go?'

'No, you're all right. Just be a bit nicer to her, that's all.'

Daryl hems up her face again, all nice and tight. 'OK. But forgetting your anniversary after only five months doesn't exactly bode well now, does it?'

'Yeah, well, neither does shit stirring,' I snap.

Neither of us can look at each other for ages after that. A girl comes out from behind the bar and sets up a mike on stage. She's cute – bleach crop and a tight zebra print T-shirt. She taps at the mike to make sure it's working, then switches on a tape player. Salsa music starts up and Kat comes back from the loo.

'Listen, Kat,' I say before she can sit down. 'I've told Daryl why you're mad at me, that I forgot our anniversary. She was going to go but I told her she's all right. That's right isn't it? She's all right.'

Kat pinches up her nose like she can smell something bad. 'Yeah,' she says slowly. 'You're all right.'

*

The minute the cabaret starts, I know it's him. I mean, I know it's her. With the lights down and the make-up you can't really tell. I mean, you can tell it's all an act. But what you can't tell for sure is whether it's a 'she' being a 'he', or just a 'he' camping it up.

But it's definitely the same one. That traffic cop. The one who gave me the funny ticket, you know, the flyer offering classes on how to walk like a man? I've tried to ring him loads of times since to find out more about it, but I just keep getting his machine.

Tonight, instead of his cop uniform, he's wearing a frilly white shirt, leather trousers. His hair's tied back with a red bandana and he's got a tiny goatee right in the middle of his chin like a gravy stain. But he still struts about like he owns the place. Still got that fake American accent.

Carlos the Latin Lover bounces across the stage, grabs the mike. The applause dies down. 'Thank yuh. Thank yuh very much,' he says.

Just like Elvis.

'I'd like to begin with a little Tom Jones number. My own special tribute to your bee-u-di-ful country,' he says.

'It's Not Unusual'. He's got all the moves – leg wags, hip swivels. The works. Like Keith, only about a million times better. Right in the middle of the second verse he stops, prances up to a group of queens near the front and thrusts his pelvis in their screaming faces. Then he's straight into his stand-up routine – Mr Sleazeball over from America, hot to trot for all the Welsh girls. His jokes turn the air so blue, it's ultraviolet. I can feel my face tingling in the dark. To end the first half he launches into 'What's New, Pussycat?' Sings it deep and slow, taking off his shirt to show his hairy chest – and full brown breasts in a black leather bra. He finishes by pulling a banana from down the front of his trousers, licking it up both sides like an ice-cream cone and biting off the top.

The audience goes ballistic, mobs him as he runs out the side door. And before my head can have a chance to argue, my legs are pushing me through the crowd and up the stairs after him.

Carlos's dressing room is the room they normally use for line dancing. Stinks of fags and sweaty feet. Grey floorboards. Fold-up grey chairs are stacked in piles against the long wall and there's a bench down the far end where the caller stands and shouts out the steps. When I open the door Carlos is standing in front of a mirror propped up on two empty beer barrels, stripped right down to his underwear. He doesn't turn round when I walk towards him. Just carries on binding his breasts with a bandage, black eyes watching me through the mirror.

I stop three feet behind him and hold out the flyer he gave me, my hand shaking to match my voice.

'I've come about the course,' I say. 'You said I could have a discount.'

He doesn't say anything so I keep talking. I remind him how we met. Go into all the details. In fact, I'm gabbing on so long, Carlos has finished his bandaging, wiped off his beard and patched up his foundation by the time I'm through. But he still says he doesn't remember me. So I explain about Keith. About how I want to learn to do Elvis. How Carlos is a much better Elvis than Keith, even when he's doing Tom Jones.

Carlos nods his head at that. 'Elvis is the King of drag kings,' he says. Then he glances down at my flyer. 'OK, I'll buy it. Looks like my handwriting. You can have your fifty per cent. The next course starts here, Wednesday at seven.'

'The thing is . . .' I say, 'I can't really afford it. Even with the discount.'

'So? I'm not a charity. Get a job.' Carlos reaches in his bag for an eyebrow pencil.

'I've got one. I start next week. But I won't get paid for a month and anyway I'm putting everything I can into my GTFO Fund,' I say.

'Excuse me?' he says, his eyebrow pencil hovering just above his upper lip.

'My Get The Fuck Out Fund. I'm saving to go to London to be famous.'

Carlos laughs so hard he smudges half his moustache, has to start all over again.

I don't see what's so funny about it. I'm sick of everyone laughing at me when I tell them I'm going to be famous. I mean, at least I want to do something with my life.

'Look, just forget it, will you?' I say, start walking back to the door.

But Carlos stops me. 'I'm sorry, kid,' he says. 'But you shouldn't be so sensitive. Or give up so easily.' He starts pencilling in a sideburn. 'I was laughing because I did the exact same thing at your age. Hid my money in an old shoe box.'

'Really? I keep mine in a high interest savings account.'

More laughter. I think he likes me.

'I thought I could maybe work for you,' I say. 'Be your assistant.'

Carlos starts on the other sideburn but keeps his eyes locked on mine through the mirror. 'You say your dad's an Elvis impersonator?'

'Yes. He's been doing it for years. Keith's mad about Elvis. He even called my sister Lisa-Marie.'

Carlos's eyes flick up and down. 'And what did he call you? Priscilla?'

'No. Mam had me before she met Keith. My name's Ani,' I say. 'What about you, what's your name?'

Carlos jerks his head at the flyer still in my hand. 'Like it says.'

'But you must have a real name?' I say. 'A girl's name?'

He shrugs. 'Just Carlos,' he says.

I don't push him. I bet his real name's something embarrassing. Something his mother landed him with. Something stupid like Angharad. I mean, what kind of name is Angharad?

Taking off his bandana, Carlos combs his hair into a side parting, then slicks it down with gel.

'Keith'd kill for your hair. It's just like Elvis's,' I say.

'Yeah?' says Carlos, smoothing the sides flat with his hands. 'Thanks.'

'Keith's hair's mousy brown. He has to dye it. He had terrible trouble getting the colour right at first,' I say. 'Most black dye is blue-black not brown-black, see. Keith says doing Elvis with blue-black hair is almost as bad as wearing a wig,' I say. 'He wouldn't be caught dead in a wig. Now he gets the official dye sent to him, all the way from Memphis. He orders it on the internet.'

Carlos pulls a lock out from his fringe, arranges it in a kiss curl. 'Hair is everything,' he says.

Bit by bit Carlos finishes his make-up and puts on his costume. I try to help him as much as I can. For the second half he's going to be what he calls a New York Dandy, in a three-piece suit and cravat. As he pulls on his trousers, I notice he's got a bulge in his underwear. It's not big enough to be a banana. I want to ask him what it is but I'm too scared, so I just ask where he's from. Turns out he really is American. And he's a cop too. He gets his badge out to prove it. One of New York's finest, he says. He and some mates are over here on an exchange. Something about zero tolerance. But although he lives there now, he's not from New York originally. He grew up in Iowa. Carlos says Iowa is like Wales, only with corn.

Just then the cute bar girl comes upstairs and tells Carlos it's time for the second half.

'Sorry, kid, gotta go now,' he says, checking his reflection one more time, making sure everything is perfect.

Shit. This is it. He's going to walk away. I'll never see him again.

'Yeah. OK. Bye then.'

I shove the flyer back inside my jeans, hang my chin down on my chest.

'Tell you what,' Carlos says, 'be here Wednesday night, six-thirty sharp, and help me get ready for class. If you don't kill anyone you can be my assistant for the duration.'

I practically fly down the stairs I'm so happy. I want to leap around on the stage, tell everyone my news. But when

I get back down to the bar, no one's interested in me. They're all too busy crowding round our table watching Kat being held back from scratching Daryl's eyes out by the slaphead in the biker jacket.

'I know what you're after, you bitch,' Kat screams, twisting and kicking under the guy's armlock. 'I'm not stupid, you know.'

Daryl folds her arms, leans back on her heels. 'Really?' she says. 'That's not how it looks from where I'm standing.'

Chapter Ten

Down the bottom of the drive, the first thing you notice is the green. Copper roof, spring foliage, pine trees. Russet brick walls first serving only as a base note, but then leading you up the curving drive to the splash of scarlet door in the olive annexe. Behind it, Main Building, with its tower at one end, high oblong windows, looking more like a church than a school.

But when I open my eyes, fat drops of disappointment rain down on the contours of the landscape, bleeding the colours together, draining it all away to sludge. What did that last review say? *Pedestrian. Two-dimensional. Second-rate.* I should face facts. Ten years, that was my lot. Not even that. My last really decent idea was three years ago.

Seven years of plenty and now a lifetime of famine.

I rip the sketch out of the pad, then turn the page and rip it again, right in half. I keep ripping and turning, ripping and turning, until I'm left with a sheaf too thick to break, so I crush it in my palm, squeezing until my knuckles turn white and I can feel the blood throb through the veins of my hands.

Maybe Ani's right, maybe some of it was my fault. Maybe I did let Kat get to me. Ridiculous, I know, but I couldn't help myself. The way she delighted in flaunting their relationship in front of me. Kat's arm lying across the seat, fingertips stroking Ani's neck. Kat's mouth flipping the lobes of Ani's ears, whispering hearts and flowers. Kat's tongue swabbing back and forth, licking Ani, insides out.

And Ani. Ani, the most beautiful I've ever seen her, soft and shining. Golden. The lights from the bar dancing in her hair, deepening the shadow of her collarbone.

I couldn't help myself.

But tonight things will be different. I'll make it up to her. Tonight we'll soar again. Yes, I feel better already knowing that I'm going to see her tonight. My night. Story night.

*

Supply teaching is harder than I thought. No simple matter of turning up, no lessons to plan. This week I've been teaching Key Stage 3, GCSE, A, you name it. And with barely enough time to bone up on the objectives for each level. At all levels you're supposed to illustrate understanding, investigation and imagination. You're supposed to include a Welsh dimension. So I've been talking boundaries, I've been talking relationships, I've been talking change.

I've been talking till I'm blue in the face.

Can science be represented through art?

Respiration occurs when inhaled air passes into the lungs, down smaller and smaller tubes until it reaches tiny air sacs, called alveoli, only one cell thick. Oxygen from the air travels across the alveoli cell membranes to the blood capillaries on the other side, which are also only one cell thick.

Air on one side. Blood on the other.

But what do you call the space between the two sides?

Elements of colour, shape and texture can be used to create movement. Enough movement to shock the viewer's eye.

Being confronted by so much Welsh has been my biggest shock on return. Not just the odd phrase flashing past on a road sign, but paragraphs. Pages of information saying the same thing and saying not the same thing. Twice over.

It's been so long since I immersed myself in my mother

tongue that I almost drowned the first couple of days. I couldn't believe how much cross-referencing I had to do with the English side of the page. Told myself it was just the jargon I didn't understand, but it wasn't. Slowly, though, the confusion cleared and by yesterday I was spooning sentences whole into my mouth, letting them wrap themselves around my tongue, ooze between my teeth like warm rice pudding. I didn't realise I was speaking aloud until I looked up into the baffled faces of Year Nine.

Welsh speakers are the in thing, these days. Cymraeg is definitely cool. But Newport is a border town, its loyalties are split down the middle. Yes, the Welsh flag flies from the churches and public buildings. Yes, Newport has two seats in the Welsh Assembly. Yes, the current Archbishop of Wales resides in Newport. But although the road signs are all bilingual, English is usually on top. The county name oscillates between Gwent and Monmouthshire. And TV viewers can pick up either Cardiff or Bristol stations depending on which way their aerials are pointing.

In Newport, if you're wanting to learn a second language it's probably French.

In creating art, you use your knowledge and understanding of the work of others to stimulate your own thought processes.

When I was growing up, Welsh was my family's language of choice. My mother insisted on it. My mother said all the best stories were Welsh stories. My mother's name was Eirwen. Yet another funny Welsh name. But for once it's even funnier in English. Snow White, that's what Eirwen means in English. My father's name is almost as bad, Rhodri, King or Ruler of the Circle. For years I didn't see anything strange about this. Until I was six they were just my parents' names. Bilingual children that age don't differentiate between their languages, they switch them around willy-nilly. So when I was six and my mother pulled a rosy red apple out of the Dream Box and told me the story of Snow White and the Seven Dwarfs, I thought she was telling me about the time she met my dad, Prince Charming, and how, in the Happy Ever After Land, the two of them went on to be King and Queen and have me, Daryl, their 'most beloved'.

At least that's what I told my friends at school the next day. Of course they all thought it was hysterical. After that, Welsh became my secret, if not my shame. I even refused to speak it at home for a while. My mother was livid, our battle raged for months. But she should have expected it, she should have known.

You see, Daryl's not a Welsh name. It's Anglo-Saxon.

Eventually we reached a compromise. But when I was thirteen my mother died and neither me nor Dad could bring ourselves to keep up the Welsh after that.

Then I moved to London.

I wish I had a pound for every Londoner who's told me about the time they went to Wales on holiday. How they walked into this pub and everyone was speaking English, but the minute they opened their mouths and ordered a drink the locals switched to Welsh, just to make the point. And then there's all the people who snigger at the way I say saucepan and toothbrush and here. But the ones who really take the piss, the ones who make me so angry I want to stamp on their heads until their brains shoot out of their ears, are the jokers who hawk and spit at your feet when you approach.

'That's how you say hello in Welsh,' they tell you, grinning like baboons.

Shit like that is hard to keep fighting on a daily basis. A lot of Welsh people I know in London don't even try, they just dump their accent, blend right in. One guy even makes out he was born in Bermondsey. But then again, if I was from Barry I'd probably lie about it too. I've not sold out myself, mind. Oh no. Gone the London way instead, used my Welshness to my own advantage. Or at least I thought I had. But when I watched the videotape of Dad and me on

TV the other night, the main thing that came across was how English I sounded.

Most subjects are transformed by the angle of the light which falls on them.

Even after a month I still can't get used to how friendly people are here. In London, if a stranger comes up to you on the street, you assume they're going to ask you for money. In Newport they're just commenting on how nice it is that spring has finally arrived.

I guess the bottom line is there is no bottom line, the boundaries are all blurred. The deeper you go, the closer you look, the harder it is to see. Respiration occurs as a chemical reaction when energy is released. Or rather when energy is changed from the restricted form of a chemical bond to another, freer form. When it comes down to it, all we are composed of – all of us, everything – is energy. Energy is all there ever is.

Justine Powell! Once again I have to single you out. Stop throwing clay around and sit down. Now!

*

Break time. I lock up the Art room and head up to Main Building for something to eat. As I cross the car park I notice two boys crouching over their rucksacks between the wire fence and a red hatchback. I recognise them both from my Year Seven registration group. Rhys James and David Something-or-other. Their body language screams illegal recreational activity. I walk quietly over.

'What are you up to there, boys?' I say.

Rhys, tall with blond hair, jumps then stuffs something, I can't see what, into his coat pocket. David, darker and weedy looking, shoves a small white box into his rucksack. When he turns round to face me, a thin plume of smoke drifts away behind him.

'Have you two been smoking?' I ask.

'No, miss,' they chorus.

'Right then, you won't mind showing me what's in your pockets, will you?' I say and hold out my hand.

Neither boy moves. Behind me, an audience is collecting along the grass verge. Whispers of anticipation. I ignore them.

'Come on, show me,' I say again.

Reluctantly David dips his hands into his pocket and pulls out the cigarettes.

'And the matches,' I say.

The loot handed over, Rhys skips backwards down the side of the hatchback and darts away. David tries to follow him but he's too slow. I catch hold of his hood, spin him round to face me and place my hands square on his shoulders.

'Get off him, you big fat bully,' yells Rhys.

Laughter and nudges from the crowd.

'Yeah,' says David, wriggling under my grip. 'Fuck off me.'

I glare down at him. 'What did you say?'

'I said fuck off me,' he says again, but his bravado cracks halfway out.

I pull the little shit nearer, anger popping in my ears. But then I hear a snigger from behind. Sensing my hesitation, David seizes his opportunity and twists my arm back and up until I'm forced to pirouette underneath, to keep my balance. As I turn I stumble over the straps of his rucksack trailing on the ground, fall forward, landing with a thump on my right hip.

The next thing I know Rhys and David are standing over me, their faces white and frightened. My hands hurt like hell and when I look down I see bits of skin hanging off, the palms pockmarked and crusty with gravel. Rolling up into a sitting position, I push myself to my feet using just my knuckles like a gorilla and limp up to Main Building. Both boys bolt away in opposite directions across the yard. As he runs David's coat slips down off his shoulders and the orange lining of his hood pokes out at me like a giant tongue.

The staff room is empty, thank God, except for Louise sprawled across three chairs, eating an apple and leafing through the paper. I drag myself over to the first-aid cabinet above the sink, then flop down opposite her and dab gingerly at my elbows with TCP-soaked cotton wool.

Louise glances up from the paper, her eyes widening in surprise. Her black and white wrap-around skirt has unwrapped itself, exposing the muscle of her thigh.

'Whatever happened to you?' she says.

'Don't ask,' I say, running my fingers up my arms, checking for further damage. 'I reckon I'm just not cut out for this teaching lark.'

'Sure you are,' Louise says. 'Robert says the kids don't know what's hit them, all the work you've been doing.'

'So how come I'm the one with bloody knees? Look at me,' I say, lifting up my skirt, 'and I'm supposed to be going out tonight, too.'

Louise grins at me knowingly. 'Is this why I've hardly seen anything of you lately? Got yourself a hot date, have you?'

'Kind of,' I say.

Since I came back home Louise and I have seen quite a bit of each other. Once, twice a week we've gone out – pizza, the movies, that sort of thing. Nothing unusual but still nice. Very nice. We're becoming real friends again. There's just one subject I haven't broached yet . . .

'Someone special, is it?' says Louise. 'Have you shagged him yet?'

I keep my eyes fixed on my wounds.

'No, nothing like that. It's only been a few weeks. We're just enjoying getting to know each other. You know, playing it slow.'

'What's there to know? You either fancy someone or you don't. It took me three hours to get Greg's knickers off. That's about as slow as I ever want to play it,' she says.

'It's complicated,' I say, flicking bits of gravel off my right knee. 'I'm not sure anything's going to happen. I might just be making a colossal fool of myself.'

Louise shrugs. 'Just throw yourself at him. Then if nothing happens, well, at least you'll know where you stand.'

'Suppose so,' I say.

Oh, this is ridiculous. I should just come out with it. I've been trying to tell her for weeks now. All those cosy little chats at her flat, waiting for the right moment. Well, here it is. And it's not like she's going to be shocked or anything. Look at her, she's reading the *Guardian* for heaven's sake. Anyway, she probably already knows. She probably worked it out way before I did, at school. She's probably just waiting for me to confide in her so she knows our friendship is secure, has reached that deeper level.

'What's his name?' asks Louise. 'Do I know him?'

'Actually it's a woman,' I say, all of a rush. 'Her name's Ani. I don't think you know her, she's quite a bit younger than us, she's an art student at Cardiff and we haven't done anything yet because she's seeing someone else at the moment, but I don't think it'll be for much longer. I know she likes me, she really likes me, she keeps inviting me out with her, with them, all the time and she wouldn't do that if she didn't like me, would she?'

The tick of the clock on the wall. Louise staring at me, mouth hanging open.

'You mean you're ...'

'I'm gay,' I say.

'But you wear skirts, make-up. You don't look like a ...'
And she casts her eyes downwards, notices the flaps of her skirt hanging loose, picks up both edges and folds them one over the other across her lap, then weights her modesty carefully down with her hands.

Maybe it's the sting of the antiseptic but all of a sudden I'm not nervous or embarrassed any more, just sick to death of her fake liberalism, her smug marriedness.

'A lesbian? You can say it, you know. It's only a word, it won't kill you.'

'I know… it's just, it's just such a surprise,' she stammers.

This makes me laugh so hard I snort all over my chin and hand. 'Oh come on, it's all over the place these days. TV, films, books, you name it.'

'Not in Newport,' Louise says firmly.

'Please,' I say. 'Newport's got its fair share, all right. I had two of them cruising me in Commercial Street last Saturday morning.'

'I just meant I don't know any.' Louise blushes. Then, tucking a stray hair behind her ear, she leans forward and, still holding her skirt together with her elbow, takes hold of my snot-sprayed hand, understanding burnishing her eyes. 'I'm sorry,' she says. 'I'm not handling this very well, am I? What I'm trying to say is it doesn't change the way I feel about you. It doesn't matter.'

I snatch my hand away. 'It matters to me,' I say.

Chapter Eleven

Next Saturday morning. I'm a barista. That's what you get called when you can work the espresso machine, when you've passed the course. Me and the other new girl, Hayley, had to be over on Queen Street before eight this morning so we could be baristas by lunchtime. Took for ever. Before we could get our hands anywhere near the espresso machine, Sharon the trainer had to do all the theory stuff first. Droning on and on. Boring crap about strengths and roasts, how many zillion times bacteria reproduce in ten minutes. Just when I thought she'd finally dried up and we could have some fun, she started listing all the cakes and sandwiches we'd be serving.

Cream cheese bagels
Almond croissants
Mozzarella and sun-dried tomatoes on ciabatta

But my favourites are the hazelnut biscotti. I've had three of those. And the little bags of chocolates in the shape of coffee beans.

The espresso machine looks ever so complicated, all those buttons and handles. But it's dead easy really, when you get used to it. You just have to set your routine up right, from the beginning. The trick is not to fill the portafilter too full before you tamp down, remember to stroke the ears to get rid of the excess grains. And you've got to be quick. The shots shouldn't take more than twenty-three seconds to come out, run like honey off a spoon. Once the shot is in the cup you have to serve it or pour in the milk within ten seconds else the crema, the foamy head bit, loses its lustre.

I'm not really sure what the lustre is. I thought it was the espresso going cold, but it would take more than ten seconds for that to happen, wouldn't it? Don't suppose it really matters though, as long as it's done right. Sharon reckons I'm a natural. She says I have totally grasped the knack of listening and responding to the coffee and helping it reach its highest flavour potential.

Hayley's useless. When you're on the machine you're supposed to call the orders back to the person on the till so they know you've got them. But Hayley keeps mixing everything up and she never gets the angle of the jug right when she has to foam the milk. The one time she did, when the foam rushed up the side, the silly cow was so scared she dropped the jug, sending boiling hot milk all over the place. So Sharon told her to stay on the till. But Hayley's even crap at that, keeps jamming it. I mean, what moron can't work a till? Sharon's so pissed off with her now, I reckon she's just waiting for Hayley to do one more stupid thing so she can sack her, which will be good because then Kat can come and work here instead like we planned.

I fucking love this place. I love the way they let you sit here reading the books without buying them. The way they've got the newspapers hanging off the walls on long wooden poles. Even the uniform's cool. The colours match the cups and you can mix and match them any way you want. The brighter the better, Sharon says. So today I'm wearing the red apron, the orange T-shirt and the green baseball cap.

Carlos really took the piss when he saw me, called me a colour-blind uniform slave.

Like he can talk!

But he likes it really, eats in this place all the time back home, he says.

Carlos reckons this café is EXACTLY like the ones in New York, right down to the napkins.

*

Talk about busy. I've been grinding and tamping non-stop since two. I'm shagged out. But by the time Daryl comes in at five it's all gone quiet again, just a couple of stragglers not yet gone home for their tea.

As soon as I see Daryl – even though I knew she was coming – even though I asked her to come, my stomach starts to fizz like there's this tiny little worm, red hot, spinning round inside me. Bringing it all back to me – how she was on the phone Thursday, too fucking weird for words. Acting like I was cancelling our wedding or something, when it was only supposed to be a drink, for goodness sake.

I guess I should have known she was weird from all that flying business last week. I mean, look at her now with no coat on, hair plastered down in rats' tails, soaking wet from the rain outside. Her shirt's so wet, it's two-tone. Tidemark right across her chest and arms. She's such a sight the two last customers look up from their books and stare. But Daryl just keeps coming, like a tank – up and over the counter, flattening me, then crashing through the wall and toppling down to the street outside.

She doesn't even bother to say hello, just jumps straight in. I'm expecting more aggro, more whingeing, but what I get completely floors me.

'I'm sorry about last week, Ani. My behaviour was totally out of order,' she says. 'I had far too much to drink. But that's no excuse, I know. Can you and Kat ever forgive me?' Splattering raindrops across the counter, she stands there staring at me like her legs will collapse if she takes her eyes off me for a single second.

101

I'm so gobsmacked I can't speak. Out of the corner of my eye I can see Hayley rubbing a cloth slowly up and down the steam wand, her giant Spock ears flapping in the breeze. So I pull myself together.

'It's OK, we were all pissed. I had a raging hangover all day Sunday,' I say. 'And I'm sorry about cancelling on you Thursday. But after what happened I thought it best if Kat and I were on our own. Just for a few days.'

This is a big lie. Kat wants me to tell Daryl to bugger off completely. Giving me real earache about it, she is. But if I do that I'll never get my shit together in time. So I've got to keep the two of them separate, just till things blow over. I've got no choice.

'What can I get you?' I say, trying to make my face look like her gawping doesn't bother me.

For a second she doesn't catch my meaning, so I jerk my head up to the menu board behind me and light slowly dawns.

'Oh, right, yes,' she says, 'Regular cappuccino, please.'

Pointing her to the table opposite, I move over to the espresso machine, giving Hayley my best fuck off and die stare on the way. Hayley goes beetroot and starts loading the dishwasher up with dirty cups. Bet you a fiver she cracks at least three.

Right, two regular cappuccinos coming up:

pull down dosing lever, tamp coffee into filter,
stroke ears and hook into the machine, OK.
Steam milk, espresso down twenty-two seconds, great,
jug in left hand, hold back foam with spoon,
pour, pour,
brush foam in.

Perfect.

I take the coffees – yellow saucer, red cup for Daryl, green saucer, blue cup for me – and a clean tea towel over to the table. As I sit down I notice some moron has scrawled the initials P.H. on the table in blue biro. Next to them is a booklet: CENTRE FOR VISUAL ARTS in thin white letters along the side. The cover's a photo of a life-sized naked Barbie doll on a desert island with cactuses. I lick my finger and try rubbing the letters out, but they've been scratched right down through the varnish into the wood. And this café's only been open a month, too. Bloody vandals. Can't leave anything nice round here.

I give up rubbing and flick through the booklet instead. The inside pages are half English, half gobbledegook.

'What d'you get this for? Didn't they have it in proper English?' I say, dropping the booklet back down on the table again.

'Yes, of course, but I need the practice,' says Daryl.

'Waste of time if you ask me,' I say.

Daryl peels her wet scarf off her neck, scrapes her chair back from the table, bends forward until her head is right between her knees, then rubs her hair hard with the tea towel. When she sits back up her face is bright red and her hair is all fluffed up around her head in tight curls.

It's not that she's not cute. Just too weird and intense.

'Didn't you do Welsh at school?' she says, pats her face and neck dry, then drapes the towel over the back of her chair.

'Oh yeah, the teachers were always going on about it, how useful it was. They even told us about this tiny place the other side of the world...'

'Patagonia?'

'That's it. They made this huge deal about it. See? You can travel the world and speak Welsh, they said. Pathetic it was.'

I reach over and grab some cookies off the counter – stem ginger and acacia honey – been saving myself for them. Yummy.

'I take it you were never interested in going,' says Daryl. 'To Patagonia?'

'As if!' I choke on my cookie and start a coughing fit so loud that Sharon, over by the stairs, stops talking to her mate and turns round to see who's dying. Daryl slaps me on the back and the cookie goes down the right way.

'Who wants to go to some crazy place in the jungle where they probably marry their brothers?' I say, great big chunks of cookie still sticking in my throat. 'Time warp, too, I bet. They probably all still wear those stupid pointy Welsh hats in Patagonia,' I say.

Daryl laughs, dunks a cookie in her coffee, then stares over at the bookshelves next to us, sucking on her cookie with a dreamy expression on her face.

'What is it about Welsh culture that it gets pushed deep inside to the most inaccessible places? You think it's disappeared altogether but somehow it manages to hang on, clinging to the cliffs of your subconscious.'

See what I mean? She talks like that all the time, like she's in some saddo documentary programme on BBC2. I bet she's got a stupid pointy hat at home, too.

'Go on then, how many times have you had a conversation in Welsh since you've come home?' I say. 'Not reading books, actually talking to someone?'

Daryl lifts up one shoulder.

'There you are, see. I bet you don't even think in Welsh,' I say.

'No, not really,' she says. 'Sometimes something reminds me of my childhood and the odd phrase comes into my head, like snatches of a song that...'

I can see she's getting that moony look on her face again so I shove another cookie at her gob, quick sharp. She takes the hint and eats it.

'Anyway, Cardiff's the capital city. You can't not have Welsh spoken in the capital,' she says when she's finished munching.

'Maybe. But it's all got way out of control,' I say. 'Keith – my stepdad? – his mate Brian works for the Social over in

Maindee and he says there's a woman in his department who insists on speaking Welsh all the time, even when she talks to people just down the corridor. She'll talk English to them down the pub all right, but not when she's working. When she's working it's nothing but Welsh and the official interpreter. Now is that barmy, or what?'

'It's the principle,' says Daryl.

'Principle! If she was from North Wales, *Welsh* Wales, maybe. But she's from Newport like the rest of us. It's all just a big wank, and so's she.'

Then I realise what I've said, can feel the blotches come out on my neck. So I yank my cap over my eyes, run my nail up the curve of the P. Frill of blue dirt shooting up my thumb. When I look up again Daryl is leafing through her art booklet like nothing has happened. She catches me peeking, stops reading and smiles.

'What happened at your workshop Wednesday night?' she says. 'Was it any good?'

I tell her we're taking it step by step, that all we did last week was practise being loud and taking up space. You know, like men do on buses, sitting with their legs wide apart as if their balls are so huge they can't possibly bring their knees together to give you room to sit down. Not that we've got on to balls properly yet, though. That's the week after next, after make-up. We only touched on them when we were practising sitting.

Carlos says the trick is not to wear your balls too high. Most drag kings use rolled-up socks, which are OK generally, but condoms stuffed with cotton wool give a much more accurate shape and texture on squeezing.

That got the gigglers in the group going, I can tell you.

Our homework this week is to stare at men's crotches. We have to study exactly where the bulge lies when men are seated, how their jeans fold, and how the bulge moves when they're standing. I've been trying it out all day today. But I haven't had much luck so far. Most of the men who've come in here have had their coats done up because it's raining, and the ones who haven't have been wearing baggy jeans. It's very frustrating. At the end of the course Carlos says we're going to have a drag king contest and the winner can perform with him downstairs in the club on the following Saturday night.

I have to win. I have to.

'I'm sure you will,' says Daryl.

I don't say anything, just scrape up the last of the foam with my spoon. The chocolate tastes like chalk and grit all mixed together.

Daryl glances at her watch. 'I have to go soon,' she says. 'I promised Dad I'd pick him up at six. On the phone you said you had something to ask me?'

I shift in my seat, clean the rest of the crud out of my nails. 'The thing is . . .' I say.

'Yes?'

'You know I was telling you about this end of year project I've got to do for College . . .'

'Yes.'

'I really wanted to do something different, something eye-catching . . .'

'Sounds great. What do you have in mind?'

'Well, that's just it . . .'

'What is?'

'I'm a bit stuck and I was wondering if you'd be able to help me, give me some ideas,' I blurt out, all in a rush.

Daryl's face looks like she's just come up with the Thunderball on her Lottery ticket.

'What about your family?' she says.

'Oh, they're no use. They know nothing about art.'

'No, I mean you could use your family,' she says. 'Keith's Elvis gear, the furniture. Anything you can get your hands on.'

And then she's laying it all out for me, all these fantastic ideas. She's got the whole thing sorted in about three minutes. It's amazing.

Pop art with a whole new spin. In this post-postmodern world you can break all the rules, she says. Anything goes. I don't know why I didn't think of it myself. We'll set the whole thing up in a loft. Not in Chelsea, nothing radical ever happens in Chelsea any more. Somewhere in the East Village, off St Mark's Place maybe. In the daytime it will be an art gallery, like a drag king doll's house. Only life-size, with whole rooms as installations. And, at night . . . at night the dolls will come alive. It'll be like nothing that's ever been done before. I mean, Carlos told me about that club on 13th Street. But it was only open at night and it's closed down completely now.

Daryl raps her spoon on my knuckles. 'Earth to Ani, Earth to Ani,' she says.

'What? Oh, sorry, I was miles away.'

'So I noticed.'

She makes ready to leave, stuffing the Art Centre booklet into her bag.

'Why don't we go down to London for a few days, check out all the latest exhibitions? You might pick up some ideas,' she says. Then her smile stretches right across her face. 'We could stay at my flat,' she says, 'if that would be all right with you, of course.'

Kat's face flips up in front of my eyes with a snap. But I push it back down again.

'All right?' I say. 'It's awesome.'

Fucking awesome. I can't believe Daryl ever wanted to come back to Wales. If I had a flat in London you wouldn't see me in Wales for dust. I bet her flat is dead arty too – paintings and stuff everywhere, even in the bathroom. I bet that's exactly what it's like.

We make arrangements to meet up the next day, to make proper plans. Daryl reckons we'll have to stay down in London for at least a week to do all the galleries, there's that many of them. Then she leaves, and I'm just dreaming of what it'll be like until ten minutes to closing when a bloke comes in for some tea. And I can't believe my luck because he's wearing a pair of purple trousers so tight you can see his dick pinned against his thigh like a squashed slug. When he goes to sit down I follow him over, wipe down his table, then accidently-on-purpose drop my dishcloth on the floor so I can see how the slug looks in the sitting position. But the sleazeball catches me looking and starts rubbing his hand up and down his crotch, moaning.

I scramble up off the floor as quick as I can, kick out with my foot. I mean just to give him a fright, catch the chair leg. But my foot misses and I kick him hard on the shin, making him squeal like the rat he is.

Pervert.

Chapter Twelve

Every word of my stories is the truth, the whole truth and nothing but the truth.

And if you believe that, well, God help you.

What a beautiful morning. Dad's garden in the spring sunshine, the wisteria creeping up the pergola, its trusses casting rippling shadows across the lawn. Ani and me, strolling around the garden, admiring the early irises. Tiffany windows. Celebrations of birdsong showering down from sycamore trees.

Ani and me, sitting under the pergola, drinking coffee and talking about art.

Ani, sitting in the spring sunshine, not talking about Kat. Ani's face, bloated with tears, not talking about turning up here at five past eight, three hours early, banging on the door to be let in. Ani's mouth, not quite smiling at Dad making her breakfast while I frantically pull on some clothes. Ani's eyes, never looking directly into mine, welling up the one time I mention Kat's name.

Now just Ani, leaning back against the post of the pergola, telling me whopping great stories about life in New York, how awesome it is. Awesome being Ani's new word. Awesome being Carlos.

Me, wanting to kill Carlos.

But how can you kill someone who doesn't exist?

At twelve o'clock Dad comes back from church and says he's going over to Cardiff to check on the mud puppy, wants to know if Ani would like to meet Newport's very own scientific phenomenon. Ani thinks it would be awesome. I wonder who on earth would want to be stuck in some mouldy biology lab all afternoon when they could sit in spring sunshine instead. But Dad insists I come, says he has a surprise for me.

I hate surprises.

You'll like this one, Dad promises.

Down by the car I let Ani take the front seat. Dad reaches over to unlock the back door.

Ani and Dad. Dad and Ani. His clipped grey head. Her curved cheek. She, chatting away. He, listening, nodding.

This is how it could be. This is how it should be.

If it weren't for Mum.

'Do you think it's weird?' Ani asks. 'Dressing up and pretending to be somebody else? Kat does. Kat reckons me and my family are completely mad. She says we freak her out.'

'Kat sounds like she's scared of what she doesn't understand,' Dad says.

We drive up the motorway, past Tredegar House. Captain Morgan's rum. It's raining now, the drops sharp and hard, forcing the spring sunshine over towards Twmbalam, and when I open the window the wind roars like a motorbike through the gap. A giant cumulonimbus towers above St Melon's like a forger's anvil. Hovering inches above the flat-iron top, through the single patch of clear sky, is the moon.

'Look at that cloud,' I say, leaning forward to push my face between the plastic headrests. 'If you climbed up and stood on top, you could touch the moon.'

'Do you know what clouds are made of?' Dad says.

'Candy floss and cream cheese?' Ani giggles.

Dad shakes his head. 'That's the fluffy white ones, but the ugly grey ones, they're made up of all the swear words

110

people come out with over the course of a day. That big black one's yours, Ani,' he teases.

Not true, of course. Truly, clouds are chips of ice so small the air currents easily keep them billowing in the sky. Around these tiny truths, even smaller facts of nitrogen, oxygen, carbon-dioxide are colliding, arguing, clinging to each other for support. None of them can survive for long on their own. Mother Nature is not too fond of free radicals – too quirky, too explosive, too unstable. Only the plodders, the inerts, remain single all their lives.

But there are only traces of those, thank God.

Have you ever wondered why the atmosphere doesn't all float away? All that constant bumping and grinding, you'd have thought the gases would have all scarpered by now, boldly gone where no gas has gone before.

It's all down to gravity, of course. Every child knows that.

But escape is not impossible. Scientists have shown – don't ask me how exactly, maths was never my strong point – that if you launch a ball up at an initial speed of 6.98 miles per second or greater, it will keep rising. And rising.

You don't believe me? How do you think they launched all those probes out into deep space? It took a lot of work though. 6.98 miles per second is pretty damn fast.

Of course, most of us never reach the escape speed, and those of us who do are usually nowhere near enough the edge to get away before we crash into an acquaintance and get distracted, go hurtling off in another direction, down again, or sideways, forgetting we ever wanted to leave in the first place. But the truly determined can always make it. Stands to reason. If NASA can get a man on the moon, a couple of oxygen atoms can make it out into the wide black yonder.

Have you ever wondered what we'd find when we got where we were going?

Aristotle used to tell this story that the world was made up of four shells, the four elements of matter. Earth, Water, Air

111

and an invisible outer shell of Fire that can only be glimpsed on stormy nights. Beyond these shells, Aristotle said, was not the endless vacuum of interplanetary space, but an eerie fifth element, a quintessence, vastly superior to the other four. *Aether*, a physical representation of perfection.

According to Aristotle, if you want to reach perfection you have to keep climbing. But it's not easy. Most people, even if they make it as far as the edge, don't have the courage and strength of purpose to break through the ring of fire.

Ani runs her fingers down the window, traces the outline of the cloud.

'I do,' she says, 'I will.'

Then she twists her neck and looks back at me.

'I mean, I would if it weren't just a story,' she says.

Dad parks the car in St Andrew's Crescent and we battle the wind through empty Sunday afternoon streets to the University. Dad striding ahead while Ani and I lag behind, peering into dark Victorian windows, trying to uncover their secrets. At least the rain has stopped, thank God. Don't you just love Welsh weather?

'I wish I lived in a house like that,' Ani sighs, pointing to the biggest, then she tells me how awful it is living with her family, how she's desperate to leave.

But when I ask her why she doesn't move into a student house she just shrugs, says she can't afford it.

'They can't be that expensive, not if you share,' I say. 'Check out the noticeboard at the student union. You'll find somewhere.'

'I can't afford anywhere,' she sneers. 'It's all right for you, you've got a flat in London.'

'A basement studio in Hackney doesn't make me rich or posh,' I say.

'And what about that big posh house up Allt-yr-yn your dad lives in?'

'The Vicarage? That doesn't belong to us. That belongs to the church.'

'Doesn't matter. You're all still posh. You're all so posh up Allt-yr-yn you don't even wash your cars on Sundays,' she says.

Waiting to cross Park Place, my eyes trail down Ani's body as she presses the button on the pelican crossing, then shoves her other hand down the front pocket of her jeans, jangling her loose change. She looks like she could take over the world today. Legs splayed, shoulders back, stomach pushed forward. No sign of her earlier distress. When she steps across the road she actually swaggers.

'It's my new boots,' she says when I ask her what her secret is. 'They're men's. Carlos says it's really important to wear men's boots because men's boots are wider than women's, even when they're practically the same model.'

Then she stamps her foot on the ground and rocks both feet from side to side as if to show that's the only way her feet could possibly touch the edges, the boots are so roomy.

'And it's true. The minute I put them on I felt like I was standing on the ground for the first time, like nothing could get in my way,' she says.

'Tough girl, heh?' I say.

Ani hooks her thumbs through the loops of her jeans, flicks back her eyes and rolls her hips.

'You betta believe it, sister,' she drawls.

'Awesome,' I reply.

'Come on, you two, stop dawdling,' shouts Dad from all the way over by City Hall, his cassock flapping against him, outlining his legs.

As Ani and I run giggling past the National Museum I wonder if my sculpture is still on display or if it has been locked away in some basement, out of sight, out of favour.

Up Edward VII Avenue, the University buildings stand like elephants at the circus, all polished up and trumpeting their longevity and stature. Dad stops outside the Bute Building, former palace of engineering and now Schools to Architecture and Journalism.

The Bute Building, with its landmark red dragon flying from the roof, holding a red iron cog in its paw. Where else would you hide a mud puppy?

'Just Mike's little joke,' says Dad. 'Besides, we could hardly keep it at the Biology Department, could we? That's the first place the journos would look.'

He gallops off across the grass. 'Come on,' he yells from the corner. 'Mike told the caretaker to keep the side door open for us.'

But the side door remains firmly locked so Dad goes off in search of keys while Ani and I sit down on the kerb to wait.

To pass the time I regale Ani with stories of my artistic life in London. Stories about admiring people who tell me I am the Barbara Hepworth of my generation. Stories about how many times I've been thrown drunk and disorderly out of the ICA bar with the best of the Britpack. Stories that show just how cosmopolitan and over the top London can be. As good as New York, any day. Story piled upon story, bubbling up from deep inside, streaming out of my mouth like all the bottles of free champagne I make out I've drunk at the Groucho Club.

Ani laps it all up, hunkering close to me, her whole body jiggling with excitement. Wide eyed, she laughs at my punchline, throwing her head right back. I wrap my arm around her waist and pull her towards me. She tastes of birdsong and spring sunshine.

But the moment our lips touch she freezes in surprise, then goes limp. At first I think she's joining in, but from the little jerks her body makes each time I probe, the lack of friction, I soon work out she's just playing dead until the danger passes.

Bereft, I let her go and she jumps to her feet, moves two arm-lengths away, wiping her mouth clean with her sleeve.

'Sorry,' I say, holding out my arms to her. 'Ani...'

'Stop it. Stop staring at me.'

'I'm not.'

'You are,' she says. 'You're always doing it. I can't breathe for the way you look at me all the time.'

'I can't help it. I like looking at you,' I say.

'Well don't. It's creepy.'

Ani starts to walk away, then she stops. As she turns back the sun breaks through the cloud bank and the light draws promises across her face. She sits down next to me again.

'We can still go to London like we planned, though, for my project?' she says, looking up at me through her fringe.

'Of course,' I say.

She smiles, leans over and flutters her lips against mine.

My stomach churns. Maybe there is hope, after all.

Dad returns with the caretaker's keys and we enter the labyrinth of Bute, flicking switches one block at a time, each switch waking a strip of neon with a flash of expectation.

The mud puppy, when we reach it, is no dragon, however. There are no young virgins lashed to the bars of its cage, waiting to be sacrificed. No monstrous roars. Just a pathetic, bleached-out creature trapped inside a smooth-walled tank, shivering despite the heat lamp. It crouches like a small cat on its own private beach, above a smaller tank of water, not swirling muddy river water, but still and clear. Chlorinated.

'There you are, then,' Dad says. 'What do you think of that?'

'I think it looks lonely,' Ani says.

'It's OK. Just needs time to settle,' says Dad, reaching down and stroking the mud puppy's tail.

Ani asks Dad to tell her the mud puppy's story again. I fidget around, looking for something distracting on the walls, the floor. But there's nothing. Just white airtex tiles, banks of computer monitors. Ani hanging off Dad's every word, legs swinging gently, banging against the footbar of the lab stool.

God, what am I doing? She's such a child.

Dad pauses in his lecture and the two of them peer down into the tank again.

'It doesn't do much, though, does it?' Ani says. 'Just lies there.'

'It's making evolutionary history. Isn't that enough?' Dad says.

Evolutionary history, presumed in one form or another since Aristotle's time. Not by Aristotle himself, mind. Oh no, Aristotle was barking up completely the wrong tree on evolution. Get this, Aristotle actually thought that worms spontaneously created themselves out of rotting apples. I mean, I ask you.

These days, of course, we know it's the old, old story of natural selection and gene mutation. Diverse adaptive responses to environmental pressures – you know the drill. Fish – amphibian – reptile – bird – mammal. That's evolution for you.

And for me?

Evolution. From the latin – *volvere*, to roll. *E*-volution. *Un*-roll. But who said the unrolling has to be always in the same direction or in a straight line? Did you know there's a type of fish that can breathe air? Or that scientists recently found the remains of a dinosaur which had a four-chambered, double-pump heart with a single systemic aorta like a mammal's, instead of the usual three-chambered double aorta of the reptile heart?

The biological environment of our planet is patchy to say the least. Different modes of life are required for different habitats and sometimes, shock horror, the habitats become so different so suddenly that a species has to transform itself pretty bloody quickly, and not over the generations some experts would have us believe. Sometimes the change happens overnight.

What about that first brave Australopithecus who stood up on her back legs one morning and thought: Hey, the world looks much better from up here? All right, so it took a few centuries for her to become Homo erectus. But not to stand up. That just took a couple of seconds.

How do I know all this? How do you think? Listening to Dad tell it over and over, until it permeates my brain, a kind of intellectual osmosis. He never lets up. Listen to him now describing how mud puppies mate...

The males have an elaborate courtship ritual, a lot of strutting and gill-flaring. During the performance, the male deposits masses of sperm-containing jelly on to the river bed, then the female...

Oh, you don't want to know about what happens next. That really is disgusting.

By the way, don't for one minute think I've given up on the mud puppy being a dragon.

As far as I'm concerned, if a fish can have lungs and a dinosaur a human heart, then dragons can come back to Wales.

'Can I touch it?' asks Ani.

'Gently now,' Dad nods.

Ani lowers her hand into the tank. But the tips of her fingers have barely touched the mud puppy's back before she jumps away with a scream, stumbling off the stool.

'It's all slimy,' she shrieks.

Dad laughs. 'Of course it's slimy,' he says. 'All amphibians have moist skin. That's why they have to stay in or near water, to protect them from drying out. Go on, try again. It won't hurt you.'

Gingerly, Ani puts her hand back down inside the tank, strokes the mud puppy quickly once, then relaxes, smiles, strokes it again.

'There now, it's all right, it's all right,' she croons.

I wish I was that skin.

Back outside, the wind has strengthened to gale force nine and hailstones bounce off the tarmac. But Mike Llewellyn-Jones, Dad's partner in mud puppy crime, is still waiting for us under a golfing umbrella with my surprise. Scruffy and bald, formal in his shirt and tie even though it's Sunday, he chirps at me like an over-excited budgerigar, fighting to be heard above the elements.

Apparently he had a dinner party last night for some American businessman who's interested in sponsoring the mud puppy as part of some dubious publicity campaign. Mike showed him the tape of me and Dad on TV, including the clips of my work, and this guy was very interested, thought it would be a great angle to take.

'What would?' I shout, not sure I've heard him right over the wind.

'You, as local artist and co-finder of the mud puppy,' Mike yells, dancing on his toes like a schoolboy with his first dirty magazine. 'He wants to commission a piece of work from you. What do you say to that, then?'

I don't know what to say. I just stand there, eyes tearing from the wind, heart too full to speak.

This could be it. My big chance. Chance to create something *real*. Something that will make everyone sit up and take notice, once and for all.

While I'm gulping and blinking, Dad steps in, pumps Mike's hand. 'Very good of you, Michael,' he booms. 'Very good of you.'

'It was nothing, man. Credit to you, she is. Bloody marvellous.'

'How about that then, Daryl?' Dad says, turning to face me. 'A big commission! You'll be famous, love. Famous!'

Standing next to him, a grin exploding across her face, Ani reaches over to take hold of my hand, squeezes it and doesn't let go.

Chapter Thirteen

So it's official. New York City is definitely the place to be if you want to see drag kings in action.

Carlos took me to this totally awesome bar on East Houston – way over between Avenues A and B – which has drag king shows every week and, even when there isn't a show or games like there were last night, the kings still get dressed up and go there just to hang out or shoot pool with their mates.

It was so cool. The cover charge was ten bucks for kings, fifteen for everyone else. I had to work late, was still dressed in my civvies, all my gear stuffed into my gym bag, ready to change in the loos. So I gave the bouncer the full fifteen. But she just handed me the five back, straight away!

Why improve on perfection? she winked, stroking my palm. Then she said I should stick around so she could buy me a drink or anything else I wanted. A diamond maybe? Or an apartment?

I was going to tell her she could have me for a Ferrari. But Carlos pushed me past before I could get my mouth even halfway open. Said he would have to keep a much closer eye on me in future, seeing as I was such tempting shark bait.

Honestly, he's worse than Mam sometimes.

Getting my look together was easy. I just used my family, like Daryl said. That picture of Bampy from when he was courting Nana? Proper Teddy boy, Bampy was. I backcombed my hair, slicked down the sides with Keith's Brylcreem and, hey presto, a star was born.

The make-up and sideburns were a bit of a nightmare, though. Even with a whole week's practice. But luckily the bar lights were dim so no one could see the bald patches, extra splodges of spirit gum.

I wore Bampy's lime green suit, trimmed with black velvet, because Nana said it showed off my hair the best. When I tried it on yesterday afternoon, Mam and Nana both burst out crying, said the likeness was amazing. And afterwards Nana let me have all Bampy's best Teddy stuff. Brought it round for me this afternoon when I was out, over Daryl's. She was going to give it all to Keith but he's too old and fat. So now it's in a big pile on my bed.

After tea, I'm sorting through the pile – Bampy had so many shirts I'm running out of hangers, have to double, even triple them up – when I hear this weird shuffling noise behind me. It's Kat creeping up the stairs, along the landing, a giant mouse in jeans and new trainers. When she reaches my room she stops, leans against the doorjamb – half in, half out – twisting strands of her hair together then wrapping them round her ear and sucking on the ends like she always does when she's nervous.

'Hi,' she says, her voice all cracks and whispers, then clears her throat, tries again. 'How's it going?'

I just keep sorting. But when Kat reaches into her pocket and pulls out a pack of gum, my hand freezes on the hanger halfway up the sleeve of Bampy's best blue velvet coat.

Cow! She's not getting round me with a stick of gum. No way. Not this time. I mean, I might not have been exactly honest with her about not seeing Daryl any more, and I know I haven't been spending the kind of time with her she thinks I should. But I'm the victim here. I'm the one with bruises on my arms.

Moving my cowboy boots to one side, Kat sits down on the edge of the bed, left leg folded under her.

'We need to talk,' she says.

'That's not what you said last night,' I say, making my eyes look like I've just discovered dog shit over new shoes. 'Last night you said you were never going to speak to me ever again.'

'Yeah? Well I was mad at you,' she says.

I stalk over to the wardrobe, my arms full of jackets and dump them on the rail, banging each one down then pushing it over – bang, push, bang, push – as loud as I can.

'It's late and I'm tired and I don't want to talk to you,' I say.

'Just piss off, will you?' I say.

But Kat stays right where she is.

'I need to know what's going on,' she says. 'Between you and Daryl, I mean.'

'Bloody hell! How many more times?' Spin round to face her. 'Nothing's going on except you being a paranoid cow all the time.'

'No?' she whines.

'No!'

Kat jumps up off the bed.

'So how come you're always hanging out with her then? And that freak Carlos! He's another one who's after you.'

'Carlos! Are you nuts? He's got a girlfriend in New York. Talks about her all the time. Bores the knickers off anyone who'll listen to him. Carlos doesn't fancy me!'

Then I bend over and snort out these great big belly laughs, like that's the most stupid thing I've ever heard, just to piss her off.

Which it does. But not exactly how it's meant to. Instead of collapsing in floods, Kat comes charging up to me, jabs her finger into my arm. Right on my bruises!

'You fancy him, though, don't you? Don't you? You fancy him,' she says.

121

'Ow! Get off me, will you?' I yell, shoving her away. 'What is it with you and that finger. I'm going to be black and blue in the morning. Again.'

'All right, all right,' Kat says, leans back against the dresser. 'But there's definitely something going on between you and Daryl, I just know there is.'

Talk about bitter and twisted. How many times do I have to tell her?

I move over to the window. A lovely warm breeze lifts up the hairs sticking to my forehead. We'll be able to go outside without coats on soon. About bloody time. I fucking hate winter.

'You're telling me Daryl's never tried it on with you? Ever?' Kat says, coming up behind me, still glaring.

I try my best to look into her eyes, I really do.

'I knew it!' she hisses. 'I just knew it!' Then she stares out the window into the black space where the playing field is meant to be. Hard grey shutter falling over her face.

'But she kissed me. I didn't kiss her back,' I say.

Kat's head snaps round so fast her ponytail whips across my face.

'She kissed you?'

Me and my big mouth.

'Yes, but I didn't kiss her back. I told you.'

'You didn't tell her to fuck off either, though, did you?' she snaps, walking off again, as far off as she can get.

'I'm just trying to keep Daryl sweet so she'll help me and Carlos set up the club,' I say. 'Carlos thinks...'

But before I can finish, Kat has covered both her ears with her hands and screwed up her face like an angry raisin.

'Shut up!' she yells. 'Shut up! I'm sick to death of hearing what that bull dyke thinks.'

And then I'm not sorry any more, not dying inside. I'm just boiling.

'Yeah? And I'm sick to death of you judging me all the time! Telling me what to do, who I can talk to. Well, get this!' I yell, punching my left hand with a crack. 'It's none of your business who I talk to. And if you can't stand that, well you can just FUCK OFF!'

I scream the last two words so loud, we both stand there blinking in shock. Kat recovers first.

'OK then,' she shouts, storming over to the door. 'If that's how you feel, then I bloody well will! I've got better things to do than hang round here,' she says.

'Fine by me!' I say.

And I march back over to the bed, pick up the nearest shirt and fold it, tucking the sleeves into the back of the neck, trying to stop my hands from shaking.

'I won't be back,' Kat says, hand poised above the doorknob.

'Bye!' I wave.

Kat wrenches the door open and for one second I think she really is going. But then she just stops and stands there, staring out into the hallway. After another second, she turns round, comes back over and sits down next to me on the bed. She picks up Bampy's best white shirt and lays the sleeve out along her right knee, acting all casual. Except for her left leg which wobbles up and down like it's made of jelly.

'This is nice,' she says, smoothing the cuff down with her hand.

'Yeah, it was my Bampy's. I wore it last night when I was out with Carlos.'

And then I'm telling her all about MeowMix, about the Blind Date game, the karaoke contest, the all-king gigs every Wednesday night.

'You should come with us next time,' I say. 'You'd love it. The bars in New York are much better than they are here.'

From out of nowhere, Kat starts laying into me, twice as hard as before, punching me on the arms, the shoulder, elbowing me in the ribs.

'Shut up, you liar! Shut up!' she shrieks.

I try to grab hold of her arms, pin her down. But she just

headbutts me in the chest. We topple over sideways, her on top, still punching and screaming.

'Liar! Fucking liar! You were never in New York. You were never there!'

Somehow I manage to slide down, clamber out of her way. Shuffle backwards across the floorboards, keeping my arms straight out. Try to fend her off. Kat's usually a crap fighter, I've always seen her off easy before. But today she's all flying feet and fists. Every time I try and stand up she swipes at me broadside, kicks my legs till I fall back down again. Till all I can do is crouch down against the back wall, my feet going like a seesaw as she comes at me again, and again, and again.

'Liar!' she screeches, taking a flying leap and landing right on top of me. Pulls out a chunk of my hair.

'I was there! I was!' I fight back.

As sudden as she started, Kat stops dead in her tracks, sits back on her heels, panting. 'When?' she says.

'Last night, with Carlos. I told you.'

'Last night you were in New York with Carlos?' she says, looking at me like I'm the one who's gone mad, not her.

'Yes,' I say.

'Last night, you were in New York City. New York City, America, in a drag bar, with Carlos?' she says.

What's the matter with her, is she deaf or something?

'Yes,' I say.

'How?' she says. 'Go on, tell me. Tell me how you can be here all yesterday afternoon with me, in New York City with Carlos last night, and back here again today?'

I can feel my heart knocking at the bottom of my throat.

'Concorde?' I say.

Kat grabs my make-up bag off the dresser, holds it high above her head, then hurls it at me as hard as she can.

'Liar!' she screams.

The bag misses me by a millimetre, bouncing off the wall then splitting open, scattering its contents all over the floor and me.

'Watch it, that lot cost me a week's wages,' I say.

I run around, picking everything up:

Spirit gum
Red, blond, gold facial hair
Five o'clock shadow

I had to order that specially over the internet because all Mam's eye-shadows have glitter bits in them and how many men do you know with sparkly cheekbones?

Meantime Kat is pacing up and down my room, ranting on about what a freak I am, how I'm living on the other side of the galaxy, how nothing I do or say makes any sense any more.

I keep trying to open my mouth, say something. But Kat won't let me get a word in edgeways.

'You're out of your fucking tree!' she yells.

But then the fight goes right out of her and she flops down on the bed, ruining all my neat piles. I try not to weaken but the sight of her rubbing her hands up and down her thighs, crying, is too much for me. So I sit down across from her, face the wall opposite.

'They'll take you away if you're not careful. Lock you up,' Kat says.

'It's a free country. I can do what I want,' I say.

'But you really think you were there,' she says.

'No I don't.'

'You bloody do! It's not normal.' She jolts the bed so our bums rub up against each other.

'You're not so normal yourself, you know,' I say.

'How d'you mean?'

'Well, you're going out with me for a start.'

'That's different,' she says.

'How exactly?'

'I don't know. It just is, all right?'

I give up, move back over to the window.

There's no getting through to Kat when she's like this.

My room looks really great from this angle, though, even with all the mess. Almost exactly like in the photo. It was definitely the right thing to do, moving my bed round like that, stereo speakers either side of the bookcase. Improved things one hundred per cent. Like the magazine said, you don't have to have dozy things like crystals and wind chimes to have feng shui. It can still work.

'Don't you care that everyone is laughing at you?' Kat says.

My leather waistcoat. Baseball cap I nicked from work.

'No, I guess you don't,' Kat says, wiping her nose with the back of her hand.

Think I'll go back to the bar tonight. Carlos says I should go twice a week minimum, check out how the best kings move – like they're on a stage even when they're just having a few quiet drinks with their mates. Our whole lives are performance art, Carlos says.

It's such an awesome place. Way out there. As soon as I walked in I knew it was exactly what I wanted. It was ... the only way I can describe it is it was like I'd been sitting in the dark for years and someone had finally come in and switched on all the lights. So much light.

'Too much,' says Kat.

'What?'

'I said it's all too much for me.'

'What is?'

'Everything.'

'Oh,' I say.

'I'm not like you,' Kat says.

'Like what?' I say.

'Like this,' she says, swatting her arm over the bed, across Bampy's Teddy shirts, his drainpipe jeans.

'I told you, that's just a laugh,' I say and walk over to her, put my arms round her neck. 'I wouldn't do anything to hurt you, you know that.' I say.

126

Kat nods but she doesn't hug me back.

'Well stop looking so miserable, then!' I say, stroke her hair.

'I can't help it,' she sighs and squirms out from under my arm. 'Being with you, it's too hard for me, Ani,' she says.

I wonder if that bouncer woman will be there again? She was giving me the eye all night last night. Staring at me over her pool stick, smiling and licking her lips. Great big butch thing she was. Bit of a bruiser, now I come to think of it. Ugly yellow teeth too.

'You wouldn't want me to lie to you,' Kat says.

Maybe I should get Daryl to come with me tonight. Daryl will understand. She'll be able to see what I want, help me work out how to fit things together. Maybe she can even put in some of her own stuff. Like that mud puppy piece they were all talking about. That would be great.

We can still be friends, though, can't we?' Kat says.

After Kat's gone I stand there for ages staring at the photo of the two of us, last New Year's Eve, arms round each other, smiling. At least I think we're smiling but I can't tell now because the picture's gone all blurry. And then I can't look any more. I can't even stand up. I just slide down the wall onto the floor, pull my knees up to my chest.

I don't care. I don't need her. I'm going to be a star, a great big star in New York. People will come from all over the world just to see me, to tell me how great I am. And Kat'll be stuck here. Stuck in that poxy garage. She'll be sorry then, when I'm a star. You'll see. She'll be really sorry then.

Chapter Fourteen

The banner strung out across Commercial Street says *Gateway City* in curly purple letters. The banner's corners are extended white cord. The bottom right-hand corner has come loose from its mooring and flaps angrily in the breeze, slapping at the heads of the children passing underneath, who jump up and try to swing from the single thread drooping down towards the pavement.

The day is soft. But there is no trace of mud, not any more. Commercial Street has been fully pedestrianised. People walk back and forth in random patterns. Free to choose between independence and interaction. Free to fantasise about achieving city status.

I am too early. Even after a month, still on London time. Leaving forty minutes to get into town, to get anywhere, when it only ever takes ten. But opposite the Westgate is a wrought iron bench painted the dark green and gold of local authority. So I sit down, next to a woman in a blue checked skirt, to wait. The woman smokes two cigarettes in a row, lighting one cigarette off the other, the smoke blowing all around, into my eyes, into my hair.

I close my eyes, lean back against the bench and allow the weight of my fatigue to seep out through my pores. Only three more days until the weekend, until school is out. Then no more coil pots, no more detention duty, no more knotted ties. The woman shifts in her seat next to me, lights up a third cigarette. Behind us, some man is laughing and talking at the same time. A long gurgling tune with a joke so funny he can barely reach the punchline.

'All right, love. Had a long day?'

I open my eyes up to Dad standing over me like a tall black crow, clutching his briefcase bulging with Tuesday afternoons: pyx and sacrament, stole, overdue library books.

Tuesday afternoons are hospital visit afternoons.

'Having a long week. Detention duty,' I say, standing up and swinging my rucksack up onto my shoulder.

Dad clucks sympathetically. 'Well, why don't you go home?' he says. 'Give you a chance to relax. It was nice of you to come and meet me, but I can easily walk. Big night, tonight,' he says.

'No, it's OK. There's something I want to talk to you about,' I say.

Away from home, away from the memories.

Dad checks his watch. 'Right then. I just need to catch the library before it closes, then I'm all yours,' he says.

We walk back up Commercial Street, left past Iceland, through the subway into John Frost Square. The whole time we're walking I'm talking to myself; cajoling, willing myself to be brave.

Why am I such a wimp? I've tackled scarier subjects than this before. Like when I came out to him. I was absolutely petrified, convinced he'd go all Leviticus on me. My first year at college, I sat him down at the kitchen table, girded my resolve and blurted it out. When I'd finished, Dad put down his tea, stared at me silently for what seemed like centuries and then finally said:

'So that's it. Well, thank God for that. I thought it was, something I'd done.'

I should have known. My dad just isn't the fire and brimstone type.

Granted, it took a while for the reality of the situation to sink in. There were definitely one or two sticky moments. For the first couple of months he kept leaving me copies of those old Government AIDS ads. You know the ones I mean. All tombstones and gloom. No comment, no questions. Just the ads cut out of newspapers and laid out flat on my bed where I would be sure to see them. It was Dad's way of showing me he cared, just Dad trying to understand. So I found an article pointing out lesbians as a low-risk group, spread it out on his bed and everything was all right again.

For a while, at least.

As we walk past the Chartists' mosaic, I turn to Dad. 'Dad, do you think we're posh?'

Coward. Coward. The Chartists knew how to fight for what they wanted.

He stops and stares at me. 'Good grief, whatever gave you that idea!'

'Just something Ani said on Sunday,' I say, pulling my coat around me, folding my arms. 'About Allt-yr-yn being posh compared to Bettws.'

Dad laughs. 'Welsh posh, maybe. But it's not quite the same thing, is it?' he says, slipping his arm around my shoulders. 'You really like Ani, don't you, love? Special, is she?'

I nod, look over at the mosaic again. *300 Constituencies of Equal Numbers of Electors*. Flurries of angry mouths.

'She's too young for me, I know,' I say.

Oh, for God's sake, just say it, will you? Stop pussyfooting around. This can't go on any longer. You know it can't.

'What does that matter? Your mother was eight years younger than me,' Dad says. 'The important thing is how you feel.'

'Right,' I say.

My mother.

This is how it must be.

I button up my coat buttons, then unbutton them all again.

Who am I trying to kid? This is much worse than coming out.

We cross the square. The air smells sluggish, tired and oppressed under sheet-metal sky. So much sky. Not like London. In London you have to climb up high to see anything more than a patch. In Newport the sky is always the first one to be there, the first to give you its version of events. It bends over to greet you, insisting, absolutely bloody insisting, you hear it out.

Dad disappears inside the library and I sit down on yet another corporation bench to wait. The bench is hard but I am weightless, curled up inside my coat. For a second I am hungry, then I want the loo. Just for a second, then nothing. No more backbone pressing through the wooden slats, no more body, no more feeling. I try to focus my thoughts on this evening. A big commission means the possibility of more to come, means selling more existing work, means, oh yes please, another chance. And I'll be successful this time.

I try to think about success, but I am weightless and all I can think about is Mum.

Mum, Saturday mornings, hiding the chocolate biscuits in the cupboard over the washing machine so they'd last the week, then getting them down again at tea time and letting us eat them all anyway.

Mum, brushing my hair, pulling it up into bunches so tight they made my eyes go slitty, fixing the bunches with ribbons to match my dress.

Mum, buying me endless supplies of colouring books, telling me to go right ahead and colour outside the lines.

There are things you regret that you try not to regret but they just eat away at you.

She was the most important person in my world and he lied about her.

The lengths Dad went to, hiding Mum's suicide from me. Told me it was a car accident. A hit and run. But I was

131

thirteen. I wanted to know. I wanted to know everything.

I wanted to see where it all happened. So Dad took me – to a known black spot at the top of Malpas Road, where he told me the story of how some anonymous driver, probably drunk, had jumped the lights, ploughed straight into the driver's side, straight into Mum, while she was turning left. How she hadn't stood a chance. He even let me tie a wreath onto the traffic cone, helped me write a protest letter to the mayor. It worked. Three months later the council put in a filter lane.

He kept up the stories for six years.

Then I found the note

and the floor fell away.

I know, now, he did it to protect me. I know, now, he did it because he loved me. But, then, I said some terrible things to him, unforgivable things. Then I didn't say anything at all.

For nine years.

I couldn't bring myself to look at him. I couldn't bring myself to even think about him.

For nine years.

And now,

time to forgive? Time to move on?

I'm trying. But there's this glass wall between us. I want to take a hammer and smash it down, but how can I? She's my mother.

Dad comes out of the library and plops down on the bench besides me. 'That's that done, then,' he says. 'Now what was it you wanted to talk about?'

My heart goes bang and all my good intentions stick in my throat.

'I...er...you, um see...I...'

Dad tried his best to fill the hole Mum left behind her. He tried so hard. Buying me my first packet of tampons the day I got my period. Standing outside the bathroom door shouting encouragement while I grappled with the instructions. Driving me all the way to Bristol to find a

132

suitably glamorous outfit for my first real date. Comforting me three weeks later when the boy dumped me because I wouldn't let him put his tongue down my throat.

'This is about your mother, isn't it?' Dad says, picking up my hand and holding it between his, playing drums on my fingers like he used to when I was little.

I nod, too taken aback to speak.

'Thought so,' he says.

This time I don't hesitate. I seize my chance.

'So many secrets, so many lies,' I say.

'Yes,' he says. 'And all my fault. But at the time...'

He lets go of my hand and leans forward, resting his arms on his briefcase. His strong hands. His brown briefcase.

'You loved her so much. I thought, if you believed it was an accident...'

'I wouldn't blame myself?' I say.

Dad twists round to look at me. His grey eyes. Then turns and stares straight ahead again.

'Exactly,' he says.

I scrabble around in my pocket for a tissue.

'When we lost your mother the only thing that went through my head was if you ever found out how she died...' He shakes his head.

I place my hand on his arm, can feel him trembling. I want him to look at me again, but he doesn't move.

'You thought she was perfect. I didn't want to take that away from you,' he says.

'But why didn't you tell me the truth? Once I'd got over the shock?' I say.

'I couldn't. I'd kept it up for too long. I knew that if you ever found out the truth, well, I'd lose you too,' he whispers.

He still won't look at me. His clipped grey head.

'And I did, didn't I? For such a long time.'

We both sit motionless, staring into space. The town clock chimes the hour and on the fifth stroke the face splits apart with a creak. From the clock's centre, three steel

133

angels on bicycles float down, pumping away furiously, trying to stretch the tendons anchoring them to the ground. Pumping and stretching, thinner and thinner, until the tendons are straining to breaking point and

the two halves of the clock snap together again, trapping the angels inside for another hour.

Funny how your feelings for somewhere change over the years. Nine years ago, the mere thought of Newport made me want to scream with frustration and cower in terror all at the same time. And even when I arrived back a month ago, I felt like I was wandering around with my shoes on the wrong feet. But now it's...

Nobody would ever call Newport beautiful. The train that brought me here brought me the long route, through the Cotswolds: Bath – Stonehouse – Gloucester. Soft yellow stone in verdant countryside. Bright river Wye. That's beautiful. Newport is sixties industrialism laid over Victorian gothic. Not enough money. But still it's...

Still it's home.

'I was so angry with you,' I say.

Dad twists round again, looks at me at last. But as soon as he does I can't look back. Instead I concentrate on the way the green stitching on my rucksack contrasts so well with my jeans.

'I know,' he says.

Really well. I should get a shirt or something in the same colour.

'And her,' I mumble down into my chest.

'I know,' he says.

'I mean, how could she leave us like that? Didn't she love us enough, didn't she love me enough?' I say fiercely, finally meeting Dad's gaze.

His grey eyes.

'Of course she did,' he says.

'But she couldn't have.'

'She did. She loved you very much,' he says, then stands

up and walks up and down in front of me a couple of times, sighs and sits back down next to me again. 'She just wasn't happy,' he says.

'She was a coward. She was always saying we should follow our dreams, but she didn't have the guts to follow hers,' I say.

'No! Don't think that, don't ever think that! She was ill, depressed,' he says. 'It just wasn't recognised. Nobody talked about depression in those days. She kept it a secret, she was ashamed. If only she'd said something, hinted, maybe we could have done something.'

'She never even said goodbye,' I say.

Dad takes hold of my shoulder, squeezes it.

'The important thing is you're here now,' he says. 'We can begin to put all the hurt behind us now, just remember all the good times.'

I look up into his eyes, feel his strong hand pressing down.

I want to laugh in his face. I want to tell him it's not that simple. I want to tell him about the years of counselling I sat through to try and understand. I want to tell him that part of me still hates him – and her – for what they've done. I want him to tell me why. I want to tell him I love him, I forgive him, but first I want him to tell me why. I want him to wipe away all my tears with his hanky like he used to and tell me why.

'Hey, love?'

I could end this right now. I could just turn my back and walk away. I could tell him exactly what I think of him and then just walk away, jump on the next train out of here. Away from the lies, away from the pain. I could walk away and never think about him again. I could be free.

'Daryl?'

'Yes, of course we can,' I say.

Dad bends over, hugs me tight. I count to three, then pull away, but Dad is too full of relief to notice. All smiles, he stands up and tucks his shirt further into his trousers.

'Well, we can't sit around here all evening. Got to charm this rich Yank into giving you that commission,' he says.

*

Robert W Koch, Vice-President (Information Services) of Corona Systems Inc., Newark, New Jersey, comes into the bar of the Celtic Manor Hotel at seven o'clock sharp to make me an offer I would be a fool to refuse and seal the deal with champagne. Bob Koch, who has spend the best part of four days eating five-star dinners and reducing his handicap, in between back-to-back business meetings, is now in the mood for some homespun cooking and some of our fine Olde English ale. Dad and I, who have spent the best part of twenty minutes goggling at cocktail lists and salivating over dinner menus, in between mouthfuls of peanuts, do our best to swallow our disappointment with our Premier Cru and drive Bob Koch out and up the Chepstow Road to the Croes Wen Inn near Penhow.

'They do the best steaks here,' Dad says. 'They do the best steaks in the whole world here, don't they, love?'

'Yes,' I say, fiddling with the green wooden table marker, wishing we could just get on with it. 'They do great steaks, here.'

'And Daryl should know,' Dad says. 'My Daryl's been all over the world, haven't you, love?'

We choose a table opposite the log fire and the three of us order our steaks, start drinking our beer. All of us preferring medium rare, Bob Koch and Dad on pints, me, the designated driver, with just a half. The minute we're settled, Bob Koch launches into his ideas for my commission.

His ideas!

Apparently, what is needed is something that brings together our two great nations but which is also symbolic of our individual roots.

Oh, please.

'We want something real, you know?' says Bob Koch.

'Something everyone can understand. Nothing too abstract, nothing too way out.'

'I can't create to order,' I say.

'Sure you can, you just need time to think about it,' he says.

'How long have I got?'

'Three months.'

'Three months!'

Leaning back in his chair, Bob Koch pushes up the sleeves of his golfing sweater – pastel diamonds, silver-hair-covered arms – gulps down another inch of his pint. 'Like I said, we don't want anything too elaborate, and you already have your inspiration. The mud puppy,' he adds, in case we'd forgotten. 'We'll make sure there's a ton of publicity.'

Then he mentions a sum that makes me think maybe I can do it, after all.

'She can do it, Bob. Daryl's full of ideas,' Dad says.

I run my hand up and down the plane of my glass. Smooth. Cool. Supercooled. Most solids have a crystalline nature, but not glass. Glass is always liquid, chaotic. But then frozen in time.

Too brittle. Too fragile.

Bob Koch glances round the room. 'This is such a great place. Traditional, you know? So English,' he says.

'Welsh,' I say.

'Daryl,' Dad hisses.

'Excuse me?' says Bob Koch, silver brows furrowing up into a receding hairline.

'Wales,' I say. 'This is Wales, not England. England's ten miles that way.' I point towards the window.

Bob Koch shrugs and sucks up the last of his Brains, wipes his mouth with his napkin.

'Whatever. We'll give you free rein. Just fax me next week with your ideas,' he says.

My ideas. For the first time in months I am brimful of ideas. I can see them in my mind's eye: full of energy and movement. At the moment still fragile. Needing to be treated carefully to survive. But with a little heat, a little air, they are soon reconfiguring, transforming themselves in size and shape.

Chapter Fifteen

Saturday morning. Keith's big day. Daryl and I head over to the Dolman early, about lunchtime. But it's still three hours after Keith and Mam and Lisa. Everyone is very nervous.

Because it's a special occasion, I'm all dressed up. Bampy's blue velvet jacket, black drainpipes. I raided Mam's wardrobe last night and found a white shirt with big lacy cuffs which fits just perfect now I've decided to go for light 'burns and a small goatee like the one Carlos wears. Carlos says a drag king doesn't need masses of facial hair. The merest hint presumes masculinity, he says.

'You look like little Lord Fauntleroy, all grown up,' says Daryl, answering the door.

See, she knows all these famous people.

Daryl looks pretty good herself. Girly, but good. Cropped purple top and matching trousers underneath a miniskirt made out of some shiny pink sari material. Red velvet waistcoat with mirrors all over it. Loads and loads of silver bangles, all up her arm.

'First time I've not seen you in black,' I say. 'That colour really suits you. You should wear it more often.'

Daryl's face blushes to match her clothes, but she covers it up by grabbing hold of my arm, spinning me round like we're dancing.

'Your wish is my command, Prince Charming,' she says. 'Now, summon forth your coach and horses and take us to the ball.'

I wish I had even half of whatever it is she's on, sometimes.

We head up Kingsway and park right outside the stage door. Double yellow lines. But it's OK because I've got Nana's Orange Badge. The stage doorman peers out of his hut, lets me through with just a nod, but stops Daryl before she can get both feet on his step.

'Performers only past this point, love,' he says.

Quick sharp, Miss Goody Two Shoes turns back, starts walking round to the plebs entrance. I grab her arm, drag her back in.

'Be a sport and let her through, mate,' I tell the doorman. 'It's an emergency. Her husband's forgotten his wig and he can't go on without it. You should see him, got a head like a rubber ball, he has. Not like me,' and I flick my fringe up, show him my lovely low hairline.

The doorman sucks air in through his teeth. 'Go on then, but don't be all day about it,' he says.

'Thanks, mate, you're a star,' I say. Then me and Daryl run up the corridor before he can change his mind.

As we turn the corner, the doorman yells out at me. 'You're never going to win, son, you know that, don't you? Not unless you do something about that flaming hair of yours.'

Just what I need, another comedian.

It's the same when we get to the dressing room. Big sign on the door saying *Men Only*. And when I walk inside, all the Elvises think I'm a boy, they all think I'm here to perform. Even though Bampy's blue velvet jacket is tight across my tits. Even though I forget to deepen my voice when I ask if anybody's seen Keith.

All the Elvises have to use the same dressing room, the Crowd Dressing Room. Pete, the stage manager, won't open up any of the other dressing rooms, the ones with more facilities, because they're just for the stars and the judges say all the Elvises are equal before the competition. The Crowd Dressing Room looks exactly like the corridor only bigger and squarer. Breeze blocks painted white. Concrete floor. Concrete smell. No windows. Along the wall near the door there are four dressing tables with different sized mirrors, with a row of hooks for coats on the opposite wall. And that's it. The Crowd Dressing Room is really the Prisoners' Dressing Room.

Prison crammed full of Elvis. Elvis is definitely alive and has taken over the whole building. No sign of Keith, though. Daryl and I search all through the dressing room, the auditorium, backstage, the bar. Nothing. In the end we find him in the Green Room, with Mam and Lisa, in disguise in his joggers and trainers. Elvis still folded away in his suitcase.

'There's no point getting ready. It's going to be hours yet,' Keith says. 'All this concrete is playing havoc with my sinuses.'

I introduce Daryl to Mam and Keith and she immediately gets in their good books because she calls Mam 'Mrs Morgan' and Keith 'Mr Morgan', insists on giving Mam her London address and telephone number for when we're away.

'Don't worry, Mrs Morgan, I'll take good care of her,' Daryl says.

'Call me Lorraine,' Mam says.

Pass me a bucket, I say.

Keith asks me to help him check through his set with him. I walk over to the table where he's spread out his song sheets, just as Mam tells Daryl she's worried about me.

'She's always in a dream world, making up stories about New York all the time. And, as for all this dressing up like a man...'

'Yes, she takes after your husband on that, doesn't she?' says Daryl.

141

That makes Mam laugh out loud. 'Yes, I suppose she does. But that's just it, it's a hobby for Keith. OK, some people might think he's a bit crazy and maybe he is. But only at weekends. He knows when to stop. He doesn't think he really is Elvis,' she says. 'With Ani, I'm not so sure.'

'Ani just gets a bit carried away sometimes,' says Daryl. 'It's the artist in her. She'll be all right.'

I can't listen to the rest because Keith is going on about Pete the stage manager and his equality rules again. Turns out Keith can't have Mam and Lisa as his backing singers like he planned, in case it gives him an unfair advantage over all the other Elvises. Keith wants me to go backstage, try and persuade Pete to let Mam and Lisa go on anyway. Keith thinks I'll be able to get round the rules because I know Pete from way back. From all those shows I was in for dancing.

Yes, all right. You got me. I used to go dancing. Ballet and Old Time Ballroom. Too embarrassing for words, I know. But I did it.

It was all Mam's idea. Mam thought ballet lessons would make me graceful. Mam said I walked like a duck. But it didn't work. The only thing I ever got to be was a tree. A sodding tree, stuck to the ground and waving my branches around in the wind.

Pete the manager is over by Stage Right, trying to untangle the rope and tackle for one of the light barrels. I try and persuade him, tell him how cute Mam and Lisa look in their matching outfits. How hard Lisa's been practising. I really go for broke. But Pete's not having any of it.

'Sorry, Ani,' he says. 'Rules are rules. No backing. No extras. No gimmicks. Now do me a favour and sod off, there's a love. I've got three flats to hang still and a broken mirrorball to fix.'

I go back up to the Green Room to tell Keith the bad news. He takes it like a man, but Lisa starts up grizzling right away. She can whinge for Wales, my sister. She won't shut up till Keith promises her a cheeseburger, extra fries

142

and a strawberry milkshake. Mam and Keith take Lisa off for her bribe. They invite Daryl and me too, but seeing we've got the Green Room to ourselves for a bit we stay behind, pull some chairs together and just chill.

'I wish I could talk to my dad the way you talk to Keith,' Daryl says, puts her feet up on one of the chairs. 'You're so relaxed with each other.'

'What are you on about? Your dad's great,' I say, stretching my arms above my head and yawning. 'Dead easy to talk to.'

'Not with me he's not.'

'How come?'

'He did something terrible when I was younger,' she says. 'And we've never really been able to get past it.'

'What did he do that was so bad?'

'He lied to me,' she says.

'Well, I guess everybody lies sometimes, even vicars,' I say.

'It was a big lie,' she says.

'Oh,' I say.

And we sit there. Daryl all sniffy and teary, staring down at the carpet, bangles jingling on her arm. Me just looking round at the photos stuck up on the walls, all round the Green Room and out in the hallway. Black and white photos of all the plays the Dolman's put on over the years. All the actors, directors. Nobody famous, though.

'Maybe he can't talk to you because he's embarrassed,' I say. 'Maybe he is sorry, but he's ashamed too. So ashamed he can hardly talk about it. Maybe you should make the first move,' I say.

'I did,' says Daryl and raises her head, looks me in the eye. Big fat tear running down her cheek.

'When?'

'Tuesday.'

I wait for her to give me the whole story. But she just leans forward, her body all tense and fidgety like she's about to run away.

143

'And?' I say.

'And he thinks it's all fine now. He thinks we've cleared the air,' she says, starts pulling her bangles over her hand, one by one.

'But you don't?'

'It's just hard to forget everything, that's all. Saying sorry, even if you really mean it, well it just isn't enough sometimes, is it?' she says.

I shift in my seat, look over to the door where two of the Elvises are larking around in the corridor, singing 'American Trilogy' in two-part harmony.

'What?' says Daryl.

'Nothing.'

'No, go on, say it,' she says.

'You won't like it.'

'Just say it.'

'Promise you won't get mad at me?'

'I promise.'

'Well, it's just that . . . well . . . don't you think you're being a bit hard on him?' I say. 'I mean, don't you think that maybe just seeing you every day makes him remember, will always make him remember? Don't you think the only way to change that is for you to say it's OK? Show him you think he's really a good person? I mean, he is a good person, isn't he, your dad? Really.'

And I think of my dad, my real one, and how he never comes to see me and how he hasn't even sent me a birthday card. Not one, not since I was seven.

'At least you know your dad loves you,' I say. 'Whatever he did before, whatever he said before, he really loves you, your dad. Anyone can see that. Your dad thinks you're the best thing since sliced bread.'

The whole time I'm talking, Daryl is just looking at me with her mouth open. Until I can't stand it any more and I dry up, twist my ring round my thumb. 'I told you you'd be mad at me,' I say.

'I'm not mad at you,' says Daryl. 'I'm just wondering how you got to be so wise so young?' And she leans in and kisses me.

On the cheek. But just as she does, Kat walks in through the door with that Gareth Matthews from the chippy. And they're holding hands! I can hardly believe it. I mean, there I was thinking that fight we had last weekend would blow over, that she would come round. There I was thinking of ways to make it up to her. And all the time, she's going round with poxy Gareth Matthews. Cow!

But I should have known. I should have sussed. I mean, look what happened about the coffee shop. They had some more jobs going this week, and Kat was top of the waiting list. But when Sharon rang up offering her the job Kat told her that she wouldn't be caught dead working with a load of boring books and a load of boring people. Honest, that's what she said. I know because Kat's mam told my mam all about it in Sainsbury's on Thursday. Kat's mam said she was mortified how rude Kat was. Kat's mam couldn't believe Kat would rather stay in that dirty garage than hang out in a really lovely place like the coffee shop.

And now we all know why, don't we?

Lardy-arse Gareth Matthews is why.

When Kat sees it's me, when she sees Daryl with her arms round my shoulders, Kat's wrapping her own arms, her legs, everything all round lardy-arse Gareth Matthews.

So I grab hold of Daryl, kiss her again, on the mouth this time. Tongues and everything. And all the time I'm kissing Daryl I'm looking over her shoulder to see if Kat is watching. Which she is, and getting really mad, too. So I throw myself into the kiss even more, shut my eyes.

'Wow,' says Daryl when we come back up for air. 'Whatever did I do to deserve that?'

'You just wait,' I say, making my voice all sexy and low. 'You just wait till I get you down to London,' I say, looking over for Kat again but she and Gareth have disappeared.

Daryl just stares and stares.

*

After years more waiting, no sign of Kat, the competition finally begins and Daryl and me go down the hallway to the auditorium, Daryl telling me about the sketches she's done for my living doll's house installation.

'Nothing too elaborate, just a few ideas,' she says. 'You'll have to fill in all the detail yourself, of course. Draw them in your own style. I don't want your tutor thinking you've been given an unfair advantage over the others. Well, not much of one anyway,' she winks.

'The others?' I say.

'Your fellow students.'

'Oh, right.'

Shit, I forgot I said this was for college. It's all moved on so far since then.

We bag the two rows of seats by the side of the main door. Horrible orange covers. Wait for Keith, Mam and Lisa to come back from changing. There are fifteen Elvises in the competition. Each Elvis can perform for ten minutes. So with all the sets, two intervals and the four finalists repeating their sets all over again, that's nearly five hours of 'Suspicious Minds', 'Polk Salad Annie', 'Blue Hawaii' and 'American Trilogy'.

You can't even get a drink. The bar doesn't open till six. Poxy licensing laws.

After an hour, all the Elvises start blurring into each other. Till only the really bad ones stand out. Like Gareth Matthews for a start, who looks a right pillock in a shag-pile wig and a jumpsuit belted so tight he looks like a sack of potatoes tied in the middle.

You can always tell how serious an Elvis is by his outfits. The really dedicated ones, the ones who want to go professional one day, like Keith, they study old photos and

146

films, then copy the clothes as close as possible. And it's not easy. The embroidery and the studwork Elvis had was very intricate. You should hear Keith and his mates when they get together. They're worse than a bunch of girls. Look at them now, whispering through the sets about the length of this Elvis's trousers, gossiping about that Elvis's pompadour. In between the acts they brag about all the good deals they've got on material samples and the skill of their dressmakers. Without giving any names away, of course.

A Chinese Elvis comes on. One of Keith's mates knows him, he's the manager of the restaurant next to Vacara's fish shop. He's so bad he's almost good. Sings 'Blue Hawaii' in a Chinese accent and instead of the proper boots he's wearing trainers. His black jumpsuit is covered all over in ruby studs, even his crotch. And when he turns round the studs spell out ELVIS all across his back.

'Good job too,' I say. 'If it wasn't for that you'd never know who he was supposed to be.'

Mam, Daryl and Lisa fall about laughing. But Keith's dead angry, whacks me across the back of the head, tells me to show some respect. For the Chinese guy, and for the King, he means. Makes me feel really ashamed.

Then it's Keith's turn. He gets up from his seat and we all kiss him good luck, even Daryl.

Keith walks to the end of the row, turns and bows. 'Now there's going to be a lot of swooning and screaming in the next few minutes, ladies,' he says. 'But don't let that scare you. It's just a result of my animal magnetism.'

So we all scream and swoon as he walks off in his Aloha Eagle. Cock of the Walk. The gold stars on his legs glinting in the spotlights. Joyce managed to fix up that tear so it hardly shows, and she also made him a matching cape to cover everything up, just in case. He takes the cape off at the beginning of the first number, 'Suspicious Minds', and the four of us stamp and scream some more. Keith bows again, blows each of us a kiss, then starts to sing. Me, Mam and

Lisa swaying and singing along with him.

He's really good. Great concentration, perfect grinding finish to 'Minds', lunges, karate hands, sexy frowns all the way through his set.

'He's going to make it,' Mam whispers. 'I just know it. He's going to get through.'

But then it all goes wrong. The next Elvis who comes on, right after Keith, doesn't come on Stage Left like the others, but rises up from underneath, using the hydraulic ramp, up onto the apron, clouds of dry ice all around him, throwing rose petals out into the audience. Nobody has heard of him before, nobody knows anything about him, except that he's streets ahead of Keith. He's streets ahead of everyone. He wriggles and screams, thrusts and jives. And his voice is amazing. Just like Elvis. Better than Elvis.

The stranger's set goes a full two minutes over the maximum ten allowed. And he requests a minute's silence at the end of 'Trilogy' in memory of the King. But even before the set's halfway over, the muttering starts. About how he's a cheat, a professional in an amateur competition, got an agent, money behind him. About how he's had a nose and chin job to look more like Elvis. And when the supposedly broken mirrorball starts turning in the middle of 'The Wonder of You', sending diamond chips slashing through the dry ice, things get really nasty.

'Disgusting I call it,' Mam says, hiding Lisa's eyes from a build-up of pelvic thrusts. 'This is a family show.'

'What about showing respect?' I say.

'There's nothing respectful about that,' says Keith. 'Who is this guy anyway? Dirty sod. Does anybody know who he is?'

I just keep my head down.

Keith doesn't win. He doesn't even get into the top three. No prizes for guessing who the winner is.

Carlos.

*

Pig sick of Elvis, Daryl and I walk up the drive to Daryl's house. Daryl turns the key in the lock, opens the front door, then stops dead, tripping me up. I push her forward but she won't move. Just stands there, ears straining, like she's trying to tell if the house is breathing.

'Something's wrong,' she says. 'Listen.'

'I can't hear anything,' I say. 'What is it, what's the matter?' I say.

She puts out a hand to shush me. We creep heel-toe, heel-toe through the hall, down the utility area, me holding on to her waistcoat, past the washing machine, the fridge-freezer, turn the corner into the kitchen.

And there's Daryl's dad sitting on one of the chairs, except he's not really sitting, more slumping, halfway on, halfway off, his long skinny legs splaying out in front of him, his feet all higgledy piggledy, his face slack down one side like the elastic's gone out of his skin, with this awful whiny rattling noise coming out of his mouth, but it's his eyes, his eyes that are the worst.

There's Daryl's dad trying to stand up, move towards Daryl, except he can only make it about an inch off the chair before falling forward, crashing down onto the floor, his face turning this awful grey-blue colour, first his lips, then his whole face, and then the whiny rattling noise is stopping, and then there's no sound at all.

There's Daryl screaming at me to get an ambulance, rushing towards her dad, but the telephone is up on the wall and I can't seem to get my arm to work, I'm having to really concentrate to make my arm lift itself up and pick the phone up off the wall, dial 999, and when I'm holding the phone to my ear I'm really scared because I've never had to dial 999 before, and what if I say the wrong thing?, but just as I think this, the operator is asking me what service I want in a soft slow voice, and then I hear myself speaking.

'It's Daryl's dad, he's fallen on the floor. He's gone this funny colour and I think he might be dead.'

And then there's me crying down the phone and begging the operator to send the ambulance quick because I think Daryl's dad is dead, and then the operator is speaking to me again in that soft slow voice, asking me to calm down, taking the address, telling me not to worry, telling me that the ambulance is on its way, telling me to put the phone down and go outside, and look out for the ambulance.

And so I look over at Daryl to tell her that the ambulance is on its way, but Daryl is not looking back at me, she is on her knees, next to her dad, and then Daryl is pulling her dad's head up and back, putting her hand under her dad's neck, opening her dad's mouth with her fingers, placing her lips over her dad's lips, blowing air out of her mouth into her dad's mouth, so then I put the phone back on its hook, and go outside to look out for the ambulance.

I guess this means we won't be going to London now.

Chapter Sixteen

It takes seven and a half minutes for the paramedics to arrive.

Ani waits out in the middle of the road, in the heavy rain, to flag down the ambulance, then shows the paramedics into the kitchen, dripping water over the tiles.

The paramedics inspect Dad all over, check for a pulse.

Blur of needles, tubes and blankets. Dad, being strapped onto the stretcher, laid out on the trolley, carried down the drive. Neighbours, opening their curtains, switching on their porch lights, asking if there's anything they can do. Ani, shutting the dog out in the kitchen, fetching Dad's pyjamas.

And me?

I'm just standing there, feeling my insides freezing in time. I bite the ends of my fingers, shake my hands in the air. But the frost continues creeping up my arms, along my body, down my legs, until I am cracked right through.

Now, there's only the rubber pump of the ventilator pushing air in and out of Dad's lungs. The beep of the heart monitor on the wall. Ani always next to me, so close I can feel the muscles in her thigh jerk as her leg presses into mine. I can feel the hairs on her arms prick the back of my hand. I look down at my hands. They seem to be worrying a plastic cup to shreds. I try to keep them still but they've developed a life all of their own. Ani moves behind me, wraps her arms around my waist, lays her head against my shoulder and squeezes out a reassurance.

Why is everybody so quiet? I've never known the world so silent. Why is nobody screaming?

But there is only the rubber pump of the ventilator pushing air in and out of Dad's lungs. The beep of the heart monitor on the wall.

I want to sing a song, recite a nursery rhyme, the shopping list, anything to block out that bloody rhythm. I want someone to pinch me, tell me none of this is really happening. I know none of this is really happening. It's all just a bad dream. But at the same time I know I'm wide awake. I know I have to face this.

The doctor arrives and I force myself to focus on his mouth, try and make sense of what he is saying.

...suffered a cerebral embolism, a massive stroke to the brain...

No kidding. I was there when Dad fell unconscious to the floor and his face turned purple.

...can't breathe on his own. We think his chest muscles are paralysed...

I was the one who gave him mouth to mouth while we waited for the ambulance.

...all we can do now is wait...

Wait for the drugs to start working. Wait to see if Dad will breathe on his own. Wait for Dad to wake up.

The NHS makes its excuses and backs out of the cubicle. Ani goes off to fetch me yet another cup of tea while I slide down into the nearest chair, concertina my chest down into my stomach and stare straight ahead.

What a humiliation Intensive Care is. The body in the bed isn't my dad. My dad is tall and athletic. My dad has thick grey hair and prominent cheekbones. This slack-jawed, balding imposter with plastic tubing poking out of his mouth, hand – even his dick, for God's sake – this isn't my dad. This whey-faced, drooling alien lost in a pile of

NHS-stamped pillows isn't my dad. Any second now my dad is going to come striding through those doors over there and ask what the hell's the matter with me. Did somebody die?

I turn my head towards the doors, hold my breath and count to ten. But nothing happens, no one comes in.

I shut my eyes tight until the world turns purple with flashes of orange and slide my cross – my mother's cross – up and down its chain one, two, three times. But nothing happens, no one comes in.

Oh, this is ridiculous. I am acting like a six-year-old, praying for a miracle. But I don't believe in miracles.

I walk over to the far window. In the street below, a man is standing waiting at a bus stop. Waiting for a bus to carry him away to his life, somewhere out there. Not in here, though. There is no life in here. No future. Dad is going to die, I know he is, and it's all my fault.

I don't know what to do.

It's all my fault.

Somebody tell me what to do.

Ani comes back in with the tea and catches me halfway out the door.

'What is it, Daryl?' she says. 'Where are you going?'

'I need some oil,' I say.

'What?'

'Oil. Oil.' I can feel my head bobbing back and forth like a chicken, so I try to hold steady. 'I need some oil,' I say and continue walking down the corridor, but Ani holds me back.

'Why do you need oil?' she asks.

'Isn't it obvious? If Dad is going to die, then I need to anoint him.'

Ani's face is a joke. But I've lost my sense of humour.

'Your dad's not going to die, I just know he isn't,' she says, trying to turn me back inside the Unit, back towards Dad's bed.

But I push her out of the way. 'I need some oil!' I shout. 'He's my dad and I need to anoint him, all right?'

153

Ani backs away in shock and the duty nurse looks up from her notes, scowls at me from behind tortoiseshell glasses and raises her finger to her lips.

I am breaking her rules with my noise.

I want to smash my fist into the nurse's smug fat face. I want to wrap my hands around her scrawny neck and squeeze. My father is lying here in a coma, will probably never wake up again, but God forbid I should cause a scene, show how I feel. God forbid I should...I should...disturb her fucking coffee break with my embarrassing emotions.

But, like a good girl, I just uncurl my fingers from the door handle and lower my voice to a whisper.

'It's important,' I say, hardening my heart against the tears in Ani's eyes. Then I take a deep breath and walk over to the nurse's station.

Focusing on the hairgrip pinning the nurse's cap to her hair, I slide my mother's cross up my sweating neck and back down again, one, two, three times, then slide my eyes down the nurse's fringe and onto her face.

The nurse lifts her arm and pats her head to check the cap is secure.

'Can I help you?' she asks. Offset by her uniform, the nurse's voice is like frozen sea water.

'Do you have any oil?' I ask, keeping my voice stiff and formal. 'I'd like to anoint my father.'

'I see. Well, the hospital chaplaincy usually tends to patients' religious needs. We serve several denominations here: Church in Wales, Catholic, Methodist. We also have a rabbi. I'd be happy to call someone for you.'

A single tear drops onto the black tiled floor near my right foot. I scrub it away with my shoe.

Damn it. I won't cry. I won't.

The nurse leans over her desk and hands me a tissue.

'You know,' she says, thawing a little. 'We can keep your dad on life support for as long as necessary. There's plenty of time for you to call your own priest.'

I blow my nose, letting my hair fall forward to hide my face.

He is his own priest.

'I know,' I say from behind my curtain. 'But it's something I need to do for myself. I mean, it's something I need to do for my dad. Don't you have anything I can use?'

'Hang on,' says the nurse and, bending down under her desk, brings out a small black handbag, then rummages around in it for a few seconds before handing me a plastic bottle half filled with a thick liquid.

I read the label:

Oil of Olay
Complete Care
Moisturising Fluid

The bottle sits squat in the palm of my hand, the white plastic flat and opaque against the pink round tips of my fingernails. The label is curled up at the edges where dribbles of oil have seeped through and dissolved the glue. It is frequently used. An everyday item.

Pouring some of the oil into the palm of my hand, I place the bottle carefully on the ledge above Dad's bed. The label's trademark gold disc glints in the light spilling out from the overhead strip.

I try to get Ani to move round the other side of the bed, so Dad will be surrounded by prayer. But I am crying too hard to speak so Ani tangoes blindly back and forth under my near-hysterical waving until she works out what I want her to do. When she is finally in position I hook a little of the oil onto the tip of my thumb and lean over Dad. But then freeze halfway.

'I can't remember the words,' I hiss.

It's been years since I set foot in a church. Nine years.

'I don't think it really matters,' Ani whispers back. 'It's the thought that counts.'

A dribble of oil runs down my thumb and lands on one of the plastic sensor patches taped to Dad's chest. As it falls I catch a whiff of the scent. It smells of my mother.

And then, suddenly, miraculously, I know what to do. Calm and certain, I drag my thumb down the centre of Dad's forehead, across to his left temple, then across to his right temple, reciting as I go.

'I anoint you, Dad, in the name of the Father, the Son and the Holy Spirit.'

Then I rub the remaining oil into my hands exactly the same way as Mum did – along each palm, up over the back, wiping the traces away on the inside of each wrist.

Now there is nothing left to do but wait.

Ani and I sit together, listening to the rubber pump of the ventilator, the beep of the heart monitor on the wall and, to pass the time, I tell us the story of when I was nine and Dad and I were walking down by Fourteen Locks and I tried to walk across the top of the lock gate but tripped and fell in. I tell us the story of the time Dad and I found a blackbird nest and came back twice a day for a week, waiting for the baby blackbirds to hatch. How blackbirds nest in that part of the woods every year.

Ani also tells us stories, about how mad her parents get about Elvis and how her mum wears a TLC necklace which she says Elvis gave her but which she really got out of a magazine.

We tell each other all the stories we can remember.

Then neither one of us can think of any more stories to tell.

The nurse comes over to check on her patient. I watch as she changes Dad's urine bag and smoothes out the wrinkles on the bed. Professional. Detached. But then, as she turns to leave she stops and brushes the back of her left hand along Dad's cheek.

'There you are, my lovely,' she croons. 'That should make you more comfy. Can't have you crossing your legs now, can we?'

She looks across at me and smiles.

'Everything OK?' she asks.

'Yes thanks,' I say. 'And thanks again.'

'No problem,' she says, then pauses. 'Look, it's going to be a while yet and you've been here for hours. Why don't you go home and get some rest? We'll call you if there's any change.'

I don't want to go. I don't want to leave him. But I am so, so cold.

I reach forward and place my hand over Dad's.

'Dad? Can you hear me, Dad? Dad, I'm going to go now, just for a little while. Just to change my clothes, grab something to eat. I'll be back soon, Dad. Don't worry. I'll be back soon.'

*

I am still freezing. The heat of the shower is no relief. Immediately the water hits my shoulders, all its energy dribbles away. I lean back against the tiles and watch the water sluice across my breasts, down my stomach, thighs, down into the drain.

Flicking the heater off, I climb out of the shower and towel myself roughly, trying to get some circulation back, then drag myself into the bedroom, Dad's bedroom. Mum's bedroom. The room is dim and cold. It smells sharp and clean, like furniture polish. On one side is a walnut wardrobe with a full-length mirror. On the other side is the window and, in front of it, my mother's walnut dresser and crystal rose bowl. At the bottom of the bed is a walnut blanket box. I sit down on the side of the box, opposite the mirror, and run my hand along the box's bevelled edge, staring at my reflection in the mirror, remembering what lies inside. All my mother's favourite things. All the things Dad could never bring himself to throw away. All the things Dad would never dream of throwing away. Jewellery, scarves, photographs.

Suicide note.

You just need to reach down inside the Dream Box. Say the magic words.

Behind me, I feel rather than hear Ani approach. I turn round to face her.

My shivers tell her everything she needs to know.

'Let it go, just let it all go,' she says.

And with that she kisses me. Or rather we kiss each other. And deep underground, the fires jump and spit. Tiny atoms of hope leaping and colliding, moving so fast their energy is clearly visible. At first it is just a faint glow above the horizon. But soon green and red pillars of light climb up into the sky, waving and swirling in the wind, then stretching across to form a curtain which ripples with static electricity. Flowing and folding, the curtain changes colour from red to orange, green, violet, all the colours of the rainbow, mixing and flickering, weaving into each other. And all the time the heat inside is building until, with a flash, the curtain is rent apart. Lightning rays explode in all directions, searing holes in the sky through which the spirits of the dead peek down from the celestial regions. Reflections of heavenly warriors, drawing the storm away and throwing down a rainbow ladder to span the abyss and lead us safely over to the other side.

ELEMENT III

Mud Puppy 'Twinning' planned

Worldwide interest continues to grow in the unfolding story of Newport's very own scientific phenomenon – the mud puppy that can breathe air.

In an unprecedented token of civic friendship, the mayor of Newark, New Jersey, has reportedly offered the mayor of Newport the gift of a female mud puppy as a mate for the male found in the River Usk last month. It is hoped that in breeding the two mud puppies together, experts at the University of Wales will be able to further understand the evolutionary miracle that the world is currently watching with bated breath.

Speculation is also growing that New Jersey computer software giant, Corona Inc., is planning a commercial joint venture here in Newport which could bring hundreds of new jobs to the area. A Corona spokesperson confirmed that private discussions were underway with an as yet unnamed Newport company, but would not be drawn on the details. Should the joint venture go ahead, it will go a long way to secure Newport's position as the Silicon Valley of the UK electronics market.

South Wales Argus
Tuesday 20 April

Chapter Seventeen

Tuesday afternoon and the plane touches down five minutes early: five-oh-two pm, not five-oh-seven pm, like the captain said. Can't see any houses yet, though. Can't see New York. We left Gatwick at three, so even though it's taken over seven hours to get here, it's like it's really only taken two. It's like I've got a whole extra five hours in my life.

As long as I don't go back. And I'm not, ever. Going back, I mean. I'm going to stay right here in New York and be famous.

The inside of the terminal is empty. A giant big empty warehouse with little booths all down one side and rows and rows of those zigzag things they have in Post Offices. Where is everyone? Where are all the people, the commuters? I thought everybody in America went everywhere by plane? But there's just the people off my flight, and that was half empty. The Americans, they've all gone up to the booths for American passports only. There are loads of them so they can get through dead quick, the Americans. But the rest of us, the aliens, we only have two booths and miles and miles of zigzags.

I'm busting for a wee but I can't see any loos, so I just walk towards the alien booths. The zigzags go practically the whole length of the terminal, and you have to walk back and forth five times.

Stand behind the red line. Have all passports and documents ready.

There are four aliens waiting in front of me, behind the red line. Four aliens and then I have to know what to say.

Three.

Two.

One.

'Passport and ticket, please.'

I hand the booth man my passport, ticket and the postcard with Carlos's address on it. *673 E. 7th Street, Apt 4FG.*

The booth man doesn't look up, he just says, 'Business or vacation?'

Above the booth man's head is a yellow flag with some sort of crest – two women dressed in funny old clothes and a shield: *Liberty and Prosperity.*

'Vacation,' I say.

The booth man's eyes look up at me, down at my ticket, up at me again. 'How long will you be staying?' he says.

'Two weeks.'

'Two weeks?'

'Two weeks.'

'So how come you have a return ticket dated October 15?'

When the booth man asks me this, my heart goes bang and my underarms break out in a sweat. But I don't know why. I mean, it's not like I'm breaking the law. The guide-book says the law says I can stay in America for ninety days as long as I don't work. And I've sold my car and everything. So I don't need to work.

Ninety days. That's ages. I'm bound to be famous in ninety days.

I look the booth man straight in the eye. Little round glasses.

'It's an open ticket, all right? It was the cheapest I could get. But I'm only staying two weeks. I've got to go back then. For my exams,' I say.

The booth man raises his eyebrows a bit but doesn't say

anything. Just carries on tearing along the dotted line of my arrival card. Then he stamps the card and my passport, sticks the card on top of the pile of other arrival cards, tucks my ticket and the postcard with Carlos's address on it inside the front cover of my passport and slides the passport back across the counter towards me.

'Nice trip,' he says, not looking up at me again. 'Next.'

I put my passport and my air ticket inside the front pocket of my rucksack, but keep the postcard with Carlos's address in my hand, hold it out in front of me.

673 E. 7th Street, Apt 4FG
NY, NY.
New York. New York.

The other side of Customs is a lot busier. People everywhere. So many people I can't see Carlos. I can't see him anywhere. Even when I stand down at the end, where the white lines of the ramp meet the two yellow end lines, the ones that tell you where Customs ends and America begins, I can't see him. I stand stock still with my feet on the two yellow lines, twist my head left and right, but I still can't see him. I can't see him anywhere.

And then I'm shaking and sweating and everything's gone blurry. The faces, the walls, everything. Blurry and sweaty. Because he said he'd be here. He promised me. I made him write it all down. I made him repeat out loud to me what time I was arriving and then I made him write it down. Five-oh-seven pm local time, Newark airport, Newark, New Jersey. He said he'd be here. But he's not. He's not.

I should find a phone. That's what I should do. What time is it at home? Mam will tell me what to do. I should find a phone and ring Mam. Where are the phones? Where are the fucking phones?

I step forward off the yellow lines and that's when I see them, behind a big white pillar. Three big shiny silver phones, all in a row with half-bubble glass booths hanging over them.

I'm so glad to see them I practically run over to them and just when I reach them I hear someone shouting out my name.

It's Carlos. Sitting on one of the chairs opposite the phones. Hidden by the pillar.

He was here. He was here all the time!

God, he looks good. White T-shirt with the sleeves folded up over his shoulders. Red kerchief round his neck. Behind him, coming towards me as well, is a girl wearing a blue leather coat. Not a jacket, but a long coat. And long blue boots too. Even though it's summer.

That must be Carlos's girlfriend, Thalia.

Carlos waves and strolls over towards me, rolling off the balls of his feet.

I stand still and wait for Carlos and Thalia to reach me.

Thalia doesn't roll. Her heels are too high.

'Ani,' Carlos says. 'Good flight?'

Thalia doesn't say anything, just smiles at me. Thalia has glittery purple lipgloss on her lips and long, straight, silky hair. She's the spitting image of Kat.

I wish Kat were here.

'You know,' I say, hold my rucksack tight across my chest. 'Boring.'

'You hungry? Wanna grab a coffee or something before we get going?'

'OK,' I say.

Thalia smiles at me, whispers something in Carlos's ear.

'Right. Yeah,' Carlos says, looks over at me again. 'Thalia says to tell you she's sorry she can't welcome you properly. But her strep throat is real bad just now.'

Thalia smiles again, mouths something at me. Can't really tell what it is so I just smile back at her.

What's strep throat when it's at home?

Thalia smiles a third time, then whispers to Carlos again. Carlos nods.

'Unless you wanna go right now,' he says. 'Thalia reckons you must be tired.'

'Yeah,' I say, put my rucksack back down on the trolley, my big suitcase which has all Bampy's stuff, lean my leg against my small suitcase, which is full of all my normal stuff. 'A bit.'

'So let's go,' says Carlos.

I still really need the loo but I don't want to say this and anyway, Carlos is already striding off to buy the bus tickets, leaving me and Thalia to push the trolley out of the terminal and down the slope to the bus stop. Thalia still not talking, just smiling.

The bus stop is full of people loading luggage, buying tickets. But inside the bus is cool and quiet. No toilets, though. I slide down into two seats halfway up. Carlos and Thalia sit down in the seats opposite and straight away start tickling each other, playing around just like me and Kat used to do. But I don't care. I just put my rucksack down on the aisle seat, lean my head against the window. The seat backs are blue and yellow checks. They're so tall I can't see the people in front of me or behind me. But I can hear them, chatting and laughing. I can feel them kicking me in the back as they sit down, pull down the seat trays.

The driver gets on, shuts the bus door, shuts in the cool, the quiet, and backs out of the bus stop. And then we leave.

We leave the bus stop and head for New York.

New York. New York.

My brain tells me I should be looking where we're going. I should be looking for New York. I should be looking everywhere. But I am so tired all I can do is lean my head against the windowpane, close my eyes. Try not to think too much about the toilet.

When I wake up we're driving along a main road. A motorway. Motorway signs are green here, not blue. The licence-plates are different too. Light blue for the Garden State. Red, white and blue – Statue of Liberty. Cars are queuing up outside the bus window. Bigger and shinier than any of the cars at home. They're all going the other way, though. On the other side. On our side, the wrong side, the right side, the road is nearly empty.

'B and T crowd,' Carlos says, pointing his finger at the car queue. 'Pack rats.'

I know I should ask him what he's talking about but I'm too knackered. So I just lean my head against the window again, stare at the cars.

The bus speeds up, past lots of water, then goes uphill to where there are trees and petrol stations and billboards advertising more cars. We go through a toll. Signs for a tunnel. Coming downhill towards the tunnel, the hedgerow dips down further and further and then there it is, right in front of us! The Empire State Building. Exactly like it is in the movies. And there's the Chrysler Building, and the World Trade Center. All of them rosy, rosy pink from the sun behind us. It's like magic! No, it's better than magic, it's like a miracle.

But the best thing, the best thing ever, hanging next to the Trade Center towers, taking up almost the whole sky. Huge and red and fiery, like a giant blood orange...

'There you go, kid,' says Carlos. 'We fixed that moon up specially for your arrival. Welcome to New York,' he says. 'Welcome to the rest of your life.'

*

The apartment is empty when I wake up. Empty and dark. I sit up in bed and turn on the lamp, check how I look in the mirror.

Fucking nightmare, that's how. Fucking monster from the deep lagoon.

How I feel too.

My comb and toothbrush are laid out on the top of the little basin between the bed and the door so I slide up off the bed, wet my hair down, clean my teeth until the giant swamp monster disappears. Above the sink there's a picture

168

of a cat. All splodgy and awkward, just like the pictures our Lisa used to draw when she was little. The ones Mam always made such a big fuss of, sticking them up on the kitchen wall like they were Picasso's or something.

Still, at least our Lisa used to use colour. This cat is just black and white splodges. Like the rest of the place.

Everything in this apartment is black and white. White walls, black furniture, black and white rugs, black and white pictures. Black and white window blinds. Black and white everything. Except the floor, which is little wood diamonds. Like a giant jigsaw puzzle, only with some of the pieces missing.

I go down the hall, past Carlos and Thalia's bedroom, past another splodgy picture, some sort of African mask thing, to the living room. Well, it's the living-dining-hall-and-kitchen-room really. There's not many doors in this flat. Carlos took most of them off to let in more light. The only windows in the whole place are one tiny one in each of the bedrooms, which face straight out onto a brick wall so are no bloody good and the two big ones here in the lounge.

Poky or what?

But I musn't complain. I mean, it's not like I'm paying rent or anything. And anyway, it's just temporary, while I get my bearings. I'll soon get my own place. A proper New York loft. I'll have loads of light then.

In the kitchen, propped up against the microwave next to a packet of bread rolls, there's a note from Carlos.

Hi, Ani.
Hope you slept OK. Me and Thalia have gone over to Stingy Lulu's. The place we were last night?
Meet you there.
Oh, and we bought you these to make you feel at home.

Enjoy! C.

169

I pick up the bread rolls.

Thomas' English Muffins

What the fuck's a muffin?

They taste all right though, sort of sweet. I eat three, toasted with some red jam with no bits in it so you can't tell if it's raspberry or strawberry and crumbly white butter that comes in a funny stick pack. Then I get dressed and head over to Stingy Lulu's.

My first time outdoors on my own in New York. Even though it's gone nine and getting dark, a gang of kids is playing baseball in the street outside, yelling at each other in a funny language. They look about our Lisa's age, maybe a bit older. I can't really tell because they're Chinese. When I walk past them they stop still like statues and stare at me till I'm way past their pitch line. Till I'm all the way over the other side of Avenue C.

Carlos tells everyone his apartment is in the East Village, because the East Village is trendy. But it's not really, it's in Alphabet City. Carlos says he has enough problems without people knowing he lives in Alphabet City. Carlos says Alphabet City is totally safe now Giuliani has cleaned everywhere up, but you try telling people that. Especially cab drivers.

New Yorkers go everywhere by cab. They're really cheap compared to back home.

On the next corner there's a shop with a metal shutter pulled down tight. The sign above the shop is some funny square black writing and below that KOSHER WINES in big black letters. Blue and red Chinese graffiti splashed across the shutter. Above the sign is a metal balcony with a red geranium on it in a big old white paint tub and above the balcony is a metal ladder leading up to another metal balcony and another. These are the fire escapes. Carlos and Thalia and me have got one outside our apartment. All New York houses have them. It's the law. Carlos says he couldn't believe it when he first came to Cardiff and saw that the houses don't all have balcony fire escapes. Don't we care if we all burn in our beds?

Our fire escape is Carlos's thinking place. But it's really his smoking place. Carlos is forever climbing out the apartment window and squatting out on the fire escape, even when it's raining because Thalia won't let him smoke in the house.

Thalia has asthma.

After Avenue B is Tompkin's Square Park. This used to be where they had loads of riots. Carlos says there was even a song about it. But now it's been cleaned up too, like everywhere else. Well, almost. There are still a couple of meths drinkers sitting on a bench near the gate. But I'm not scared because right next door to them is a cop car with two cops in it, keeping an eye out for trouble.

Wonder if they're Carlos's mates?

'So, you wanna hold my snake?'

I jump straight back from leaning against the railings. A bloke is standing right up close next to me. A really creepy-looking bloke with white stringy hair and dirty jeans tucked into rubber boots. He holds out his arms to me and lying across them, Oh my God, lying right across them and round his neck, I can't believe it, it's a giant fucking snake!

The snake is thick and white with pale brown patches all down its back and it doesn't move, even when the man holding it lifts it up again and holds it out to me about six inches from my face.

'So, you wanna hold it or what?' the snake man says.

'No, I don't want to fucking hold it, what do you take me for?!' I yell, back away quick sharp.

But I can't go far because the railings are right behind me and the loony and his snake are right in front. I twist round looking for the cop car. But it's gone, and so have all the meths drinkers. The street is totally empty except for me, a mad bloke and his snake.

I look down at the snake. The snake looks up at me. Pink eyes.

171

The snake man takes another step towards me.

'I told you to keep that thing away from me, it might bite.'

'No it won't. And even if it did it ain't poisonous. It's a python. An albino. Very rare,' he says.

'I don't care what the fuck type of python it is, just keep it away from me!'

I'm yelling at the top of my voice now.

It works. The snake man looks hurt but steps back again.

I look round me again. Still no one else around in the street. Nobody else around in the whole fucking world.

'Hey, where you from?' asks the snake man. 'You've got an accent. You from England?'

I don't believe this. Is he crazy, or what?

'Thought so. I could tell from the way you say fuck. You English say fuck so politely.'

One hundred per cent certifiable, this one. Any second now the men in white coats will come along and recapture him.

'I just love English accents.'

Better keep the nutso talking, though. Till someone comes.

So I say, 'Why are you walking around with a snake, anyway?'

'I just like it. It's like my thing,' says the snake man.

'How long you been here in the Big Apple?' he says.

'Two days.'

Any second now...

'How long you staying?' he says.

Why's everyone so interested in how long I'm staying?

'Till I get famous,' I say.

And where the fuck are the white coats when you need them?

The snake man looks me up and down. One green eye. One blue eye.

'Famous as what?' he says.

'Dunno. Just famous,' I say.

The snake man nods. 'You can be anything you want in this town. You just gotta find your thing.'

I keep my eye on his thing, make sure it isn't going to bite me. Under the streetlamp, the patches on its back are almost pink. I put out my hand to touch it, but then change my mind.

'So where do you get an albino python from anyway?' I say instead.

'Omaha,' says the snake man.

'Omaha?'

'Omaha.'

'Where's that then?'

The snake man jerks his thumb backwards over his shoulder. 'Midwest,' he says.

'Oh right. I know. That's where Iowa is. That's in the Midwest, isn't it?'

'Kinda,' says the snake man.

I look at the snake again. 'My friend Carlos, the one I'm staying with? He's from Iowa,' I say.

'Go on, hold it,' the snake man says, stepping up to me again.

'No ta,' I say.

'Go on.'

'No, really,' I say. 'You're all right. I have to go now, anyway. My friend, he'll worry about me if I'm late. He's a cop. He gets really worried about me, being so new and everything,' I say.

And I pull my rucksack up onto my shoulder and take a tiny step sideways, like I'm ready to be off. But it doesn't work. Snake man doesn't move. He just stands there staring at me.

We stare at each other.

Then, suddenly, quick as a flash, the snake man leaps forward and I can't believe it because he's lifting the snake up and dropping it round my neck! Right round my fucking neck! My hands jump up but it's no good because the snake is already on me, I can feel it on me, the weight of it, its skin, wrapped all over me, around me.

I want to smack out at the snake man, tell him to get his thing the fuck off me, but he's fading away, look see?, he's fading away. Till it's just me and the snake. Nobody moving. Nobody breathing. All I can feel is the snake. Crackly dry skin. Scales inside my mouth.

Then the snake flexes a muscle and a ripple runs along its back, over my shoulder, behind my neck, and right through my head. And I'm thrashing and sliding down the railings, over the pavement and off down the street.

Running for my fucking life.

Chapter Eighteen

'PRAISE THE LORD!'

I get called in by the hospital at six thirty-five. Dad is acting up again. Extra loud this morning, says Sister Anne.

'PRAISE THE LORD!'

You can hear him all the way down in the cafeteria, she says.

'LET THE EARTH HEAR HIS VOICE!'

She hates to bother me so early but the other patients are beginning to complain and it is all rather getting in the way of breakfast.

'PRAISE THE LORD!'

It happens nearly every morning now. This morning it began at six with 'Onward Christian Soldiers'. Normally they manage to calm him down after a couple of verses with tea and toast, but on his bad mornings, when he's really agitated, well, you know there's only one thing that works and much as she'd love to be able to do it, well it's just that it takes so much time and there's so much to be done before Doctor makes his rounds and

I pat her forearm to reassure her and push open the door.

'PRAISE THE LORD!'

Dad sits bolt upright. He doesn't look a pretty sight. Hair sticking up, false teeth hanging loose, cheeks flushed with blood and smeared with breakfast. And all the toast crumbs, the marmalade, the transcendent bliss, none of it can hide the hollowness of his cheeks, the bone scraping against the underside of his skin.

Dad pauses in his singing and I can tell he's looking at me, even though his eyes are closed.

'Hello, Dad,' I say.

'PRAISE THE LORD!' he replies, flashing his gums.

A bit wobbly after the stroke maybe, but still a decent tenor. After forty-three years of dithering, my father has finally been blessed with utter conviction. It's just a shame he doesn't know it.

'LET THE PEOPLE REJOICE.'

I look round the room. Clean. Comfortable. Controlled.

Dad couldn't stay on at the Royal Gwent. He wasn't sleeping. Actually no, that's not true. That's just the story I tell everyone. But you, you deserve the truth.

'SO GIVE HIM THE GLORY,'

Truth is, it was the other patients who weren't sleeping. Things got so bad they were having to sedate Dad almost every day.

It's much better here. He's much calmer.

I sit down on bed, which is so high my legs dangle off the edge. Leaning across Dad's legs, I pick the Bible up from the trolley table. 'Where were we?' I say, opening it up at the marked page.

'GREAT THINGS HE HAS DONE.'

'Ah yes, Proverbs.' And I start reading, loudly.

'*Ages ago I was set up . . .*'

Immediately Dad falls silent and listens.

'*. . . at the first, before the beginning of the earth. When there were no depths I was brought forth; when there were no springs abounding with water. Before the mountains had been shaped . . .*'

It's funny how Wisdom is a woman in the Old Testament, isn't it? I mean, let's face it, women don't usually have a good press in the Bible, do they? Especially not in the Old

Testament. Holds women responsible for just about everything, the Old Testament. When it mentions them at all, that is. But here it is in black and white. Wisdom and the Holy Spirit. Both *she*.

And that's not the best bit either.

The best bit, or so the story goes, is that God created Wisdom before she created anything else.

Before the earth, before the waters, the clouds, volcanoes.

Before the primordial soup.

Before the fluctuations in the quantum field became a condensed mass of fundamental particles of energy-matter which, in a constantly expanding space, coalesced into the present observable universe.

Before all that came Wisdom.

'*Delighting in the human race.*'

More fool her, if you ask me.

Of course, there are other stories. There always are. Dante tried to convince everyone that Virgil was more than sufficient a guide through the circles of hell. Only at the very threshold of heaven did he concede a helping hand from Beatrice. And even Aristotle rejected feminine intuition for the cold, hard drive of logic.

But that's philosophers for you.

And for me?

I just never manage to see down the road far enough. Take this business with Ani and New York. I sure as hell didn't see *that* coming, did I?

Wisdom – daughter, lover, designer. Providing experience, intuition and, above all, order, with the lightest of hands, the most gracious of touches.

All else that is needed is the power and creativity to apply them.

Is that all?

Yet even so, I sometimes wonder at the wisdom of wisdom. I sometimes wish we could give all this self-awareness stuff a miss and move on life through instinct, like cats.

Less human. More being.

Dad flings his arm up over his head and mutters something. Potatoes, I think. At the same time his left cheek starts twitching uncontrollably.

The stroke has weakened most of Dad's muscles. But it's the muscle of his memory that has suffered the most. It's not just the singing. He can't carry out any proper conversation, or at least any that involve something more than a moment's reality. His thoughts circle in his mind like an LP record, round and round in the same worn grooves, playing over and over, then skipping across to a different track altogether.

The worst part is, I think, that sometimes he knows he's not remembering. Every now and then glimpses of the old Dad pop back up through the haze and he is transformed.

Right then, as if on cue, Dad stops muttering, opens his eyes and looks at me, grey eyes sharp as knives.

'I saw your mother this morning,' he says.

Despite myself, I feel my shoulders tightening. But I keep my voice matter-of-fact. 'Oh yes?' I say. 'How was she?'

'Oh, you know your mother, busy as ever. She brought me a cake. A Victoria sponge.' He smacks his lips together. 'Made a bit of a pig of myself with it, I'm afraid. Paying for it now, mind. But it was worth it. Never could resist one of your mother's sponge cakes.'

See what I mean? It's like this day after day. But I have to keep trying. The doctor told me that the more conversations Dad and I have, the more I jog his memory, the more sense he should make. Eventually. So I come here every day and tell him all our memories.

Some days I can talk for hours. Some days I can barely talk at all.

My first memory is one of fear. When I was still very much a baby – two at the most – my mother stopped bathing me in the plastic baby tub in the lounge in front of the electric fire and made me sit in the proper bath upstairs.

178

To keep me from drowning, she only ever filled the bath up an inch or two with water and I would sit shivering, staring up the avocado sides to the tangerine tiles above. At the end of every bath, Mum would pull the plug and the water would swirl under my legs and down the plug hole. And every single time I would try to scramble out, screaming with terror. But the sides were always too high and too slippery. I had no choice but to wait the eternity for my mother to reach down and pick me up, wrap me up in a towel and cuddle me until everything was perfect again.

My mother would always laugh at my antics even as she comforted me. Because, of course, she knew what I didn't – that I wasn't going to wash away down the plughole with the water.

She had the wisdom.

I still haven't learned. But I expect you've worked that one out for yourself by now, haven't you?

Thought so.

Dad starts to thrash about again so I carry on with Proverbs. But it's no use, he's soon off.

'GOD IS LOVE,' he shouts.

'Shush, Dad, shush. You're disturbing everybody.'

But it's no use.

'LOVE IS OF GOD,' he screams.

Sister Anne pokes her head round the open door, fingers to her lips. I smile, wave the Bible weakly at her and she retreats, closing the door firmly behind her.

'A-MA-Z-ING GRACE.'

Oh no, here we go again.

I wheedle and plead with him for a full five minutes but it's useless. There's only one thing that works. So I pick the Bible back up.

I suppose you think it's ironic, that it happens to us all eventually. Role reversal, I mean. Dad is now the child and I the adult. He spent all that time, all those years, protecting me, and now it's my turn to protect him. Well I can tell you it's nothing like that. He's still my dad. In his actions, his facial expression, the look in his eyes – he's still my dad. Even with all this bloody singing. The way he stops halfway through a hymn, takes a sip of tea, then blithely carries on. That's my dad all over. Just slower and a bit blurred round the edges.

The tables may have turned slightly, but the past has not been erased.

And the future?

Well, as Dad will probably shout out any minute now, if you want to make God laugh, tell Her your plans.

After only fifteen more minutes of reading, the crisis is over and Dad has dozed off, still propped up in a nest of pillows, snoring gently and dribbling out the corner of his mouth. I get up off the bed, slide past the trolley table to the side cabinet and pick up the water jug, pour some water into a plastic beaker, then dip the corner of Dad's flannel into the beaker and gently wipe all the goo off Dad's face. Dad doesn't move. Even when I comb his hair down until it's sleek and shiny again. Sitting back down on the bed, I turn my eyes away from my father's slackened face and stare out at the square of blue sky through Dad's window. I keep my eyes on that blue square and try to keep my thoughts at bay.

'Have you done all your homework?' Dad says, waking up as quickly as he dropped off.

I twist round to look at him again. 'Yes, Dad,' I say.

'You know what your mother's like about you getting your homework done.'

'Yes, Dad. Dad...'

'I know she's a bit strict with you sometimes, love. But she's got your best interests at heart, you know that, don't you?'

'Dad...'

'She's right and all. You'll never get that place at art college you're always going on about if you don't do your homework.'

'Dad, I want you to do something for me.'

'But you're a good girl really. I know that. And so does your mother.'

'Thanks. Dad, I want you to do me a favour. All right, Dad? Dad?'

'Well, what is it?'

I jump, then clear my throat. It gets me every time, this sudden shift back into reality.

'I want you to lie back and think of somewhere calm and peaceful.'

'Peaceful.'

'That's right, Dad. Calm and peaceful.'

'Cottage.'

'That's it, Dad. Lovely. A lovely cottage, somewhere calm and peaceful. By the sea maybe. That's it, Dad. I want you to think of a peaceful little cottage by the sea on a beautiful calm day.'

'Where is it, this cottage?'

'What? Oh yes...um...The Mumbles, yes that's it. The Mumbles. Remember the Mumbles, Dad? You always liked the Mumbles, didn't you? I want you to think of that cottage we used to stay in, at the Mumbles.'

'No.'

'What?'

'No, it can't be by the sea. The cottage. It can't be by the sea.'

'Why ever not?'

'Oh come on, love, use your imagination. The sea, water, that's sex, isn't it? I'm not going to calm down much thinking about sex now, am I?

'That's always your mother's trouble too. The Mumbles, specially.

'She always wants to throw all her clothes off and dive straight in.'

*

Coming out through the door to reception – more like a hotel than a hospital, with sofas and percolated coffee – I pass a woman with short auburn hair and a massive black bruise arching backwards across her cheek from the bridge of her nose to the row of silver loops in her ear. It looks like she's been battered by a crowbar. But as I walk past she yawns, lifts up her hand and rubs her right eye like a child trying to stay up way past bedtime and I see the blemish is more to do with mascara than mayhem.

*

By the time I get home from Dad I'm totally exhausted. All I want to do is sleep, be by myself. But of course there's no chance of that because Louise is in the kitchen washing up last night's dishes, fixing my lunch, generally being useful.

Generally being a pain in the bloody arse.

Hearing me approach, Louise spins round from the sink, a cheery caring smile pinned to her face, and waves the kettle at me. 'Hi, you're early,' she says. 'Fancy a cup?'

I set the car keys down on the breakfast table very, very carefully. 'No thanks,' I say.

'Sure?' she says. 'It's no trouble.'

I know I should be grateful. I know she's only trying to be kind. It's just that everything is so bloody organised, so bloody *neat*. The worktops, the kitchen floor, they all sparkle. The living-room carpet has been hoovered to within an inch of its life. She's even polished the chair legs, for heaven's sake. It makes me want to scream. It makes me want to rip the neat blue ribbon which exactly matches the stripes in her neat blue jumper off the bottom of her neat brown plait and wrap it tight around her neat pink throat.

But of course I don't. I just snap, 'Yes I'm bloody sure, OK?' at her and then immediately feel guilty when she flushes and turns away, tears in her eyes.

'Sorry,' I mutter.

'That's OK,' Louise says tightly, wiping the dishcloth round and round inside a wine glass until it squeaks.

I walk over to the sink, lay my hand on her shoulder. 'No, it's not OK,' I say. 'It was bloody rude and I'm an ungrateful cow especially when you're bending over backwards to help me. I'm sorry, Lou, it's just, well,' I pull out a chair and flop down at the table, run my hands through my hair. 'If I get one more offer of a cup of tea, one more home-baked cake, one more casserole, I think I might kill somebody.'

Still not looking at me, Louise switches on the kettle, opens the cupboard above her head and pulls down the jar marked TEABAGS, dumps two bags into two clean cups. 'Yes I know, it's dreadful, isn't it,' she says. 'We have no idea what to say at times like these. I remember when Mum was in her last stages.' She pours hot water into the cups. 'Every time anyone asked me how she was doing I wanted to yell 'still dying' at them, just to see what they would do. But you can't, can you? In the end, I took to wearing big hats and dark glasses in Commercial Street, just so no one would recognise me.'

I don't know where to put myself. 'I'm sorry about your mum,' I say. 'I didn't know.'

Louise slides the two cups of tea onto the kitchen table and sits down opposite me. 'Why should you?' she shrugs, stretching over and pulling the milk out from inside the fridge door. 'It was a couple of years ago now. You weren't here.'

'And I don't know why I'm so bad-tempered and teary all the time still,' I say. 'It's been over a month now since Dad got ill.'

'You're under a lot of strain, what with teaching and the commission.'

'It's just that I feel so hemmed in half the time. And the other half, well, it's mad. I alternate between wanting to spend twenty-four hours a day with Dad and wanting to run away, back to London, back to my life.' I stare morosely down at the African violet which Louise has moved from the windowsill to the centre of the table. 'I must be the worst daughter in the world.'

'No, just human. Life goes on, it has to,' Louise says. 'If you were seven years old you'd be stamping your foot and screaming how unfair all this is, how you want to go swimming instead. But adults aren't supposed to stamp their feet. We're supposed to grin and bear it all. Even though the feelings don't go away.'

After that, neither of us knows what to say, so we just drink our tea.

'You know what we need now, don't you?' I say when I can't bear the silence another second.

'What's that?' Louise says.

'Cake!' I say. 'We need cake. Home-baked bloody cake.'

'And lots of it!' Louise says.

So we dig into Auntie Myrna's home-baked coffee and walnut sponge cake with extra thick double cream on the side. Between mouthfuls, Louise tells me there's a message on the answerphone from Bob Koch, but I can't think about that now.

'You know,' I giggle. 'A couple of months ago my dad would have died rather than spend weeks cooped up in bed with the Romans.'

'Yeah, your dad's always been on the low side, hasn't he?'

'So low, he's practically horizontal.'

'What about you?' Louise says.

'What about me?'

'Do you believe in God?'

I look up at the phone hanging up on the wall. I look at the noticeboard with the parish list stuck to it. I look at the calendar with the PCC meeting highlighted for tomorrow evening in green. Look at the light switch. At the thermometer.

'I'm not sure what I believe in any more,' I say.

'It's a very good hospital, you know, St Joseph's,' I say.

'Yes,' says Louise.

'Dad's much more settled there than he was at the Gwent.'

'Good,' she says.

'But so expensive. I can hardly believe ... '

Louise shifts in her seat. 'Now, now, Daryl. Stop fishing. You know I can't tell you who's paying for it. The entire PCC has been sworn to secrecy. Anyway, it's not important. What's important is your dad gets better as soon as possible.'

I give up. Louise always was a bit of a clam when it came to gossip.

'Anyway, it's the true meaning of the Church,' she says.

'What?'

'You know, the creed: *We believe in one holy catholic and apostolic Church*. That's what the word catholic really means: universal, open to all,' she says.

'God, Lou,' I say, standing up and scraping my chair across the tiled floor. 'You're such a bloody English teacher sometimes. Want another cup?'

Chapter Nineteen

I run and run as fast as I can up Avenue A and into St Mark's Place. As soon as I turn the corner I see the sign for Stingy Lulu's, see the Indian Chief statue outside the front door. Life-size.

I stop outside the big glass window of Stingy Lulu's, which is all fogged up on the inside so you can't see who's there, you can just see shapes moving, colours. But I don't go in straight away. Instead I walk up the pavement a little bit, past the Indian Chief statue, past a woman selling body jewellery, past a fancy-dress shop, stand against the wall of the fancy-dress shop's stoop, light a cigarette and just lean there for a bit, looking around. Above the Indian Chief's head the Stingy Lulu sign is all lit up, pink and blue. The whole street is lit up. Signs and market stalls and people. Loads of people everywhere. Every single person in the entire world is stuffed into St Mark's Place, cruising each other, cruising me.

Have to roll the icy waves down my body for two whole cigarettes before I stop shaking.

Don't want Carlos and Thalia to see I've been running. Don't want them to see me scared.

I fucking hate snakes.

But then it starts raining again so I walk back down the block, past the Indian Chief statue and push through the door into Stingy Lulu's.

Stingy Lulu's is a cross between a bar and a diner. A real old-fashioned fifties American diner. Only more so. Walking into Stingy Lulu's is like walking into a Doris Day film where someone's been playing about with the controls on the telly, turned all the colour and sound buttons to maximum, then outlined everything in black felt-tip.

Carlos and Thalia are sitting in a booth at the back drinking Bloody Marys and eating fried calamari. Carlos is wearing his new drag outfit – *Red Mario from the Barrio* – which clashes with the lime green and yellow of the booth. Thalia just in her leather coat, as usual. I walk over to them and Thalia pats the empty seat next to her for me to slide into, facing Carlos. I sit down. Then I just sit there. I want to tell Carlos and Thalia about the snake man but I'm not sure, so I just sit there. I just sit there and listen to Carlos tell Thalia about the new club again, about how great it's going to be, listen to the music coming out the jukebox. Doris Day music.

Then our waitress comes over to our table. Doris Day pink dress and apron. Doris Day blonde wig. Terrible waitress, she is. Slops the coffee around something shocking. And we never even asked for coffee. Sharon would never let me get away with that kind of service back home.

But the worst thing is when she pulls two fistfuls of sugar and powdered milk packets out of her apron pocket, dumps them down on the table, right in the coffee puddle!, and then sits down. Right next to Carlos!

Turns out our waitress has been due a break for twenty minutes and her feet are killing her on account she's wearing new red stilettos.

Turns out she's not just our waitress, she's also a mate of Carlos's.

Turns out she's not just our waitress, she's also a drag queen called Patrice.

Thalia and I say hi to Patrice, then Carlos tells Patrice all about our new club, how great it's going to be. How it's going to be more out there than anything else in the East Village, in the whole of Manhattan.

I'm not really listening. I'm too busy looking at Patrice. I can't get over how great she looks. I mean, if it weren't for the fact she's six foot one, if it weren't for her deep voice, the five o'clock shadow on her chest, you'd never know.

Then Patrice catches me staring so I look away, quick sharp, feel my ears turning beetroot.

'Sorry,' I say.

'That's OK, honey,' Patrice says. 'I like to be admired.' And she runs her hand across the top of her sweetheart neckline. Candy pink nails to match her candy pink dress. 'My boobs always were my breast feature,' she says, cups her right tit in her hand. 'Gonna hafta do something about this little one, though.'

I keep staring. 'They look fine to me,' I say.

'Nah, the nipple won't stay erect, the rubber's too soft. The left one's OK, which is just too annoying because I bought them as a matched pair only six weeks ago.'

Carlos and Thalia snigger into their celery sticks.

Patrice just carries on talking. 'It would be better if I could just put on a little weight,' she says. 'The advantage of being a fat cross-dresser is you can grow your own boobs. But me, everything I eat goes straight into these luscious long legs of mine.' And she picks up my hand and lays it right on her candy pink knee!

I can feel my whole face turn beetroot now, right up into my hair.

'Feel how silky smooth they are,' she says and drags my hand slowly up her thigh, pressing it down hard. Till the ends of my fingers poke through the holes in her fishnets. Till I can feel the skin of her candy pink thighs. And all the time Patrice is pulling on my hand, dragging it nearer and nearer towards her.

I just manage to yank my fingers free before my hand reaches her hem and I find out exactly what she's got hiding underneath her candy pink skirt. I yank my hand away and fold it safe in my lap, inside the other one, keeping both my hands well clear of Patrice's legs. Keeping my eyes well clear of Patrice's chest, keeping my eyes fixed on the jukebox over by the toilet.

Patrice sits back in the booth and sips her coffee. Winks at me.

I eat a piece of calamari. And another. 'Do you shave them? Your legs, I mean?' I say.

Carlos nearly busts a gut when I ask Patrice that. But Patrice just smiles a slow smile, licks her lips.

'Oh sure. Legs, arms, chest. And what I can't shave, I pluck,' she says, points to her eyebrows. 'I'm a very furry girl.'

'Doesn't that hurt?' I say. 'Plucking, I mean?'

Patrice looks sad for a second. 'A little,' she says. 'But you have to suffer for beauty.' Then she stops for a minute, looks me up and down, my jeans, T-shirt, flat-combed hair. 'At least, some of us do,' she says, giant bitchy smile across her face.

'Yeah,' I say, smile back even harder. 'Especially when we get older.'

But then I decide I'm not going to let Patrice get to me. I decide I'm going to tell her and Carlos and Thalia all about the snake man instead. So I do.

Just the bare facts, mind.

Got to keep my cool.

But when I tell them, Carlos and Thalia and Patrice, they're not cool about it at all. They're all really shocked, like something terrible has happened. Thalia puts her hand across her mouth and gasps. Carlos scowls.

And Patrice? Patrice just squeals.

'Oh my God. Oh my God. Oh my God,' she says. 'What did you do? Did you scream? Oh my God, I would've screamed.'

For some reason this makes me feel better about the whole thing and I really can be cool about it.

189

Now it's over.

'Well no, not really,' I say. 'I didn't do anything. I couldn't, could I?' I say and rub the condensation off the side of my glass, look over at Carlos muttering under his breath, shaking his head so hard I think his bandana is going to fall down over his eyes. 'I mean I thought it was just a New York thing. You know, like you're always saying, Carlos – anything and everything can happen in this town,' I say.

'Not like that,' Carlos says. 'That's just plain weird. If a guy had done something like that to me I'd have kicked his ass.'

'Damn straight,' says Patrice.

Even Thalia puts her arm around my shoulders, gives me a squeeze, her long silky hair tickling the back of my hand.

This makes me feel totally brilliant!

'It wasn't that big a deal,' I say.

'Are you kidding?' Patrice says. 'It was assault. Pure assault. You should sue.'

'Right,' says Carlos.

'Really?' I say.

'Put it this way, Ani,' says Thalia. 'What would you've done if someone had done that to you back home in Cardiff?'

'Dunno,' I say, sip my Bloody Mary through the straw. 'Sued them, I guess.'

Well, I might have. If I knew any lawyers in Cardiff.

Carlos picks up the bill, works out the tip, and lays the exact money down on the table, then stands up, ready to leave. 'Where did you say this guy accosted you?' he says. 'We should go find him.'

I can tell from the way he's standing that he's really getting into the idea. I can tell from the way he shoves both hands into his front pockets, rocks forward and back on his heels that he really wants to fetch a couple of his cop mates and go round, sort the snake man out. But I don't want any trouble. I don't want Carlos to find out how chicken I really was. So I tell Carlos I want another drink first. Don't I need one after all I've been through? Then, when he's got the round in, I get him to tell us one more time about this place he's found, the place he reckons is going to be the perfect venue for our new club. The club that's going to make us all rich and famous.

*

It's a crypt. A real one. You know, in the basement of a church, the bit where they used to keep all the dead bodies? Not any more, though. The last dead body was taken out in 1925 when the crypt was made into a soup kitchen to feed the poor and needy. It was a soup kitchen all through the Depression and World War Two.

'At least, that's what the priest says,' says Carlos, 'But I'm not so sure. They'd need a hell of a lot of bones to make all that soup.'

We're standing in front of the crypt door, which is big and black and old. Carlos opens the door with a huge rusty iron key, like the key to a giant's castle. Then he leads us into the crypt itself, down a spiral iron staircase.

'I don't think you should make jokes like that Carlos, not in a church,' says Patrice.

But Carlos just laughs. 'Church is the only place you can make jokes like that. God's always had a weird sense of humour. Look at penguins,' he says.

Carlos is always saying stuff about God. Carlos still believes in God. Always has done, he says, since he was a little kid. It's just that now his God isn't the same God that it was when he was growing up. His God isn't bigoted and judgemental. His God is accepting and gender-free. That's the only type of God he can believe in. The only way he can still call himself a Catholic, he says.

That and the fact that he likes to see men dressed up in frocks, of course.

When Carlos says stuff like that he reminds me of Daryl's dad. I wonder how he's doing, Daryl's dad? I really miss him. I should talk to Daryl and find out. I should talk to her anyway and tell her that Carlos has found us this crypt for our club, find out which of her sculptures she wants to show, how she wants to show them. They'll look really good, Daryl's sculptures, in the club. I've been meaning to talk to her about it for ages but I've been putting it off. Daryl hates me being in New York.

Down and down the spiral staircase we go. Going down the staircase is just like it is in one of those old horror movies. Spooky and smelly. The light from Carlos's candle the only light, flickering in the pitch black, sending ghosts up and down the wall. I can hardly move because Patrice has got hold of the banister with one hand and my waist tight with the other, so we have to slide down the steps sideways like a crab with four legs. Carlos is really enjoying himself, trying to scare us all by making howly ghost noises. Thalia brought a flashlight with her but Carlos won't let her use it, says we have to soak up the whole atmosphere first.

I just hope the candle doesn't go out.

At the bottom of the spiral staircase there's another door. A more modern one, painted white. Opens without a key. Carlos tells me and Thalia and Patrice to wait in the doorway with the candle while he takes the flashlight through to find the light switches.

With the candle shining against the white door, there's more light. It's not so spooky. It's almost normal. While we wait for Carlos, Patrice sits down on the bottom step, rubs her ankle and complains about the holes in the metal grating ruining the heels of her new red stilettos. Me and Thalia just lean against the wall next to the door, roll our eyes at all Patrice's moaning.

'What's that terrible smell?' says Thalia, wrinkles up her nose. 'Damp and dust and ...' she sniffs '... and piss.'

'Rat piss,' I say.

'Rats!' Patrice squeals. 'Where?'

'In the walls,' I say. 'Giant rats.'

'Gnawing away at the leftover bones,' says Thalia.

'Oh my God. Oh my God,' moans Patrice and starts legging it back up the steps, back up into the street. Even though we've still got the candle with us. Even though it's pitch black up there now. After about five steps Patrice realises me and Thalia are not running after her. That we're still at the bottom of the steps. That we're laughing at her.

Patrice stomps back down the stairs again.

'You're such a baby, Patrice, you'll fall for anything,' I say.

'Yeah, yeah, all right you got me. You got me good,' she says. 'But shut up about rats, will you? I fucking hate rats.'

Just then the lights come on and we can see the whole crypt now. Brick arches, bricks all painted white, leading away in front of us, leading away for ever. Giant brick pillars holding everything up. Patrice and Thalia and I step into the crypt, walk down the brick corridor. Under our shoes, the carpet is green and dirty. Worn out. Concrete floor shining through in places. Off the main corridor more arches lead into other arches. The whole crypt all arches. Most you can walk through, except the arches up against the end walls. These are like caves, cave arches stuffed with old boxes and broken chairs.

The bad smell is coming from one of the cave arches. The middle one. The smell is so bad you can hardly believe it. It is so bad you have to pinch your nose with your fingers, remember to breathe through your mouth. There's no way we can have a club in here with that smell. How the hell are we going to fix it?

Carlos climbs up the pile of rubbish into the cave arch, up onto the old boxes, pulls down some chairs. Shines the flashlight at the back wall and behind the chairs you can just make out a tiny ventilation grid, holes all clogged and dusty, leading out onto the street.

'There's one of these in every arch,' Carlos says. 'We can hire some air-conditioners, stick them up here and, hey presto, no more smell.'

'You're so clever, Carlos,' says Thalia. 'You think of everything.'

Yeah right. Like that's really going to work. Like we're not going to need air-conditioners the size of the Empire State Building to get rid of this smell.

I leave them to their fantasy, walk into the centre of the arches where there's a big space around four pillars, bare floorboards. Good for dancing. And that's when I see the bar.

A life-sized bar fully made up between two arches with glasses, optics, beer pumps, everything. It's even got ashtrays and beer cloths.

And a sign behind the bar saying: *Be sure brain is in gear before engaging mouth*.

The minute I see the bar, the sign, is the minute when I start to believe it can really happen, is the minute when I stop worrying about if we're really going to make it, if we're really going to be famous.

The minute I see the bar I can see everything.

I can see the chill-out room, made out of one of the caves on the bar side, only clean and with seats, orange and red seventies covers, chairs and tables laid out in little groups. I can see the bricks painted smoky pink instead of white. I can see where the art will be during the day, the life-size dolls that come to life when the people come at night.

I can see the long narrow room at the back where we can store everything, put all the coats and stuff.

I can see the pool table pushed up against the wall. No cues or balls yet, but the baize is OK. And the toilets, already set up.

The more I see it, the more I like it. No, love it. The whole place is perfect. That's what it is. Fucking perfect. Too fucking perfect for words.

Even the smell isn't too bad, when you get used to it.

But we've got loads to do yet, and we need to get busy. Carlos sends Thalia and Patrice off to measure all the arches, count all the exit signs. I'm not sure why exactly. Something to do with fire regulations I think. Meanwhile, Carlos and I sit down in the chill-out room and look at the figures. Carlos has got it all worked out. The number of people we can get in. How much to charge at the door. How much to put on the bar prices. Even with the rent, even with the bar wages bill, we're still going to be rich. We're still going to be rich and famous!

Chapter Twenty

When exactly is it do you think that knowledge becomes understanding?

*

The sun is shining out of the rearview mirror, blinding me, so I pull the car to a stop on Usk Way, get out and take a look around.

Desolation as far as you can see, rolling south to where all the land stops, to the edge of the sea.

Smell of salt mud and diesel.

Wind gusting down the road, following the course of the river, wrapping itself around my ankles, shaking my hand.

Pebbledash houses with broken windows lined up opposite derelict prefabs.

Gates of South Dock.

Boarded-up Victorian pub with peppercorn tower.

Mission to Seamen.

Sprouting purple buddleia.

Smell of salt mud and diesel.

Two kids leaning over the wire fence, fishing in the river for something exciting. I smile to myself, then turn my back to the water, against the wind. An old woman in a dirty yellow mac, carrying a plastic carrier bag, crosses the road and hobbles up the pavement towards me. As she leans on her walking stick her left hip rolls forward, her leg dragging slightly behind.

'You going over the bridge, my lovely?' she says, stopping just a foot in front of me. Then she takes the last step forward, lays an arthritic hand on my arm and looks up at me, the whites of her eyes yellow with age. 'Cadge a lift?'

Smell of dried sweat and urine.

Gagging, I go to step away, then remember my manners and step back again, trying only to breathe through my mouth, trying to withdraw my skin from under all the points where our clothes touch.

'Where you headed?' I say.

The old woman raises her stick and points straight across the river. Collar of her coat frayed and worn. Stringy grey hair stuck flat to her scalp with grease and dandruff. 'Over by there. The cripple shop,' she says.

'You're in luck. That's where I'm going too.'

'Ta ever so.'

We turn and stagger towards the car, the old woman leaning heavily on my arm, me still breathing through my mouth.

'Do you want to know my name?' the old woman says. 'It's a joke.'

'Go on, then,' I say. 'What is it?'

'It's Agnes, Agnes Day,' she says. 'Get it?'

'Baaaa,' I say.

Agnes giggles. 'What's yours, then?' she says.

'Daryl,' I say.

'What does that mean?'

'Just Daryl,' I say.

'Funny name for a girl, that,' Agnes says.

'Funny girl,' I say, and hold the passenger door open for her.

I last went over the Transporter Bridge as a kid. My memory of it is very blurred. All that's left is a small burn of excitement, a long wait, and the feeling of being way up high. In reality the gondola hangs low over the water. So low that now, at high tide, it feels like if you pushed your

197

fingers between the holes in the grating, you could trail them along the surface of the river, as though you were punting on the Thames.

Agnes and I clamber on board and sit waiting for the fun to begin.

The gondola, the gates, the driver's lookout tower, everything is painted bright blue. Everything is flagged and turreted, relentlessly cheerful. Even the covered pedestrian area has ornate iron benches to sit on, lashed to the side as if we were a ship on the high seas.

And we are on a ship of sorts. A ferry through the air. The hallmark of a bygone era now reduced to a fairground ride.

Roll up. Roll up. Fifty pee each way. Only five left in the world.

It's smoother than you think. The metal cables creak, then shudder. Like a train moving off from the station. Instead of sails, twin towers of steel mark the six hundred foot span. Towers which can be seen from miles around. Towers which are preserved on picture postcards, souvenir tea towels, monuments of civic pride.

Beneath our feet the river leaks out into the sea. And in less than two minutes it's all over.

Isn't it always the same story?

The Independent Living Centre is expecting Agnes. One of the health visitors tries to persuade her to take a bath but she's having none of it. She just wants to take me on the grand tour of all the latest equipment available for the modern stroke victim.

Shower seats
Stair lifts
Motorised armchairs – with or without commodes
Twenty per cent reduction on many items for Orange Badge holders

In the end it's not the wheeled Zimmer frames that get to me. It's not even the incontinence pads. It's the shelves full of adapted cutlery: the easy-grip knives, the elongated forks, the spoons with the handles stuck on at right angles. All in bright primary colours. They remind me of the cutlery in my Wendy house. The one my dad made for me when I was seven. A proper one, not a shop one, with proper furniture and a big yellow daisy painted on the front door. Mum and Dad stayed up all night painting that Wendy house so it would be ready for me bright and early Christmas morning.

I leave the Independent Living Centre without buying anything.

I leave with tears in my eyes.

I leave Agnes road-testing the latest hydraulic chair lift. 'Weee,' she cries sliding up and down and back and forth. 'Weeee.'

*

— Hey Daryl, Bob Koch again. Sorry to hear your bad news. We're all thinking of you here at Corona, and praying your dad gets better real soon. Don't worry about a thing. There's still plenty of time before the opening. Just call me when you feel up to it and we'll catch up.

The most important truth I learned about art I had to learn all by myself, without the benefit of tutors, of books, instructions. The most important truth about art is the most important truth about life. The most important truth about art is what you think you are doing is not what you are really doing. What you think you are doing is sketching, blocking, carving, moulding. What you think you are doing is thinking, moving, speaking, breathing. What you are really doing is none of these things. What you are really doing is all of these things. What you are really doing is telling a story.

Of course, before you even begin to tell the story, you

have to know you've got a story to tell. Then you need to work out exactly who is in the story, how to tell the story and –

and this is the crucial bit –

just exactly who it is who is telling the story.

For years I thought I was the one doing all the telling.

For years I was lying to myself.

Then I thought maybe it was the art that was telling the story, guiding my big dumb blind deaf hands, unfolding the mystery slowly, carefully, until the shape of itself emerged blinking into the light.

I found much truth in this.

So did my critics.

But the real truth, the whole truth, the absolute God's honest to goodness downright salt of the earth truth is that it is the story which is telling the story.

The story always surpasses the understanding of the artist. Even the great ones.

But the story is never going to let the artist off the hook by allowing the artist to abnegate all responsibility. Not that the story couldn't do that if it wanted to. Oh yes. And the artist knows this very well. From the beginning. The artist knows it would be a piece of cake for the story to take over completely, to show the artist by the dazzling brilliance of its own making what little talent the artist has in her own right, what a sorry excuse for a human being the artist really is. The story could do all this and more, with its eyes closed and its hands tied behind its back.

But where's the challenge in that?

Instead, the story grabs both the art and the artist by the throat and pins them up against the wall, forces them to interact with one another, to communicate. This is not easy. There is an awful lot of wrestling and spitting, scratching and crying, pleading, cajoling, swapping tales back and forth. But the story doesn't give up. Even when things look really bad. The story keeps keeping up the pressure, making both sides tell their lies until they finally reach the truth.

Truth is always in the story. Truth is in all the choices made.

Truth is, we only ever know we made the right choices when the story is fully told.

Isn't it always the same story?

*

When Dad sees Ani striding in through the door clutching a bag of grapes and waving the latest copy of *Newsweek* madly about in front of her, his smile stretches wide across his face – stretches as wide as the smile stretched across my own face the first time I saw Ani.

'Reverend Jenkins, Reverend Jenkins, look at this,' she bursts out before she's even properly through the door. 'Look, you're on the front cover, with the mud puppy. Look, see? You're famous!'

Dad pushes himself up off the pillows, the bed creaking underneath him. 'Mud puppy?' he says, his mouth twisting up into a frown.

Ani thrusts the magazine into his hands. 'Yes, look, the mud puppy and you, there, right there on the front cover. Can you believe it? It's amazing,' she says. 'Awesome. Fucking awesome.'

And she flops down on the bed next to Dad's knees, gabbing away about the article, how it calls the mud puppy a miracle of evolution, how she's shown the article to everyone she knows and they're all dead jealous.

'It's a great picture, isn't it?' she says. 'Really looks like a dragon. Not so sure about you, mind. It makes you look like some sort of mad professor or something.'

'Watch it, young lady. You're not too big for a thick ear. And I thought I told you to stop bloody swearing,' Dad scolds and wags his finger at her, his grin stretching wider than ever.

Ani just giggles.

It's only when I see this that I realise how much I've been holding myself together, how much I've been dreading Ani seeing Dad as he is now. Dreading me seeing Dad as he is now. Over and over. It's only now that I know how, ever since Dad got ill, it's been as if I've been wearing corsets, holding everything inside me and at the same time holding everything away. Every day tying the laces tighter and tighter, tighter and tighter. Trying to keep everything flat and under control. Trying to understand Dad, trying to get Dad to understand.

I thought Ani might be able to help. I guessed she just might be able to get through to him. I never dreamed...

You won't believe the amount of begging I had to do to get Ani in here today, the first time, a whole month since Dad had his stroke. She hates sickness, she says. You won't believe how hard I tried to prepare her. How much I warned her just how bad Dad can be on his bad days, just how bad Dad can be on his good days.

But Ani breezes straight in, the first time she's been to visit at all, and Dad responds straight away. Normally, like there's nothing wrong with him. Like the stroke never happened.

Just look at the two of them. Listen.

Ani telling Dad all her stories about Carlos, about his family who live in Iowa City and run a seafood restaurant two thousand miles away from the ocean, any ocean.

Ani telling Dad all about the club she and this Carlos are planning on opening in the crypt of a church, a club that's going to be the most out there in the whole of the East Village.

Ani talking to Dad as if it's perfectly normal that his face is lopsided and slack, that his right hand and arm lies white and unmoving on top of the bedclothes like a dead fish.

Dad listening to Ani like it's perfectly reasonable that anyone would be saying all these mad things, inventing all these strange people.

Ani's body radiating joy and bewitchment as she acts out her new Tom Jones moves.

Dad laughing at the way she can't quite get the hip thrusts right.

Dad banging his good hand against his chest in applause when she starts serenading me with 'Only You'.

Me blushing and stuttering and loving every second of it.

It's just like the way it used to be. It's just like the way it should be.

With every second I can feel the laces loosen, inch by inch. I can feel the breath escaping slowly out of my lungs, feel my whole body sink downwards, root itself into the ground.

All Ani's talk about New York, about nightclubs, endlessly dressing up in weirder and weirder outfits. All the worry Ani's given me these past few weeks. All the hassle. None of it seems to matter any more. None of it is important. This is what's important. Ani and me, with Dad, laughing. Together.

'They'd love this in New York,' Ani says, pointing to the *Newsweek* article lying spread open on the coverlet. 'Everyone wants to be famous in New York. It's their thing.'

What's so wrong with a little fantasy now and again, anyway? What's so wrong with a bit of make-believe. OK, so Ani overdoes it on occasion, but we Welsh are a mystical race. We love reading between the lines. Give us mythology over history every time.

But in our hearts we know the truth. Even when it's wrapped around a story. Especially when it's wrapped around a story.

And don't tell me you've never done it either. Don't tell me you've never added a little embroidery to your life, for pure entertainment value. Plain mischief. There you are, see. We're all guilty of embellishment now and again. We all like to tell tall tales.

Ani tells Dad how worried she is about the mud puppy, how pale it looked when she went to see it yesterday, nothing like as good as it looks in the magazine. Nothing like as good as it looked when he first took us to see it at the university.

'All those tests,' she says, 'they can't be doing it any good. It's so cruel. The poor thing, it should be outside in the fresh air. Not cooped up in some poxy old fishtank.'

The muscles flicker a tune around Dad's face and, struggling for control, he flings his good arm across his chest, pointing out the window, then collapses back against the pillows, closes his eyes.

'Ani,' I say, 'leave it, will you,' I walk round the other side of the bed and fuss around Dad, plumping up his pillow, tucking his sheet back in. 'You've tired him out,' I say.

But she ignores me, carries on about what a travesty all this media attention is.

'Fishtank,' Dad says, barely a whisper.

Ani swivels round, glares at me in triumph. 'There you are, see. Your dad agrees with me. It's cruelty, plain and simple. We should call the RSPCA or something.'

For some reason, after sailing through all the New York bullshit for the millionth time, this really irritates me. 'Oh, come on,' I say. 'It's hardly neglect, is it? That thing gets more love and attention in a week than any of us get in a year. It's treated like bloody royalty.'

'It's suffering,' Ani sniffs. 'You only have to look at it to see that. You don't know, you haven't been up there. What's wrong with you anyway? It's like you don't care any more.'

I fold my arms across my chest, fall forward until my thighs rest against the side of the bed and hiss at her across Dad's chest. 'I've been busy, in case you haven't noticed. Unlike some people I could mention. Some of us haven't got time to sit around all day playing dress-up and visiting baby dragons. Some of us have to work for a living. Some of us have responsibilities. *Family* responsibilities.'

Yes, all right, I shovel that last point on with a trowel. But Ani's only been home once since she moved in the night of

Dad's stroke – to fetch her clothes. A whole month and she hasn't phoned her family once. Her mum's going frantic. Leaving all kinds of stroppy messages on the answerphone. I can tell she doesn't believe a word I'm saying when I tell her Ani will call her back as soon as she can. I can tell she thinks I'm lying to her. That something funny is going on. I wouldn't be surprised if she thought I'd kidnapped Ani and dragged her off into some weird dragon-worshipping cult that uses the Church as a cover for its heinous activities.

'We have to do something,' Ani says. 'Don't you think so, Reverend Jenkins? Don't you think we should do something?'

'Do unto others as you would...' Dad begins, sitting bolt upright again, but collapses back halfway through.

My spine ratchets up a notch and I can feel the laces begin to tighten again. 'For God's sake, Ani,' I hiss. 'Will you bloody well shut up?'

Ani doesn't say a word, she just gets up off the bed, grabs her *Newsweek*, swings her coat over her shoulder and stalks out of the room.

'Now where are you going?' I say.

I follow her out of the room, watching her back bristle as she stalks away down the corridor.

'You'll need the keys if you want to wait in the car,' I call from the doorway.

'You won't forget we're having dinner with Louise and Greg tonight, will you? I said we'd be there for seven,' I yell as she passes the water fountain.

'Fine, have it your own way,' I shout as she disappears through the end doors, then turn back into Dad's room, slamming the door behind me.

'Rejoice in the Lord always,' says Dad.

Chapter Twenty-One

We celebrate by going to D'Agostino's for beer and Coke. Case of beer each. We don't get any food, though, because we're going to order in. You can get anything you want in this town, Carlos says. Any time, day or night.

'Even rice pudding?' I say. 'Even at three o'clock in the morning?'

Carlos puts three six-packs of Coke down into the bottom of the trolley, pisses himself laughing. 'You Brits are nutcases. Why the hell would you wanna eat rice pudding at three o'clock in the morning?'

'I'm only asking,' I say, stare down at the six-packs. Kat used to buy six-packs like that. Kat used to drink eight or nine cans a day. On top of tea and coffee. She was nuts about it. Couldn't get enough of it. Kat used to drink even more than that at one time. Kat used to drink twelve cans a day. But then she got a kidney infection and the doctor made her cut right down.

'Leave her alone, Carlos,' Patrice says. 'If Ani wants to eat rice pudding at three am, she can, if that's her thing. This is New York.'

And then Patrice is bouncing off down the aisle with me hanging off the back of the trolley. The both of us taking giant swigs from our beer cans, ogling the checkout girls, shouting out advertising slogans for all the stuff on the shelves. New ones, ones we've made up specially, just to piss off the heterosexuals.

Is she or isn't she?

The trolley in front's a transvestite.

Lez Beanz Meanz.

I can't believe she's not a girl.

Just for the taste of her.

*

The apartment is empty when I wake up. Empty and dark. I sit up in bed and turn on the lamp, check how I look in the mirror.

Fucking nightmare, that's how. Fucking monster from the deep lagoon.

But my comb and toothbrush are still laid out on the top of the little basin so I slide up off the bed, wet my hair down, clean my teeth until the giant swamp monster disappears again.

Above the sink there's a picture of a face. Some sort of African mask thing, all splodgy and awkward. Black and white. Just like the pictures our Lisa used to draw when she was little. The ones Mam always made such a big fuss of, like they were Picassos or something.

Everything in this apartment is black and white. White walls, black furniture. Black and white everything. Except the floor, which is little wood diamonds. Like a giant jigsaw puzzle, only with some of the pieces missing.

I go down the hall, past Carlos and Thalia's bedroom, past another splodgy picture, a cat, to the living room. Well, it's the living-dining-hall-and-kitchen-room really. There's not many doors in this flat. Carlos took most of them off to let in more light. The only windows in the whole place are one tiny one in each of the bedrooms, which face straight out onto brick walls, so they're no bloody good, and the two big ones here in the lounge.

Talk about poky.

The whole apartment, poky and dark. Empty.

But turns out, when I look out the window, the apartment isn't empty after all.

Turns out, when I look out the window, Carlos and Thalia are sitting out on the porch.

It's not really a porch, mind. It's a fire escape. All New York houses have them. It's the law. Carlos says he couldn't believe it when he first came to Cardiff and saw that none of the houses have fire escapes. Don't we care if we all burn in our beds?

Carlos is squatting down near the railing, smoking a cigarette. He's wearing his new Mario from the Barrio outfit, which is the exact same red colour as the geraniums planted in the old paint pot. Thalia just in jeans, blue leather coat, as usual. I open up the window, climb out to them and Thalia pats the upturned bucket next to her for me to sit on.

'Hi, Ani,' she says. 'Did you you sleep OK?'

'Yes thanks,' I say.

Then I just sit there. I sit there and listen to Carlos tell Thalia about this friend of theirs who picked up this woman in a bar the other night and was really happy because, although they'd just met, it felt like they'd known each other for ever. You know, the beginning of something really special. Anyway, apparently Carlos's friend takes the woman home and the next morning when they wake up Carlos's friend tells the woman how great she is feeling, how the two of them being together feels so comfortable, familiar. The woman just drinks her coffee and smiles. So it should, she says.

Turns out the woman, although she's a woman now, she used to be a man.

Turns out that when the woman was a man she dated Carlos's friend.

Turns out they were an item for nearly a year.

'Really,' I say. 'Wow, and your friend never knew? Never suspected? That's amazing.'

Carlos busts a gut when I say this and Thalia sniggers into her coffee.

'Got you good that time,' Carlos says.

'You shouldn't believe everything you hear, Ani,' Thalia says.

I can feel my ears turning beetroot, so I turn away quick, look over at the railing, at the shop opposite. Metal shutter pulled down tight. Sign above the shop in some funny square black writing and below that KOSHER WINES in big black letters. Blue and red Chinese graffiti splashed across the shutter.

'Yeah,' I say. 'You got me good.'

Course I didn't believe the story. Not really. I knew he was joking really.

It starts raining so we climb back in off the fire escape, go into the kitchen for something to eat. Thalia gets a packet of bread rolls out the freezer, defrosts them in the microwave.

'We bought you these to make you feel at home,' Thalia says.

I pick up the bread rolls.

Thomas' English Muffins

What the fuck's a muffin?

They taste all right, though. Sort of sweet. I eat three, toasted with some red jam with no bits in it so you can't tell if it's raspberry or strawberry and crumbly white butter that comes in a funny stick pack, like a normal pack that's been cut in half lengthways.

The whole time we're eating, Carlos just sits on the sofa with his head in his hands, worrying about the budget for the club. Carlos knows all about budgets. Carlos's Dad runs a restaurant back home in Iowa City. A Mexican seafood restaurant. Carlos says only his father would open a seafood restaurant two thousand miles away from the ocean, any ocean.

Carlos says the budget won't work out. The number of people we can get in the club, how much we can charge on the door, it's not enough. Even if we rake up the bar prices thirty per cent. Even if we cut down on the artworks we display, we're not going to make it. Not with the rent, not with the bar wages bill.

The problem is the fire exits. There aren't any. There's only one one way in and out of the crypt down the steep spiral staircase. So that means we have to limit numbers, if we want to stick to the fire regulations.

'And that's not the only thing,' Carlos says, pushes the papers away from him in disgust, stands up and stalks over to the dining table. 'There's the emergency exit signs. According to the fire regulations we have to put emergency exit signs up above every opening or doorway leading to the main exit. And you know what that means, don't you?' he says, turns round and glares at us, his hands stuck up under his armpits.

'No,' I say.

But Carlos doesn't even hear me, just turns and stares out the window, keeps talking, more to himself than us. 'Practically every arch, that's what that means. And that crypt is all fucking arches. Do you know how much those emergency exit signs cost?' He picks up the bottle of vodka off the table, inspects the label for a couple of seconds, then unscrews the cap, takes a swig. 'And they say we have to plumb in another two toilets, minimum,' he says. 'Fucking fire regulations.'

I don't see why we need any more toilets. I mean, there are two down there already. A Ladies and a Gents. That's enough, isn't it?

'Hah,' Carlos says, takes a second, bigger swig of vodka. 'If you want to make God laugh, tell him your plans.'

'But we can't give up,' I say. 'Not now, not after all the work we've done. We'll find the money.' I cross the rug, reach out my hand, try and get the vodka bottle from him. But Carlos lifts it above my head, out of my reach. 'We just have to use our imagination.'

'Yeah, and what would you know about it?' Carlos growls, pushes me out the way, tosses back another gulp of vodka. 'You're just a kid. Maybe when you're out of diapers you'll understand.'

'Very sorry, I'm sure,' I mutter, turn my back on him. 'I was only saying.'

'Carlos, don't be so rude.' Thalia comes up and puts her arm round my shoulder, gives me a squeeze. 'Ani was just trying to help.'

This makes me feel a bit better. But I'm still really pissed off. Still don't want to look at Carlos. Don't want to give him the satisfaction.

But then I get an idea. A really brilliant idea.

'I've got money,' I say, spin round again. 'I've got loads of money, over two thousand dollars. I've sold my car and everything. You can have that. You can have all of it.'

'Really?' says Carlos, putting down the vodka bottle.

I can tell he's really getting into the idea. I can tell he really wants to say yes. He wants to use my money to make the club. To make it all perfect. My money.

But then Thalia goes and ruins everything.

'We can't take your money, Ani,' she says. 'That's all the money you have to live on.'

Sounds just like Mam, she does.

'Yes you can.'

'No we can't. It wouldn't be fair. Tell her, Carlos.'

Carlos looks at Thalia, looks at me, then he lets out this huge big sigh. 'No, Ani. We can't take your money. You keep it,' he says.

'It's OK, you can pay me back out of the takings, out of the profits. You know, when we're rich and famous.'

At first I think this is going to work. I can see from Carlos's face that he's working it all out, working out the figures. But then, in the next second, everything changes. Carlos's face closes up again. His eyes turn into little slits and he bares his teeth like a dog, lashes into me.

211

'You stupid little girl. Don't you understand anything? The amount we need, two thousand dollars isn't going to make a spit of a difference. It'll take ten, fifteen thousand at least. It's over. It's all over.'

I want to smack out at Carlos, tell him it's not true, tell him it will make a difference, we will make it work. But I can't. I can't get my mouth to work. All I can do is back away from him, back out of the apartment, down the stairs and then I'm running off down the street.

I'm running for my fucking life.

*

I run and run as fast as I can down Avenue C and into East 4th Street. My first time outdoors on my own in New York. Carlos tells everyone his apartment is in the East Village because the East Village is trendy. But it's not really, it's in Alphabet City. Carlos says he has enough problems without people knowing he lives in Alphabet City. Especially cab drivers.

New Yorkers go everywhere by cab. They're really cheap compared to back home.

As soon as I turn the corner I see the church, see the crypt door, like the door to a giant's castle. I stop outside the big black door of the crypt. But I don't go in straight away. Instead I walk up the pavement a little bit, past the church, past a fancy-dress shop, stand against the wall of the fancy-dress shop's stoop, light a cigarette and just lean there for a bit, looking around.

A life-size cow carved out of butter walks up in front of me and starts eating black corn out of a trash can. Hanging from the cow's neck is a sign: *To the City of New York from the people of Iowa.*

Then it starts raining again so I walk back down the block, past the butter cow and push through the door into the crypt.

The crypt's a real one. You know, in the basement of a church, the bit where they used to keep all the dead bodies?

Not any more, though. The last dead body was taken out in 1925 when the crypt was made into a soup kitchen to feed the poor and needy. It was a soup kitchen all through the Depression and World War Two.

At least, that's what the priest said. But Carlos wasn't so sure. He reckoned they'd need a hell of a lot of bones to make all that soup. I told him I didn't think he should make jokes like that, not in a church. But Carlos just laughed.

'Church is the only place you can make jokes like that. God's always had a weird sense of humour. Look at penguins,' he said.

The entrance to the crypt is down a steep spiral staircase, just like the ones in those old horror movies. Spooky and dark. The light from my flashlight the only light. At the bottom of the spiral staircase there's another door. A more modern one, painted white. With the flashlight shining against the white door, there's more light. It's not so spooky. It's almost normal.

Terrible smell, though. Damp and dust. And piss.

But once I find the light switches, once I can see the whole crypt, things are much better. I can see everything now. Brick arches, bricks all painted white, leading away in front of me, leading away for ever. Giant brick pillars holding everything up. I step right into the crypt, walk through the brick arches. Under my shoes, the carpet is green and dirty, worn out. Concrete floor shining right through in places. Off the main corridor are more arches leading into other arches. The whole crypt all arches, just like Carlos said.

The bad smell is coming from one of the sidewall arches, the cave arches. The middle one.

The smell is so bad you can hardly believe it. It is so bad you have to pinch your nose with your fingers, remember to breathe through your mouth. There's no way we can have a club in here with that smell. How the hell are we going to fix it?

I walk into the cave arch, see if I can spot what's making the smell. In the middle of the arch is a huge pile of rubbish. So huge it practically takes up the whole space. I shine the flashlight on the rubbish and at first I don't see anything. Just a couple of broken chairs, a table and, shoved up against the back wall, a bundle of old clothes. Laura Brannigan poster. But as I shine the light down the clothes I can see that poking out from the bottom is, oh my God, poking out from the bottom of the clothes is a foot. It's a dead body, I can't believe it. A dead body! Right here in the crypt.

I shine the flashlight up and down the dead body. The dead body is fat and white with pale brown patches all down its back and doesn't move even when I shine the light right in its eyes.

I jump back away from the dead body but I can't go far because the broken chairs are right behind me and the dead body is right in front. I twist round looking for the exit. But all I can see are arches. The whole crypt full of fucking arches.

I look back at the dead body. The dead body looks at me. Pink eyes.

Then the dead body rolls over towards me and sits up, scratches his ear.

'So you wanna turn off that light and let me sleep, or what?' the dead body says.

'I thought you were a dead body,' I say. 'But you're not, are you?'

'Don't think so,' says the dead body. 'Dead drunk, maybe. But not dead. Not yet, anyways.' And he staggers to his feet, walks towards me. 'Want some porridge?' he says.

'Keep the fuck away from me!' I'm yelling at the top of my voice now.

It works. The drunk looks hurt but steps back again. 'I only asked if you wanted some porridge,' he says. 'You know, for your breakfast.'

I look behind me. Still nothing but arches everywhere. Nothing but arches in the whole fucking world.

'Hey, where you from?' says the drunk. 'You got an accent. You from England?'

I don't believe this. Is he crazy or what?

'Thought so. I could tell from the way you say fuck. You English say fuck so politely.'

Yep. One hundred per cent certifiable. Any second now the men in white coats will come along and recapture him.

'I just love English accents.'

Better keep the nutso talking, though. Till I can work out how to get out of here.

So I say, 'What are you doing sleeping in a crypt anyway?'

'I just like it. It's like my thing,' says the drunk. 'How long you been here in the Big Apple?'

'Two days,' I say.

Any second now...

'How long you staying?'

Why is everyone so interested in how long I'm staying?

'Till I get famous.'

And where the fuck are the white coats when you need them?

The drunk looks me up and down. 'Famous as what?' he says.

'Dunno. Just famous,' I say.

The drunk nods. 'You can be anything you want in this town. You just gotta find your thing,' he says.

Chapter Twenty-Two

I used to have this recurring dream that I was trying to get back home. From London, back to the land of my fathers. I never made it. I was always stopped by the Severn Bridge.

Each time I tried to cross the bridge – always on foot, for some reason – it would start bouncing up and down in the air like that bridge in the States, the one they always show in physics lessons. The one in Tacoma, Washington. The one where the wind came whistling down the canyon at exactly the same resonance as the natural frequency of the bridge itself, causing the whole thing to buckle and collapse.

Remember?

Well, that's how it was in my dream. Every time I tried to climb up onto the Severn Bridge it would go all wobbly, hurl me up and down. I did my best to hang on, I really did. I clung and clung, but in the end I always lost my grip. I always fell. Down and down. Down into the muddy waters of the estuary.

*

'Come on in.' Greg, Louise's husband, ushers us into the flat. 'Come on into the warm. What dreadful weather.' He's holding a silver cocktail shaker in his hand, shaking it up and down in front of him and laughing. 'Nobody would believe it was almost summer, would they?' he says.

We take off our coats, hang them up on a row of hooks just inside the door. As I bend down to lean the umbrella against the plinth, to save trailing rainwater in through the flat, Ani pushes past me and bolts off down the hall, straight into the bathroom. She's been dying for a pee since we left the house. Typical of her to wait until it's almost too late. I grimace an apology at Greg and we stroll down the hall together.

'How's things?' he says.

'Not too bad, thanks,' I say.

Not too good either, I don't say.

Every time I walk into Greg and Louise's flat, I'm amazed how clean everything is, how polished, particularly the wooden floor they've laid, covering over the Education Authority tiles. The real thing too, not that cheap fake stuff which is all the rage at the moment, but pale oak parquet, with a black inlay to set off the late-Victorian coving.

Other than maybe the giant rubber plant in the corner and the exposed brickwork, the coving is the only late Victorian feature left standing. Everything else in the flat, from the Smeg kitchen to the Eames chairs, is state of the art retro.

Including Louise's small but tasteful collection of primitive art, which she collects piece by piece from Paris by way of an exclusive little gallery in Cardiff, then mounts in simple beech frames and dots strategically around as focus points, just like they tell you to do in *World of Interiors*.

Everything polished, immaculate.

And tidy. So tidy I'm afraid to sit down on the sofa in case I crease the cushions. So instead I loiter awkwardly in front of the fireplace while Greg mixes the drinks. On the floor in the far corner of the room, between the rubber plant and the TV, below the African death mask, is a carved wooden elephant about the size of a small dog.

A new piece. Good, too.

Greg crosses the room with our drinks. 'How's your dad?' he asks.

'Not too bad, thanks,' I say, cradling the glass between my fingers and sipping slowly. Perfectly chilled, of course. And very, very dry.

'Recovering well?'

I can't look at him so I look at the floor instead.

'As well as can be expected,' I say.

Louise has changed the rugs. They used to be these dreadful coir things, hemmed with rope. But now kilims scatter in every direction. The ethnic look is obviously in again this season. Still, at least they add a bit of colour. Break up all this black and white.

'That's good,' Greg says, shuffling his feet, and I am suddenly aware of his embarrassment wafting up around me. I am aware I am not playing the good guest game as I should be. So I make a huge effort and raise my head, meet his gaze.

'In good spirits, though,' I say, as cheerfully as I can.

Greg's expression opens up in relief. 'Oh good,' he says.

'Yes,' I say and take another sip of my drink.

'Super,' Greg says, rubbing his hands together in a perfect impression of the perfect host. 'Now, what can I get you in the way of nibbles?'

He's English, of course. And posh. Not just middle class and educated like Louise and me, but proper posh. Prince Philip posh, as my mother used to say. The sort of posh that drinks Martinis before dinner on a daily basis. The sort of posh that wears a navy blue blazer and brown shoes with his jeans.

Louise tells this story of when she and Greg were first courting and she invited him over to her house for something to eat. Something simple and quick because they were going out. Not quite beans on toast, but almost. Yet, when they sat down at the table to eat, Greg still insisted Louise got out her mother's best napkins, the linen ones they only ever use at Christmas. Apparently he nearly died when she suggested they use kitchen roll instead.

Still, he's got a heart of gold, Louise says.

Where is Louise, anyway? And what is Ani doing in that bathroom?

Greg and I stand together racking our brains for something to say, *anything* to say, for what seems like hours before Ani bounds in and demands a cocktail, wants to know how you make them, wants to make one herself from scratch, and does Greg have any fags on him by any chance because she's just run out and she's gasping?

Greg lights up two cigarettes, hands one over to Ani, then opens up a large beech cabinet and retrieves the gin and vermouth, begins teaching Ani the mystery of the Martini. The backs of their heads leaning together, not quite touching, Ani's russet red perfectly complementing Greg's squirrel brown as they shake not stir.

Meanwhile, Louise finally emerges from the bedroom and starts flitting back and forth between the oven, the fridge and a state of the art beech bench table with gleaming dishes of food, her trouser suit making me wish I'd made more of an effort. As I wander over to greet her I drag my fingers through my hair, raking for bits of clay left behind by Year Ten this morning, try to smooth the creases out of my shirt.

'Hope you're hungry,' Louise says, slicing three pats of butter one by one into a bowl of couscous.

'Starving,' I say. 'What are we having?'

'Spiced leg of lamb with grilled Mediterranean vegetables in a harissa sauce,' she says.

'Very sophis,' I say.

'Very Delia,' she grins, then shoves a bowl of salad sideways for me to dress. For several minutes we stand happily side by side in silence, whipping and mixing.

Spotless stainless steel splashback.

'How's your dad?' Louise says, pouring sauce over the vegetables and couscous.

I shrug. 'You know,' I say.

'In good spirits, though.'

'That's good,' Louise says.

'Yes.'

Down the far end of the room, Ani is now rooting through Greg and Louise's video collection, pulling each video off the pile, checking the title briefly, then tossing the video haphazardly onto the floor next to her before pulling the next one down.

'And how are you? Are you OK? You look tired,' Louise says.

'I am a bit. I've been working like a dog all month, on top of Dad.'

'On this sculpture of yours? For the mud puppy?'

'No. Teaching. I've been doing a stint over at St Julian's ever since I left your place. But I could have been working just about anywhere. It's amazing how much supply work there is around.'

Louise nods. 'It's this bloody new curriculum,' she says. 'Everybody's worried that the kids haven't done enough work. So all the supply budget's going on getting as many hands on deck as poss before the exams.'

'Makes a bit of a change, though. For the liberal arts to get a look in, I mean.'

'Tell me about it,' Louise says, leaning across me for a wooden spoon. ''Course it won't last. Once the novelty's worn off and the exams are over, it'll be straight back to boring old maths and science. Or worse, job skills and internet classes.'

I smile. Some things don't change. 'Luddite,' I tease.

'And proud of it,' she grins back at me.

Greg strides over with two fresh drinks. 'What's all this about luddites?' he says, planting a kiss on Louise's cheek. 'Not you as well, Daryl. I thought it was only my wife who likes to live in the Dark Ages.'

'Well...'

'Oh don't encourage him, for God's sake, Daryl,' Louise says. 'Or else we'll never hear the end of it. Bloody scientist,' she says, pretending to slap Greg across the face, just so she can kiss it better. Then of course Greg has to kiss her back.

'Well, anyway, it's the end for me,' I say, taking the salad and ciabatta over to the table so I don't have to watch them. 'I finish my contract a week on Friday and then that's it, no more teaching for me. Or at least only the odd day. I'm going to concentrate on this commission. And Dad.'

'Oh yes, your commission,' says Greg, coming up for air. 'We can't wait to see it. How's it all going?'

'It isn't,' I say. 'I can't get my head round it at the moment.'

'When do they want it?' Louise asks.

'Two months' time. And I haven't even started it yet.'

She lets out a long whistle.

'Exactly,' I say.

Ani is now thigh-deep in videos. I wish she'd come over and be sociable. What's wrong with her? She can't still be mad at me; she was fine at home an hour ago.

'Can't you cobble something together out of stuff you've done before? You know, raid your ideas bank,' Greg says.

I sigh. God save me from software engineers.

'It doesn't quite work like that,' I say. 'You can't just fit it together like a jigsaw puzzle. You have to get inside the will of the piece. Let it become its own entity. You can't plan for that, or cut corners. You just have to wait for it to happen.'

And it has to happen. It has to. Or I'm sunk.

'And if it doesn't?'

'Let's not even go there,' I say.

Louise hands me the dish of vegetables and couscous. 'I think we're ready,' she says. 'Greg, can you carve, please? And put some music on, for God's sake. It's supposed to be a party.'

*

We sit up high at the beech bench table, perched up on matching beech barstools, which are beautiful to look at, but not at all safe to clamber onto and which murder the backs of your knees after less than half an hour.

We sit perched up high, two by two, boy, girl, girl, girl, me facing Greg next to Ani facing Louise next to me.

We sit perched. Me complimenting Louise on the food, asking Greg about the wine. Greg saying how he and Louise have just joined a wine club to find out more about these things, but this is just Sainsbury's wine of the month, still very good all the same, and only £3.49 a bottle. Louise asking me if Ani and I have got our holiday plans sorted out for the long break, now, you know, your dad seems to be on the mend it would probably do you both good to get away for a bit and not to worry at all about Dad because of course the parish would rally round, as always. Ani not saying a word, not eating a bite, just staring down at her plate throughout, pushing the food round and round the edge until, piece by piece, it goes stone cold. Me trying to catch Ani's eye, trying to get her to open up, to be *normal*, for God's sake but Ani won't look at me, won't look at anybody. She just stares down at her plate, pushing the food round and round. All you can see is the top of her head, the red-gold hairs scrunched up with mousse then slicked down with wax. All you can see is the black silk of her shirt sleeve – my best black shirt – as she pushes the food round and round the edge of her plate until, piece by piece, it falls off and onto the beech bench table.

With every piece the laces of my corset tighten another notch.

Eventually Greg steps into the breach. 'What do you think, Ani?' he says, casual as you like, refilling her wine glass even though she's hardly touched it and it only takes a drop.

Ani jumps and looks up and sideways at him, blue-rimmed eyes puzzled and blank. 'Think about what?' she says.

'Louise was just saying she thought it would be good if you and Daryl had a holiday.'

I rest my elbows on the table, lean forward over my plate. 'It's an idea,' I say, my voice scoring tight little scratches in the air. 'We could do with a break after everything we've been through. Don't you think, Ani? Hey? Don't you think?'

Ani looks from me to Greg then back to me again, then spears a piece of aubergine up off the table with her fork and lifts it up to the light, staring at it.

'Ani?' I squeak.

Still she doesn't speak. Or move. Just stares at the piece of aubergine, stares as if she's trying to see through it. Behind me, a police siren roars up Stow Hill.

'Ani?'

Ani blinks and shoves the piece of aubergine into her mouth. 'Nah,' she says. 'Can't go away again just yet. Only just got back.'

Oh please, no.

'Back from where?' Greg asks.

'New York,' Ani says, ramming a mouthful of couscous down after the aubergine, her appetite apparently returning.

I can't believe she's doing this to me. I can't believe it. I mean, it's all very well to play these games when we're on our own, when it's just family. But here, in public, I can't believe she's turning into such a . . . a . . . *liability*.

'Oh wow,' Louise says. 'New York. Were you shopping or just seeing the sights?'

'Neither,' says Ani loftily. 'It was business,' she says. 'My mate Carlos and I are setting up a nightclub over there.'

'Oh wow,' says Louise.

'Really?' says Greg.

'Yes,' says Ani. 'It's going to be awesome.'

I want to kick her. I want to kick her right off her stool, right off the bloody planet, but I can't reach her without my leg knocking into Louise's leg so I have to settle for furious glances. But, of course, Ani ignores these and me completely, just launches into yet another version of how great her club is going to be, all the weird and wonderful people and sights that will be seen there, all the different drag shows she and this so-called Carlos are planning on staging.

The list goes on and on.

Meanwhile, she's still shovelling couscous into her face like she hasn't eaten for a month, while the laces of my corset tighten. Tighten and tighten. Then, just when I think I am going to explode, she comes up with a story I haven't heard before, of how coming home from the club the other (unspecified, naturally) night, one of Carlos's police officer friends approached them in SoHo, pretended to arrest them, handcuffs and everything, then drove them round and round the streets of Manhattan in his black and white police car, sirens flashing.

Greg, who has been leaning against the kitchen wall, hands clasped behind his head, listening to this collection of sorry tales with the creases in his forehead growing deeper, suddenly sits upright again and interjects. 'I thought New York police cars were blue,' he says.

There follows a short pause of infinite duration while Greg looks at Louise who looks at Ani who looks unperturbed.

'Black,' she says firmly. 'Definitely black. Black and white.'

'That's strange,' Greg says, 'because I'm sure when we were there they were blue. Pale blue and white. You remember, Lou, don't you? When we went over last Christmas? We saw some and they were definitely blue, weren't they?'

Louise shifts on her stool next to me. 'I can't remember,' she mutters. 'Does it really matter?'

Greg scratches his nose. 'Yes, blue and white. That's it. I remember seeing a whole lot of them parked all down one street and thinking that must be why they call it *NYPD Blue*.' He leans back against the wall. 'Come on, Lou, you must remember.'

I push my head down into my hands to try and quell the

urge to run screaming from the room.

Louise's knee, pressed up against mine, stiffens then releases as she springs down from her stool. 'For God's sake, Greg,' she snaps. 'Blue, black, it's not important. Honestly, stop making such a fuss about it.'

Greg looks like he wants to labour the point but then he catches the look of pure misery on my face and changes his mind. Ani, meanwhile, just starts staring into space again. Louise collects the empty plates together.

'Who's for dessert?' she says.

*

It's a myth that you can never have too much of a good thing. Take vitamin C, for instance. Common-sense opinion is that you can take as much as you like, that you need to take lots of it to stay healthy. But, like the Roman god Janus, vitamin C has a good and a bad side. Too little, and you can get scurvy. Too much, and free radicals penetrate your cell walls, attack your DNA. The very key to life itself.

Six weeks since Dad had his stroke.

Six weeks since Ani moved in.

Six weeks.

I think I am losing my mind.

*

The study is quiet, peaceful and full of Dad. Too quiet, too full. From the bookcases to the wellingtons leaning up against the radiator to the Rembrandt print on the wall, he's everywhere. I give up pretending to work on my sketches and just swivel round in the desk chair, put my feet up on the windowsill and stare out the window, across the front patio, the rockery, down into the street below. At this time of day it should be empty. But today a woman with long blonde hair, piled up on the top of her head like a poodle, and wearing a leopard-print T-shirt and jeans that last fitted her ten years ago, hovers at the bottom of the drive, clutching a piece of paper in her hand, with an anxious expression on her face. She looks familiar for some reason, but I can't place her. She certainly doesn't look like a parishioner.

'Can I help you?' I say, opening the front door to her before she can ring the bell.

The woman jumps back in surprise. Eyes framed by so much mascara the lashes look like clusters of black thorns.

'Is this where the vicar lives?' she whispers nervously. 'The one who found the baby dragon.'

I should have known. Another tourist.

I adopt the usual tack.

'My father's not available at the moment. If you need the services of a priest, Reverend Lewis over at St John's is covering all pastoral work. I can give you her number if you like.' I turn away deliberately, half shut the door and reach for the address book on the hall table.

'No, that's not...I...Daryl? It is Daryl, isn't it. It's me, Lorraine. Ani's mam. You remember, we met at the Dolman, at the Elvis gig?'

I open the door wide again, take a closer look. 'Oh God, I'm sorry. Shit, how embarrassing. I mean, I thought I'd recognised you, but I wasn't sure. It's just that we get so many visitors at the moment, and with Dad being so ill, well...I'm sorry, come in. Please. Ani's not here, I'm afraid. But come in anyway. It's good to see you again.'

'Thanks,' Lorraine says, stepping into the hall. 'Yes, I heard about your dad. How is he?'

'Not too bad, thanks. In good spirits.'

I show Lorraine into Dad's study, where she makes straight for the yellow wing chair by the fireplace and sits down. I stay hovering by the window.

'Would you like a cup of tea or something?' I say.

'No thanks. I'm not stopping. I just came to find out how Ani is. Is she all right?'

I turn and stare out across the front patio, the rockery, down to number twenty-three where I can see Fred sitting in his chair watching TV. Behind me, Ani's mum shifts in her seat.

'Is she all right?' she says again.

I say, 'Ani?' My voice is someone else's voice, empty of sound. Empty like the street outside. No cars, not even a dog barking.

'Yes. She's all right, isn't she? It's just we haven't heard anything or seen her for so long.'

I clear my throat. 'She's fine,' I say.

Only these words in the whole street.

Forcing myself to turn away from the window, I step towards Lorraine and perch on the edge of the desk, look at her, look at Ani's mum. She looks younger than you'd expect, about my age in fact. A bit older, maybe. But not much. It doesn't seem possible.

'I'm sorry Ani hasn't been in touch,' I say. 'I have tried to get her to ring you. But you know what's she's like.'

'Too independent for her own good sometimes, yes. Do you know where she is, when she's coming back?'

'No, sorry. I don't,' I say. 'I don't know where she's gone or who she's with today,' I say, still in that weird, whispery voice.

Or when she's coming back, I think but don't say. Why she's here in the first place. Why I let her stay, move in. Why did I let her move in? I don't remember. It just happened. One minute she wasn't here, the next minute she was.

Lorraine takes a cigarette from a pack in her breast pocket, takes a lighter out of the pack, lights the cigarette, takes a long drag and drops the lighter back inside the pack, inside her pocket.

'Oh, sorry, force of habit. You don't mind, do you?' she says, waving the cigarette around in front of her.

'Actually, I...'

'Sorry, sorry, I'll put it right out.' She looks around her for an ashtray. 'Have you got...'

'I'll get you one,' I say, and go out into the kitchen for a saucer. When I get back to the study Lorraine has got up from the chair, taken my sketches off the desk, spread them out in front of her on the floor and is kneeling on the edge of the big one, leaning over it, her cigarette dangling between her fingers. I slip the saucer under her hand just in time to prevent the ash falling onto the paper.

'Ta,' she says, not looking up at me. Silver earrings swinging. Big silver hoops. 'There's some stuff here,' she says. 'Are they yours?'

'Yes,' I say stiffly. 'Yes they are. They're for a commission I'm working on. I expect Ani's told you about it. Newport Council and an American company, Corona, they're paying me to design a statue to celebrate a big business deal.'

Oh, for goodness sake, Daryl, relax. You sound like a marketing brochure.

But I can't help it. I can't get over them. Her eyes. Blue-rimmed, pupils as black as cave water.

'And, of course, to commemorate the mud puppy.'

'The what?'

'The baby dragon.'

'Oh right. Is that its wing, then?' Lorraine points her finger, and the cigarette, over the left-hand corner of the sketch.

'Um, careful. Yes, it is.'

'And what's that, some sort of pulley?'

'Yes, but it's just a beginning. I haven't really worked it all out yet.'

'It all looks good to me. I can't even draw a straight line.' She laughs and looks up at me and suddenly I see it. Right there. The molten stream of energy. Pulsating luminescence.

My legs start to shake and my chest feels like it is open to the sky, so I crouch down next to her, keep my eyes fixed on the sketch. 'I'm trying to set up a kinetic structure – you know, movement – something that complements the heritage of the town and picks up on existing themes,' I manage to say.

'You mean like that clock in John Frost Square?'

'Exactly.'

'How are you going to make it all work? With a motor, like?'

'Possibly, though I'd prefer the energy source to be more simple, more natural than that. In fact, I want the energy, the movement, to *be* the piece. I don't just want it to be part of it. I want the movement to *transform* the piece, to a whole new world of possibilities.'

I know I'm getting carried away. I know I'm losing her. But I can't seem to stop myself. For some bizarre reason I want this woman, Ani's mother, to understand. I need her to understand.

'Right,' she says. 'I see.'

It's clear she doesn't.

But I keep going anyway.

'I want there to be a coming together, but also a separation of space and mass and time. I want to show material as energy, energy as material. I want . . .'

Oh, this is hopeless. This is impossible. How can I expect someone like Lorraine to understand when I'm not sure myself?

'Do you mean,' Lorraine says slowly, thinking before every word, 'do you mean like that game we used to play when we were kids? You know, when you took a piece of string, tied a weight on the end and then spun it all round and round. Faster and faster till it looked solid, like a cone. Like you were creating a cone out of thin air. Is that what you mean?' she says.

I sit back on my heels, stare at her in amazement.

When am I ever going to learn? When am I ever going to learn how surprising people can be, how much more to them there always is than meets my eye.

'Yes,' I say. 'That's precisely what I mean. God, you get it. That's fantastic.'

Lorraine blushes with pleasure and drops her gaze. 'My Ani used to love that game when she was little,' she says.

'I think she still does,' I say.

Lorraine throws her head right back and laughs so I can see her fillings, then struggles to her feet and sits in the wing chair again, leans back and crosses her legs, lights another cigarette. Her right foot swinging back and forth.

Plastic leather slingbacks.

'Yes, she loves creating things out of thin air, my Ani. Especially stories.'

'Actually, I was hoping I might be able to talk to you about that,' I say.

The foot stops swinging.

Go on, Daryl. You can't stop now. She needs help. You know she needs help.

'Oh yes?'

'Doesn't it ever worry you?'

Lorraine has to see. She has to help.

'What?'

'Ani's behaviour. All that storytelling, the imaginary trips to New York. Haven't you ever wondered if, well, if there might be something wrong with her? Mentally, I mean.'

Lorraine's shoulders jerk upwards as she sinks down into the chair, as far down into it as she can get and then carefully inspects her manicure, nail by nail. 'What are you talking about? There's nothing wrong with my Ani.'

'Well, it's just that...'

'Are you trying to tell me you think she's crazy?'

'I just think that maybe...'

Lorraine jerks forward in her seat again, stabs the air with her cigarette. 'Because she's not. OK? No way. She's not crazy. Not my Ani.'

'No, of course not.'

'There's nothing wrong with Ani,' she says again loudly, almost shouting. 'There's nothing wrong with her. She's fine.'

Stab. Stab.

230

'But what about the stories?'

'You just need to be firm with her, that's all. Give her something else to think about.'

Stab.

'I'm sure you're right. But I really think...'

'Take her out of herself. That'll bring her round.'

Stab.

'Yes, that'll bring her round. She'll be fine then, you'll see.'

Chapter Twenty-Three

I run and run as fast as I can down Avenue C and into East 4th Street. As soon as I turn the corner I see the church, see the big black door of the crypt, like the door to a giant's castle. I stop outside the big black crypt door. But I don't go in straight away. Instead, I walk up the pavement a little bit, past the church, stand against the wall of the fancy-dress shop's stoop, light a cigarette and just lean there.

A giant red fire engine sloshes through a puddle past me, spraying lies all over me as it goes. Stops at the end of the block, by the church. Right outside the big black door of the crypt. My crypt.

So I walk back down the block, past the fire engine and push through the big black door into the crypt.

The crypt's a real one. You know, in the basement of a church, the bit where they used to keep all the dead bodies? Not any more, though. The last dead body was taken out in 1925 when the crypt was made into a soup kitchen to feed the poor and needy. It was a soup kitchen all through the Depression and World War Two.

At least, that's what the priest said. But Carlos wasn't so sure. He reckoned they'd need a hell of a lot of bones to make all that soup.

I said I didn't think he should make jokes like that, not in a church.

The entrance to the crypt is down a steep spiral staircase, just like the ones in those old horror movies. Spooky and smelly. At the bottom of the spiral staircase there's another door. A more modern one, painted white. It's not so spooky. It's almost normal.

Terrible smell, though, still. Damp and dust.

And piss.

But once I find the light switches, once I can see the whole crypt, things are much better.

I can see everything now. Brick arches, bricks all painted white, leading away in front of me, leading away for ever. Giant brick pillars holding everything up. I step right into the crypt, walk down the brick corridor. Under my shoes, worn-out dirty green carpet, concrete floor shining right through in places. Off the main corridor are more arches leading into other arches. The whole crypt all arches.

The bad smell is coming from one of the sidewall arches, the cave arches. The middle one. The smell is so bad you can hardly believe it. It is so bad you have to pinch your nose with your fingers, remember to breathe through your mouth. There's no way we can have a club in here with that smell. How the hell are we going to fix that?

I walk into the cave arch, see if I can spot what's making the smell. It's dark in here. The lights don't reach this far. But I can just about make out, in the middle of the cave, a huge great pile of rubbish. So huge it practically takes up the whole space. I shine the flashlight on the rubbish and at first I don't see anything. Just a couple of broken chairs, a table and, shoved up against the back wall, a pile of old boxes. But as I shine the light down the boxes I can see, poking out from the side, oh my God, poking out from the side of the boxes is a tail. A candy pink tail. And there's an arm, a head. It's a giant rat, I can't believe it. A giant rat! Burrowing down inside the boxes.

I jump back away from the rat but I can't go far because the broken chairs are right behind me and the rat is right in

233

front. I twist round looking for the exit. But all I can see are arches. The whole crypt full of arches.

I shine the flashlight up and down the rat. The rat is fat and white with pale brown patches all down its back and it doesn't stop burrowing, flinging the contents of each box out behind it. Clothes, shoes, books, everything goes sailing over the rat's head willy-nilly as it scrambles frantically through every box. It looks like it's searching for something it's lost. Something important.

Then, suddenly, the rat stops burrowing.

'So are you gonna bring that light over and help me, or what?' the rat says, scratches its ear.

I look at the rat. The rat looks back at me. Pink eyes.

'What are you looking for?' I say. 'Bones?'

'Don't think so,' says the rat. 'Later, maybe. Dinnertime. But not yet, not hungry yet. For now I just want my Laura Brannigan poster.' The rat pulls another box down off the pile, starts rummaging through it, but more slowly this time. 'I know I put it in one of these boxes,' it mutters. 'If I could just remember which one.'

The rat picks the box up, holds it over its head and tips it upside down. Old newspapers and dust fall out over the rat's head, feet, tail, floor. Everywhere. But still no poster. The rat sighs, chucks the empty box over its shoulder and, stretching its arms behind its back, steps out over the rubbish and walks towards me on tiptoes. 'This is no use,' it says. 'I'll never find it in all this mess. Fancy a cup of tea instead?'

I put my hands out, back two steps away, yelling at the top of my voice. 'Keep away from me!'

This works. The rat looks hurt but steps back again. 'There's no need to shout. I only asked if you wanted a cup of tea,' it says.

I look round again. Still nothing but arches everywhere. Nothing but arches in the whole fucking world. 'Just keep the fuck away,' I say.

'OK, OK, keep your hair on,' says the rat, walks over to a second pile of boxes at the far end of the cave, pulls out a kettle and two cups. 'Hey, where you from anyway? You got an accent. You from England?'

I don't believe this. This is really crazy.

'Thought so. I just love English accents.'

Yep. One hundred per cent certifiable. Any second now the men in white coats are going to come along.

Better keep it talking, though. Till I can work out how to get out of here.

So I say, 'What do you want a Laura Brannigan poster for anyway?'

'I just like her. She's like my thing,' says the rat. 'How long you been here in the Big Apple?'

Why is everyone so interested in this?

'Two months,' I say. 'And I'm staying till I get famous.'

The rat nods. 'You can be anything you want in this town.'

*

The apartment is empty when I wake up. Empty and dark. I sit up in bed and turn on the lamp, check how I look in the mirror.

Fucking nightmare, that's how.

My comb and toothbrush are laid out again on the top of the little basin between the bed and the door so I slide up off the bed, wet my hair down, clean my teeth. Above the sink there's a picture of a face. African, I think. Picasso, maybe. Black and white splodges, anyway.

Everything in this apartment is black and white. Everything except for the giant jigsaw puzzle on the floor, which has some of the pieces missing.

I go down the hall, past Carlos and Thalia's bedroom, past another splodgy picture, a cat, to the living room.

Turns out, when I get to the living room, when I look out the window, the apartment isn't empty.

Turns out, when I look out the window, Thalia is sitting out on the porch. It's not really a porch. It's a fire escape. All New York houses have them. It's the law. Carlos says he couldn't believe it when he first came to Cardiff and saw that none of the houses have fire escapes. Don't we care if we all burn in our beds?

I climb out the window and Thalia pats the upturned bucket next to her for me to sit on. Thalia is still wearing her long blue leather coat. Matching blue leather boots. Zips running all the way up the sides.

'Hi, Ani,' she says. 'Did you sleep OK?'

'Yes thanks,' I say. 'Where's Carlos?'

'Gone,' she says.

'Gone? Gone where?' I say.

'Just gone,' she says.

I can't believe it. I can't believe he's gone. Just like that, no goodbyes. No nothing. I can't believe it. So I just sit there with my mouth hanging open, staring at the houses opposite. I just sit there, twisting my ring round and round my thumb, and listen to Thalia tell me about how Carlos's dad phoned up from Iowa while I was sleeping and told Carlos that his restaurant was in trouble. I just sit there and listen to Thalia tell me how Carlos's dad told Carlos to get his butt back to Iowa as quick as he could.

Turns out the figures won't work out, they can't get the right number of people in.

Turns out they've been going bust now for nearly a year.

Turns out it's not such a great idea to open a Mexican seafood restaurant two thousand miles away from the ocean. Any ocean.

Thalia says Carlos had to leave so quick he didn't even have time to pack a suitcase. Thalia is going to pack all the rest of their stuff up and follow him out with a Uhaul.

When Thalia tells me about the clothes, about how she's already packed up all Carlos's drag outfits, his Tom Jones, his Mario from the Barrio, how they're all sitting in boxes on the bed, waiting for the janitor to carry them down the stairs to the trailer, that's when it finally sinks in. That's when I realise that Carlos is never coming back.

Not ever.

It's all over.

And that's when the tears start sliding and the snot starts pouring down my face, through my hands, dripping onto the floor. Till I'm bawling like a baby.

Thalia puts her arm round my shoulder, gives me a squeeze. But I shake her off. I won't let her try to make me feel better. I won't give her the satisfaction. Won't give either of them the satisfaction.

And then I'm thrashing and sliding over the railings, down the ladder, onto the pavement and running off down the street.

Running for my fucking life.

I will never forgive him.

Never, ever

EVER.

Chapter Twenty-Four

Two am. Footsteps on the landing. At first I think it's just the dog, but even as I think this, turning over, still half asleep, I am jerked awake by the realisation that they are human. I lie flat in bed and listen to their creep. Past my bedroom door into the bathroom, back out and across the landing to the boxroom, then into the bathroom again.

By now I am stiff and upright, straining my ears to hear, but there's nothing. No more footsteps, no running water. Nothing. Only the blood beating in my ears. I'm about to relax back down again when the footsteps return, heavier this time. Certain. Out of the bathroom, down the landing, up again, stopping outside my room then, what's that, humming?

Yes, definitely humming.

Before I can get my robe even halfway round my shoulders, the bedroom door creaks open and a silhouette shuffles into the room, humming under its breath, and switches on the overhead light.

I shield my eyes against the brightness.

Ani, dressed up like a cat burglar in black jeans and polo neck, trainers and rucksack slung over one shoulder. All that's missing is the balaclava.

'Oh good, you're awake. Hurry up and get dressed, will you? We haven't much time,' she says.

With which I'm clambering out of bed and into my robe all at the same time, catching my foot inside the duvet cover and tripping over Blackie, lying at the side of the bed.

'What's going on? Is it Dad? It is Dad, isn't it? Tell me, Ani. Tell me what's happened.'

But Ani just moves over to the wardrobe, starts pulling clothes and underwear out, flinging them backwards at me on the bed, then turns once more and glares.

'Come on. Hurry up.'

I look down at the clothes strewn across the bed and floor. All black. Apparently she expects me to be a cat burglar too.

'Ani! Tell me. What's happened?'

I go towards her, stretch out to her, try to reach her, to get her to tell me. But she still won't answer. Just slides out from under my hand and moves across to the window, peeking the curtains open two inches and looking up and down the street.

'Coast's clear,' she says, twisting round to look at me, but only a flick and then her eyes swerve back to the window again. 'Have you got the car keys by the way? Because they're not on the hook like they're supposed to be.' She runs her hand up and down the top of the radiator.

Up and down. 'Coast's clear,' she says again.

Up and down.

Clear for what?' I pull on a T-shirt, jeans. 'Clear for what? Ani! Will you please tell me what's going on?'

It must be Dad. Why else would she be making us get up at this time?

Where's my other shoe?

'Was it the hospital? Did they ring?'

That must be it. Ani took the phone into her room last night, to phone her mum. Finally.

With the doors shut, I could have missed the ring.

'Ani?'

Damn it, where's my other shoe?

'Ani!'

'Ani! For goodness sake.' I go up to her, spin her round, place my hands hard down on her shoulders so she can't get away. Then I shake her. To shake the nonsense out of her. Shake the truth out of her. 'Ani! Talk to me. Was it the hospital?'

But she doesn't react. She doesn't even blink. It's like she's asleep. No, it's like she's disappeared. It's like she's completely disappeared.

Nothing but space and time where her soul should be.

So I stop shaking her and lead her gently over to the bed, sit her down and speak to her as if I'm speaking to a very small, confused child.

'Ani. Is it Dad? Has something happened to Dad? Please, just tell me, I won't . . .'

Black circles rimming blank blue eyes.

Then she snaps back into herself like an elastic band. 'The mud puppy,' she says. 'We have to go get it.'

'What? What do you mean?'

'We have to go get it.'

Eyes fierce now, full of power, insistence.

'Why?'

Ani presses her hands together like a prayer. 'We have to go save it,' she says. Her face is twisted up and she's pulling at her jumper as if there's something nasty sticking to it.

She's beginning to scare me. Is she on something? Drugs? Is that what it is?

'We have to. We have to.'

I don't think I can handle it if it's drugs. I don't know anything about drugs.

'We have to go save it.'

No, it can't be drugs. I'd know, wouldn't I? I'd have seen something.

But whatever it is, it's clear I've got to try and calm her down. Shudders run up and down the length of her body as she rocks back and forth and she's sobbing uncontrollably now.

Wrapping my arm around Ani's shoulder, I sit down next to her, glance down at my watch.

Two twenty. Shit.

I have to get her to calm her down.

Maybe I should try to humour her.

'What sort of danger?' I say.

'What?' She looks up at me, confused and frightened.

'The mud puppy. What sort of danger is it in?'

Ani leans into my side. 'From them,' she whispers. 'The scientists. They're killing it.'

Oh please, not more adventure stories.

'Of course they're not killing it. They're studying it. They're trying to help it.'

'They are. They are. You can tell just from looking at it,' she says, tears running down her face. 'You don't know, you haven't been there for ages. You haven't seen it,' she sobs. 'You should have seen it, Daryl, when I was there today, it looked so sad, so lonely. You should have seen it. All those tests. They're killing it. You can tell. It's going to die. I know it is.'

All the time she's speaking she's getting more and more agitated until finally she's pacing up and down in front of the bed, arms flapping frantically at her sides, swallowing down gulps of suppressed emotion.

This is madness.

'It's going to die. It's going to die. It's going to die.'

Before I can stop her, she's hurtling out the door and down the stairs. I rush after her and manage to catch her on the bend.

'OK. OK. Calm down. We'll go and see it if it means that much to you,' I say.

Anything to stop this.

Immediately I say this, Ani stands still and her breathing deepens.

'Thanks,' she says, wiping her nose on the back of her hand.

Is this what she wanted all along? Is this all an act? No, it can't be. No one's that good an actress. Something is wrong. Something is really wrong.

I hand her an almost clean tissue I find in my jeans pockets, put my arm around her shoulder again.

Electric hair crinkling against my ear.

I've got to keep her calm, rational. I've got to find a way to calm her down, try to make her see sense. Face facts.

And that's when it comes to me. What Ani's mother said.

'We'll go,' I say. 'It's OK, I'm sure it is. But we'll go and have a look, just to make sure.'

'Yeah,' she sniffs.

'But we're just going to look, OK? We're not going to do anything drastic.'

Ani nods cheerfully and looks up at me, the smile widening across her face.

'Yes,' I say as we walk slowly downstairs, then go in for the kill. 'We'll go and look. But only if you promise me you'll stop all this New York business.'

Caught out, Ani freezes with one foot hovering above the step. 'What New York business?' she says.

'You know very well what business. You have to promise me that you'll stop all these stories, all this invention, about New York, about this nightclub.'

Ani hesitates, then shrugs. 'OK. Sure,' she says airily. She tugs at my arm, points at the front door. 'Now can we go?'

But I'm not so easily fooled any more. I stick to my guns, fold my arms and sit down. Right where I am, on the fourth stair down from the bend, in front of Gran's mahogany corner table.

'I mean it. No more stories about New York. No more nightclubs. No more Carlos. Especially no more Carlos. You're far too old to have an imaginary friend anyway,' I say.

Ani's eyes flit from me on the stairs over to the front door, back to me on the stairs. The door.

'Well? Do we have a deal?'

Ani's shoulders sag in defeat. 'Yes. All right. It's a deal,' she says and flings her arm down to the door again. 'Now can we go, please, or it'll be daylight before we get there?'

*

In the east, the blackness of the sky is already sloughing off like wet clay under a cold tap. The streetlamps of Edward VII Avenue arch above us, humming songs to one another and spotlighting our progress.

Keeping my eyes peeled for security cameras, I pull my jacket tighter round me, shift the rucksack from my right shoulder to my left, trying to ease the weight of my conscience, trudge miserably forward in Ani's wake.

This whole idea is ridiculous. What are we doing? What am I doing? Sneaking around central Cardiff in the middle of the night? Breaking and entering? I'm the one who's insane.

But now I've said we'll go and look, Ani won't be swayed and after her behaviour earlier, I think I'm more afraid of what she'll do if I refuse, than if we get caught. And it's not as if we're planning on stealing the mud puppy or anything. We're just going to have a look, check the thing's all right. Nothing criminal.

Oh please, Daryl, who are you trying to kid?

Anyway, I don't think I could stop her now if I tried. Just look at her, bounding up the street, oblivious of everything but her goal less than ten yards ahead.

No, this is strictly a damage limitation exercise.

'Ani,' I call. 'Wait for me.'

Amazingly she does as I ask and I jog up to her. To our left, the police station with its black squares of windows lies quiet and menacing. Above us, the flying red dragon of the Bute Building regards us with a knowing smile. Hand in hand we creep round the corner, stare into the dark of the car park.

Empty.

243

We inch down the grass verge and along the side path to the fire door, the one with the broken outside light. As we draw closer to the door, Ani doubles back behind me, unzips the rucksack, reaches in and takes out a torch and a set of keys.

'Where did you get those?' I say.

Ani's face glowing sodium yellow against the dark of her clothes.

'Ask me no questions and I'll tell you no lies,' she says, then turns and checks the locks on the fire door. 'Yale,' she says and, lifting the keys up to the light, separates all the likely contestants from the goats.

After three attempts we're in. Back inside the labyrinth. Ani has been up and down these corridors so many times now, she could walk them blindfold. I, on the other hand, still need the help of the torch and the glow of the emergency exit signs over each doorway. As we walk on tiptoe up the stairs, past a poster advertising the student summer ball, I realise I am enjoying myself. My heart is pounding, the sweat is pouring down my back inside my shirt, but not from fear.

This may be madness. But it is also exciting, exhilarating even. This is why I love being with Ani. She's impulsive, trying. But never boring. Never mundane.

We climb to the top floor, turn left and through a set of fire doors, down the long corridor towards the mud puppy's lab. But when we push open the last set of fire doors, instead of the blank-faced doors of the computer lab, we are greeted by a new security desk, complete with purple-uniformed security guard. Who fortunately doesn't see us because right at that moment he has his back turned, making himself a cup of tea.

Telephone. Teabags. Cigarette packet. Lighter.

My stomach turns over, flips inside out.

This is it then. Game over.

Silently we backtrack through the swing doors, ducking down onto our knees.

'We'll never get past without him seeing us. What on earth are we going to do?' I hiss.

But while I'm still crouched there, Ani walks calmly back through the doors and over to the security guard's desk.

The guard's shoulders move under his coat as he stirs his tea. But he doesn't turn round. Ani stands there a moment, then twists round and starts making faces at me, cocking her head to one side and poking her tongue out.

I don't believe this. Does she want to get us arrested?

I wave frantically for her to come back behind the safety of the fire door, but this only eggs her on and when the security guard finally does turn round Ani is bending over and looking at me from between her legs, waggling her hands in her ears.

'Hi, Ani.' The security guard grins.

Brown eyes squinting above puffy cheeks.

Ani stands up with a start, turns and smiles at him.

'Oh hi, Dave, you made me jump.'

Dave looks over at me peeking through the fire-door window.

'Who's this then?' he says.

Sighing, I push open the door and walk through, try to ignore the voice in my head telling me to run for my life.

'This is Daryl,' Ani says. 'You know, Reverend Jenkins's daughter? Daryl, this is Dave. He's security.'

I smile weakly at Dave. Dave nods at me.

'We've just come to have a quick decko at the mud puppy, if that's OK,' Ani says.

'Well, I don't know, Ani,' Dave says, shifting from one foot to the other. 'I'm not supposed to let anyone in there. Not while they're running the tests. The prof said things are at a very delicate stage.'

'Oh go on, please,' Ani says, simpering up at him through her fringe.

'Well...'

'Go on, pretty please. I'll be your best friend.'

'Oh all right then. But only five minutes, mind. Or you'll lose me my job.' Dave picks up the keys from out of his desk drawer and unlocks the lab door, then thrusts out his arm and holds it open for us.

Length of gold braid looping halfway up his forearm and around the cuff of his sleeve.

'There you go, ladies.'

'Ta, Dave. You're a star,' Ani says and swans on past him.

I edge up to the lab door. I can't look at Dave, look instead at the floor tiles, the fire extinguisher on the wall behind the desk. 'Thanks, Dave,' I mutter.

'So your dad's Reverend Jenkins?' says Dave.

Scuffed black boots. Steel toecaps.

'That's right.'

'I heard he was sick. How is he?'

'Not too bad, thanks. In good spirits.'

'That's good.'

'Yeah.'

As I duck under his arm, heart still pounding, hole in his sleeve, Dave calls out to Ani over the top of my head.

'How come you're here so late anyway? Couldn't this wait till the morning?'

Ani twists round and smiles at him. A beaming, innocent smile.

'Oh, we've been clubbing and we thought it would just be a laugh to have a look at the mud puppy before we went back home,' she says.

Oh please. Only an idiot would fall for that one.

'Yeah? Which club?'

'Oh, you wouldn't know it. It's a new one. Down the bottom end of St Mary Street. It's ... '

'Ani! Dave said we shouldn't take long,' I say, smiling up at Dave.

Two-day beard growth, double chin.

'We'll only be a couple of minutes. OK?' I say.

'Right you are then. I'll leave you to it.' And he closes the lab door behind him.

Inside the lab everything is exactly as it was the last time I was here. White airtex tiles, banks of computer monitors. All switched off. All quiet. No sign of tests. No bleeps. No tubes. Only the mud puppy, inside a smooth-walled glass tank, crouched down on a bed of gravel, above a smaller tank of water. Row of heat lamps.

Climbing up onto a lab stool, I gaze down at the mud puppy. It looks nothing like a baby dragon now. The creature I remember pulling from the river was sleek and plump and so huge that it would only fit into the bucket when it was doubled up and even then its tail hung out over the side. The creature I remember pulling from the river had luminous green skin with blue spots and a brilliant scarlet crest crowning its head. This skinny specimen hunched up in front of me is barely a foot from end to end, with sludge-brown skin, pale grey markings and two rust-coloured flaps of skin rising out of the place its ears should be.

But still, it is out of the water. It is breathing air.

Lonely. Weak.

But beautiful. In its own quiet way.

Behind me, Ani, over the other side of the lab, is rooting deep inside a storage cupboard.

I spin round on the stool. 'What are you doing? I thought you wanted to check on the mud puppy.'

'Hang on, it's fallen to the back.'

Ani reaches further into the cupboard until her head and shoulders are fully absorbed and, scattering staples and highlighter pens on the floor around her, she pulls out a large plastic container, turning to face me in triumph.

'I hid this in here when I came last week,' she says.

I stare as she places the container, an old Tupperware cake box with holes punched into its flimsy white lid, on the countertop next to the mud puppy's tank and proceeds to scoop out some of the wet gravel from the tank into the box with her hands.

As she layers the bottom of the box with grit, all I can do is sit there, willing her not to be stupid, silently screaming at her that we'll never get away with it. Does she really think we can just steal the mud puppy and walk out of here with it, right under Dave's nose? What about the publicity? What about criminal records? But it's no use. She can't hear me. It's all just white noise inside my brain.

Only when Ani reaches down inside the tank and picks up the mud puppy, holding it in both hands, then cradling it in the crook of her arm, whispering, 'Hello baby,' only then does my mind clear and my voice make itself heard.

'Put it back down!' I hiss. 'Put it back down.' I lean across, try to grab the mud puppy from her.

Soft damp skin under my fingers.

'Are you crazy? Put it down this minute.'

But Ani is too quick for me. Lifting the mud puppy high above her head with both hands, she holds it away from me.

'No, it'll die if we leave it here. It'll die!'

I stand up on the footrest of the bar stool, lean against the countertop for balance and stretch up to the mud puppy again.

'Give it to me!'

'No!'

'Give it to me!'

'No!'

'Give it . . . '

'Hello? Ani? What's going on in there?' Dave calling from outside.

Ani and I freeze mid-tussle. Then, taking advantage of the momentary distraction, Ani snatches the mud puppy sideways and shoves me backwards in one swift movment. I cling on to both Ani and the countertop for dear life and the three of us rock wildly back and forth. But Ani manages to shove me one more time and my lab stool topples. We fall backwards together onto the lab floor with a crash, while the mud puppy flies forward with an equal but opposite force, dropping back down into the tank, straight into the water.

Computer monitor; no heart beat; no breath.

'You've killed it!' Ani whispers.

'No, it'll be OK.'

'You have. You've killed it!'

The laboratory doorhandle turns.

I scramble to my feet. The mud puppy remains motionless under the water.

'No, we just have to get it out of the water.'

Rolling up my sleeve, I dip my hand down into the water and under the mud puppy's soft belly.

Just then the lab door swings open. 'What the hell is going on in here?' booms Dave.

Ani lets out a whoop and I turn on my heels and run. Run and run, my feet going of their own accord.

Soft damp skin beneath my fingers.

Brown eyes squinting above puffy cheeks.

Running and running until, before I know it, my feet have taken me outside, along the side path, across the grass verge, past the police station and down Edward VII Avenue.

Space and time where her soul should be.

Length of gold braid.

Steel toecaps.

Computer monitor, no heartbeat; no breath.

Computer monitor, no heartbeat; no breath.

No heartbeat

No breath

No breath.

*

Ani won't say a word to me or even look at me for the whole of the drive back to Newport. And when we reach the house she runs straight up the stairs and into her room, slamming the door behind her. Leaving me to lie awake for what's left of the night contemplating the full horror of the situation. Until the phone relieves me at eight twenty, not with a warrant for our arrests, but with a request from Malpas Comprehensive for emergency supply cover.

A Level Art exam. Extremely urgent.

Thank God for that.

But there will have to be words when I get back, Ani. Do you hear me? It isn't funny any more. It isn't cute. It's got to stop.

Do you hear me?

This has all got to stop.

Chapter Twenty-Five

I can't see anything.
All I can hear are the voices
I don't understand. Why can't I see anything?

I want to see her.

No you bloody can't.

Why won't you let me see her?

It's all your fault.

I want us to be together.

You've done this. You've done this to her.
I should scratch your bloody eyes out.

This is not down to me. This is down to you.

You've killed her!
What have you done to
my little girl, my baby?

I didn't know. I swear I didn't know.

Just their voices.

She's only seventeen. She's only seventeen.

All different voices.

I'd have never crossed that line.

Yeah? One minute she's all over her and the next...

You think you're free? You don't know what freedom is.
Tell me! Tell me what's happened.

Tell the truth. Tell the bloody truth for once.

I'm sick of being pushed around.
She needs help.

                                                    Liar!

She needs help.

                              Why can't you face reality?
You stupid little girl.
She makes up stories all the time. It's like a sickness.
                No! I know what's real.
                              There's nothing wrong with her.
                Tell them I know what's real.
You're wasting your life away.
You're just a kid.

                              Liar!

                                          Are you crazy?
                    She needs help. She's sick in the head.
    Nothing but arches. Nothing but arches everywhere.
I'm getting out of here.
                We're going to be rich. Rich and famous.
                                        Gone. Just gone.
                Put it back down!
It's over. It's all over.

                              No!
                    You've killed it!
Don't you understand anything?
                We just have to use our imagination.
It's over.

                    Why can't I see anything?
                    I have to get out of here.
                    No! I have to get out of here.
This has all got to stop. Ani, do you hear me?
                    You wouldn't last five minutes in the real New York.
                              You can't take anything for real.
                    I wish they'd all shut up.
You should have asked for help.
I should have seen it coming.

                              Why didn't I see it coming?

Just voices.

It's over. It's all over

No!

No!　　　No!　　　No!

ELEMENT IV

Mud Puppy hopes drowned

Hopes for pushing back the boundaries of scientific history were drowned last night when Idris the mud puppy retreated back underwater in the middle of a revolutionary breeding programme at the University of Wales.

Local experts continue to be mystified as to why Idris, who has been living happily on dry land since early March, suddenly decided to return to his regular freshwater habitat. 'We can only wait and see what happens next,' said Michael Llewellyn-Jones, senior lecturer in biology at the University of Wales and Director of the newly formed Mud Puppy Investigation Unit. 'But we shall monitor progress and continue with the breeding programme in the expectation that future generations will develop similar air-breathing abilities.'

Previous reports of evolutionary miracles are now being seen as premature. However, mud puppy fever continues to hit Newport in force, including a number one single by local indie band Running Dog. With its vibrant and groundbreaking scene, Newport is widely regarded as the new Seattle of the music world.

South Wales Argus
Thursday 3 June

Chapter Twenty-Six

O *Love that wilt not let me go,*
I rest my weary soul in Thee
I give Thee back the life I owe
that in Thine ocean depths, its flow
may richer, fuller be.

*

I know what you're thinking.

How did we manage to keep it out of the papers?

Louise took care of everything.

*

Louise takes care of all of them, Lorraine and Keith and Kat. She sends them all packing, then keeps an eye out for trouble, for reporters. But it was just Lorraine's idle threat.

Louise takes care of everything. She picks me up from the hospital, comes running as soon as she hears the panic in my voice, drives me back to the Vicarage to pick up some clothes, then straight over to hers to hide out.

Louise takes care of everything. I don't have to see anyone. I don't have to think. I don't even have to cope with Dad.

All I have to do is sit tight.

Greg takes care of everything, driving back into Cardiff to convince Dave the security guard, man to man, that it was all an accident. That it wouldn't help Ani one little bit if the authorities thought she had anything to do with the mud puppy going back underwater.

And it's not as if there was any real harm done. Not really. Nobody died or anything.

Nothing really happened.

It was an accident.

Turns out Greg is ex-Navy. Dave, TA.

So Dave considers his position and agrees.

No, nothing really happened.

Yes, Greg and Louise take care of everything.

Because all I can do is sit in the boxroom, in Ani's room, not moving, not feeling, just sitting there on Ani's bed, surrounded by Ani's videos and books and photographs. All about New York. Everything you could possibly want to know about New York.

Stacks and stacks.

Maps and reviews and night clubs.

Boxes and boxes.

KOSHER WINE

Stories.

All I can do is sit here, not moving, not feeling, going over it in my mind.

Over and over.

Computer monitor.

No heartbeat.

No breath.

Again and again.

Casualty: the four of us gazing down at Ani's mud-covered body. Keith in full Elvis gear. Kat a long blue sneer. Ani's mother, words pouring out from her mouth, dripping down her chin like blood.

You're a bloody liar.

She's only seventeen. She's only seventeen.

I should have known.

I should have seen.

How could you have known? Louise says. How could you? She hid it from you. She hid everything from you. She's the liar. She told you she was a student at Art College, not a sixth-former. And you had no reason not to believe her, did you?

No.

No reason.

But still, I should have known.

I did know. I knew she needed help. I knew something bad was going to happen. I just didn't know what.

And now she's in hospital, under psychiatric supervision.

After jumping off the bridge.

It's all your fault.

You've done this to her.

She needs help. She's sick. You've killed her.

And all I can do is sit here, not moving, not feeling, going over and over it in my mind.

It wasn't my fault. I didn't think she'd go that far.

I didn't know.

Away with the fairies, that one. Everyone thought so.

You'd never have let her cross that line, not if you'd known, Louise says. No one is going to believe her, or her mother. No one is going to believe them. You were only at the school for one day. Not even that. You didn't have any responsibility for her. Not really. You've got to look after yourself now. Think of your dad, your career. Look to the future, forget about the past. Stop moping and pull yourself together. What about your commission, why don't you get on with that? That'll help you keep your mind off things. Bound to. It's over. You said so yourself. She's safe. She's in the best place, where she can get some help, professional help. So forget about it. Forget about her and get on with your life.

I mean, nothing really happened, did it?

No. Nothing happened.

Not really.

I'd never have let her cross that line. Not if I'd known.

261

But then sometimes I'm sitting here in Ani's room, in the boxroom, on the bed, surrounded by her Bampy's best blue velvet suit, make-up bag. Men's shoes. And I wonder...

People should be able to take life's knocks and keep going, transform themselves, Louise says.

Survival of the fittest.

You have to believe in yourself.

Ani's in the best place now. The doctors will help her, make her see sense.

Face facts.

I should have known.

I should have seen.

They won't let me see her.

Sometimes, when I'm sitting here on the bed, on Ani's bed, not moving, not feeling, surrounded by boxes, I can see Ani sleeping and me standing in the doorway watching, as always. Watching her breath moving in and out, her skin pulsating. Luminescent. And I know.

But then my eyes fill up and I can't see her any more.

Until this morning, when I was sitting here on Ani's bed, surrounded by books and photographs, maps, her Bampy's best blue velvet suit. Men's shoes. And then I saw it, sticking out of a stack of magazine cuttings:

A postcard from the Iowa State Fair of a life-sized cow, carved out of butter, chewing on a cob of black corn. All six hundred pounds of it.

On the back was written:

Still in the booneys. Dad's restaurant is history!
But don't worry, your club is going to be awesome.
Looking forward to seeing you soon in the Big Apple.

Carlos
673 E. 7th Street Apt 4FG
NY, NY.

*

The next day my father dies.

*

We believe in one God,
The Father, the almighty...

Louise takes care of everything. She makes all the necessary arrangements. I don't have to move. I don't have to feel. The only thing I insist on is that we celebrate Eucharist at the funeral.

It is what Dad would have wanted.

... maker of heaven and earth,
of all that is...

Dad always maintained the sacraments confirmed the fullness of nature's abundance. Grain and grape transformed into bread and wine transformed into agents of change.

... seen and unseen...

And isn't that what evolution is? The creation and re-creation of new realities?

... Through him all things are made...

I guess it depends on your definition of reality.

Dad always used to say that reality is not just that which we can see, touch, hear and smell. But also that which is behind, above, beyond, inside, between, beneath all that we can see, touch, hear and smell.

And the miracle is that we can occupy more than one level of reality at any one time and in any one space.

...For us men...

The Archdeacon preaches on death being part of life and attempts a joke about how the only miracle that Dad believed in was a good malt whisky.

I'm the only one who laughs.

...he came down from heaven...

For all his doubts about miracles, Dad never really had any problem squaring science and religion. To Dad the answer was obvious. To Dad the ultimate aim of both systems was exactly the same: to tell as true a story as possible in ways that mere human beings, given all our limitations, would be able to understand.

Truth is, everything is story.

...incarnate of the Virgin Mary...

story.

...On the third day he rose again...

story.

The Big Bang, Chaos Theory –

Oh please, if they aren't stories, then I don't know what is. I guess it just depends on your definition of story.

...We believe in the Holy Spirit,
the Lord, the giver of life...

Dad always said that spirit was a story very close to breath, and to air. The air we breathe is transformed within us into our soul, into our spirit. And just as when we physically die, we stop breathing and our soul leaves our bodies, so when we lose our spirits, then although we might physically keep on breathing, we are not truly alive.

... We believe in one holy catholic
And apostolic Church ...

The church takes care of everything. Through Louise. The
PCC organises the flowers and the hearse, chooses the
hymns. The Mother's Union cuts sandwiches and womans
the sherry bottles. The Archdeacon tells me not to worry
about moving out of the Vicarage. I'm to take all the time I
need.

They do this to show they care. They do this because I
can't do anything. I can't move. I can't feel. All I can do is
stand there perfectly still and watch.

Watch my feet walk up from the church to the Vicarage
gate. Watch my hand being shaken by all Dad's friends.
Watch the platitudes come out of mouths twisted up in
genuine pain.

No one ever knows what to say at these times, do they,
Daryl dear?

What is there to say?

*We have entrusted our brother Rhodri to God's merciful
keeping, and we now commit his body to the ground: earth
to earth, ashes to ashes, dust to dust.*

*

My mother died when I was thirteen. Truth is, she gave
away her spirit.

I can't let it happen again.

I won't let it happen again.

Chapter Twenty-Seven

Tuesday afternoon and the plane touches down five minutes early: five-oh-two pm, not five-oh-seven pm, like the captain said. Can't see any houses yet, though. Can't see New York. We left Gatwick at three, so even though it's taken over seven hours to get here, it's like it's really only taken two. It's like I've got a whole extra five hours in my life.

As long as I don't go back. And I'm not, ever. Going back, I mean. I'm going to stay right here in New York and be famous.

Chapter Twenty-Eight

In the week after Dad's funeral, two things happen.

First, I receive confirmation from Bob Koch that the unveiling of my sculpture to commemorate the mud puppy has been fixed for two weeks' time.

We're going to really push the boat out, media-wise, Bob Koch's email says. *Things have all gone flat since the mud puppy went back underwater, so we need a ton of publicity to get them moving again. Appreciate it if you would fax me your sketches for Board approval* ASAP. *Then our publicity people can get to work.*

Second, Patrick, the manager of Patrick's bar in Cardiff, rings up the Vicarage with a message for Ani that the brewery have finally agreed to invest in the new nightclub, so the extra toilets can be built. It's all back on again!

*

The poster on the door of Patrick's bar is printed on neon pink paper in silver letters. Hazy photograph of Judy Garland. Or is it Joan Crawford?

Back by popular demand, the poster reads. *Show tunes as you've never heard them before. Patrice, Queen of Hearts and Flowers, brings you all your favourite big numbers every Sunday night. Tickets on the door.*

The last time I was here, Dad was alive. The last time I was here, Dad and I were on TV.

I push open the door. It is still early, so the place is empty. No one except a girl with a short blonde crop, tight black T-shirt, stacking glasses behind the bar and a large blonde drag queen in green sequins and black evening gloves, propping up the end of the bar and smoking a cigarette in a long holder.

No sign of the bar manager. I hover near the door, uncertain of what to do next.

The drag queen takes the cigarette holder out of her mouth, looks over at me. 'Can I help you, hon?' she says.

I walk slowly towards her. The girl in the tight black T-shirt finishes stacking the glasses, then disappears down the passage behind the bar. 'I was looking for the manager, Patrick?' I say.

The drag queen extends a gracious hand. Elongated fingers, silver and opal ring. 'At your service,' she smiles. 'Patrick is my male drab. I'm Patrice by nature.'

'Oh,' I say. 'I see.'

'What can I do for you, hon?'

'You left a message for Ani about her nightclub? I'm Daryl. Daryl Jenkins. Ani's been staying with me the past few weeks.'

'Oh great,' Patrice says, looking over my shoulder towards the door. 'How is she? Is she here? Have you told her the good news?'

'Well...'

'It's so fabulous, I can hardly believe it. We thought it was all over when the Council told us we needed four more toilets and then what with Carlos having to go back to the States to help out his dad.'

Candy pink lipstick over candy pink skin.

'Carlos?' I say.

'Ani must have told you about Carlos!' Patrice says. 'The whole club was Carlos's idea.'

Was it, indeed?

'Oh right, Carlos,' I say. 'That's right, he's the American traffic cop, isn't he?'

Peal of laughter from Patrice. 'Traffic cop? Never! Whatever gave you that idea?'

'I thought Ani said...'

'He had this act where he dragged up as a cop. Went down a storm with the punters.'

'Oh right,' I say. 'That must be what she meant.'

Patrice nods, lights up another cigarette. 'So how is Ani anyway? Haven't seen her for weeks,' she says.

So I tell Patrice the whole sorry tale of what happened to Ani, how she was found dazed and confused, waist deep in mud at the foot of Newport Bridge, complaining of hearing voices.

How they think she must have jumped off the bridge, or at least deliberately waded down from the Castle bank, down to the water.

'Oh my God,' says Patrice.

'Yes. I know,' I say.

I tell Patrice how the doctors are saying she was overstressed about her exams, her A Levels. They're saying she tried to kill herself. Of how she's been sectioned for her own safety.

'Oh my God. Oh my God. Oh my God.'

But I don't believe that. Not really. Not Ani. Ani wouldn't try and kill herself. She is much too much alive. She might have been stressed, confused, yes. She was definitely confused. But she would never try and kill herself. Not Ani. Never.

'How is she now?' Patrice asks.

I tell Patrice I don't know. That they won't let me see her, not yet.

'But you're going to keep on trying, aren't you?' Patrice says.

Oh yes, I say, I'm going to keep on trying.

You have to keep on trying.

I look round the inside of the bar, groups of empty tables, chairs. Stage to the right of the bar, black background curtain covered in silver moons and stars. No sign of an art gallery. No sign of a drag king installation, of dolls that come to life.

'Can I see it?' I say. 'Can I see the club? Ani's club?'

'Of course,' Patrice says. 'I'll just get the key. It's in the building opposite. You know, the church? Well it used to be a church. Not any more, though. Now it's empty. It's been de... decommissioned or whatever it is they say.'

'Consecrated. Deconsecrated. That's what they say,' I say.

'Whatever,' says Patrice. And she moves behind the bar and fetches a key. A rusty iron key. A huge key, like the key to a giant's castle. We leave the bar together and walk across the road to the church. I have to jog to keep up with Patrice's long stride. Patrice leads me through a side gate and along a slope running down the left-hand side of the church to a large oak door, painted black, which she opens with the rusty iron key.

'The club's down here in the basement,' Patrice says. 'In the crypt. A real one. You know, the bit where they used to keep all the dead bodies? Not any more though. The last dead body was taken out in 1925 when the crypt was made into a soup kichen to feed the poor and needy,' she says. 'It was a soup kitchen all through the Depression and World War Two. So they had to get rid of all the bodies.' Then she looks back over her shoulder and grins at me. Perfect white teeth. All crowns. 'But I'm not so sure,' she says.

I grin back at her. 'I know. They'd need a hell of a lot of bones to make all that soup,' I say.

Patrice laughs. 'Oh you've heard that one already, have you?'

'Once or twice,' I say.

The entrance to the crypt is down a steep spiral staircase. Going down the spiral staircase is exactly like Ani said, it is exactly like it is in one of those old black and white horror movies. Spooky and smelly. The light from Patrice's torch the only light so we walk slowly, one hand on the rusty iron banister, the other holding on tightly to one another.

At the bottom of the spiral staircase there's another door. A more modern one, painted white. Patrice opens the modern white door and we step through into the crypt itself.

And knowledge becomes understanding.

*

The day of the unveiling dawns clear and sunny. But I'm not worried. You can always rely on Welsh weather.

I put on her Bampy's best blue velvet suit, her Bampy's best dress shirt, shoestring tie. I put on new crêpe sole shoes. She would really love these shoes. I cut my hair, slick it back into a pompadour, shape the hair cuttings into side burns with spirit gum, paint on a pencil-thin moustache. Then I lock the Vicarage door, step outside and walk, legs slightly apart, head held high, rolling off the balls of my feet, down the hill, down the steps behind the railway station, under the subway, past the multistorey car park and the Kings Hotel. The entire time I'm walking, people are staring. Turning round as they pass me, stopping in their tracks. But I carry on, over the roundabout, past the Castle and into the waterfront car park. Red wave of rail.

Only when I'm facing the river, only then do I stop and look out over the water. Over the top. Over the edge.

The tide is out. Mud cascades down the full height of the river bank like sheets of corrugated iron. Mud is all there is. Mud everywhere the eye can see. Nature's abundance. Running and rolling.

Back to the sea.

Back to the beginning.

The human quest for perfection: all cultures know this story. All cultures believe in an ultimate reality from which and to which everything flows. A time and space beyond time and space. An infinite, ceaseless maturation and exploration.

How we choose to name this reality, how we choose to tell the story is not a question of fact. It is a question of belief.

There is still almost an hour to go but already quite a crowd is building. Twenty or thirty curious passers-by, and the press: local and national. Corona's publicity people have come up trumps. There's even a TV crew from Bristol. Bob Koch has laid on refreshments – white wine from California and local cheese samples, complete with little Welsh flags. Red, white and green bunting.

No brass band, though. Pity.

At least the weather is closing in. Rain clouds to the north and west competing with each other to see who can reach the river first.

Everything is as it should be. Everything is as it must be.

No one but me is looking at the sky. Everyone else has their eyes firmly fixed on the TV cameras, on the platform in front of the railing, looking out over the Castle, Newport Bridge. Everyone else has their eyes fixed on the crane behind the platform, on its great steel arm which reaches twenty feet up into the air and which will be used to winch up the casing covering the sculpture, at the moment of unveiling.

The moment we are all waiting for.

The casing, a cross between a wooden tent and a garden shed, is eight foot high by six foot long by five foot deep. It completely hides the sculpture from public view.

Secrecy is everything. Corona don't do things by halves.

I don't do things by halves.

We both want it to be a huge surprise.

My outfit is a huge surprise to both Mr and Mrs Mayor when they arrive in their official car. Neither of them knows where to put their eyes. Mr Mayor tells me that my dad would want to be really proud of me today. Really proud.

Mrs Mayor asks me if I'd like to borrow the official car to go and wash my face before we meet the press.

I just smile and drink my wine, eat my cheese.

When he finally arrives, Bob Koch isn't the least little bit fazed by my appearance. Bob Koch thinks it is all a huge joke, so funny he has to bend over and hold his stomach, a bubble of spit forming at the side of his mouth. Bob Koch thinks my appearance is just the icing we need to ensure the unveiling gets on the local evening news. Maybe even the national.

'Stroke of genius, Daryl,' Bob Koch says. 'Very artistic.'

I just smile and eat my cheese, drink my wine.

Bob Koch is a big man. Big enough to wear pinstripes. Full three-piece suit. Big enough for his Corona Inc. tie pin and cufflinks to be in eighteen carat gold. Big enough to require two minions as an escort.

Mr Mayor is a big man with a big beard. Big enough for the official car to be a Daimler.

Big enough for a full chain of office, reaching down to his navel. Trophy wife.

The unveiling is a big occasion. Big enough for Corona Inc. and Newport County Council to want to shake hands publicly.

The press cameras flash automatically in the gathering gloom.

Mrs Mayor tells us how much she's looking forward to seeing the sculpture. How she loves surprises. Has Mr Koch had chance to look round the town centre yet, to see any of the other statues we have, commemorating local history and events? There's the monument to the Chartists, the clock in John Frost Square and, of course, the great red wave behind us.

Bob Koch agrees that Newport has some fine civic monuments and he's just glad that he and Corona can play a small part in adding to the collection.

Mr Mayor wants to know why the need for all the secrecy? Can't we give just a little hint about what the sculpture looks like?

Bob Koch says he hasn't a clue how the sculpture looks in the flesh, so to speak. It was all part of the deal. Daryl here wants the moment of unveiling to be part of the whole. Nobody but the artist gets to see the sculpture until everyone gets to see it. Bob Koch says his is not to try and reason what is behind the mind of creative genius, how it dresses or how it works. His is just to pay the bills.

Mr and Mrs Mayor and the minions all laugh.

'Of course, I've seen the plans, if not the finished product. I know the general idea,' Bob Koch says. 'It always pays to keep an eye on your investments, don't you agree, Mr Mayor?'

'Of course,' says Mr Mayor.

'How true,' says Mrs Mayor.

I just drink my wine and eat my cheese. Four little Welsh flags tucked away inside my pocket.

By ten minutes to noon, the clouds have finished sizing each other up and come together directly overhead in a compromise of spitting rain. Time to get this show on the road.

Bob Koch, Mr and Mrs Mayor and the two Corona minions climb up onto the platform in front of the wooden tent. Mr and Mrs Mayor sit down on the chairs provided. The minions stand awkwardly in front of the door to the wooden tent. Bob Koch stands in front of the microphone, next to a Welsh flag-draped stand on which rests a box with a large red button. A large red button which when pressed will start up the winch and raise up the wooden tent.

The wooden tent which has covered all my comings and goings for the past two weeks.

The wooden tent I convinced Bob Koch would add precisely the required element of mystery and perfomance to the moment of unveiling, to the sculpture.

The wooden tent to which I have the one and only key.

Bob Koch taps the microphone and the crowd quietens, cameras roll.

'Ladies and gentlemen,' Bob Koch says. 'Mr and Mrs Mayor, ladies and gentlemen. Thank you all for coming out this morning to our small but important ceremony. As you know...'

I switch my gaze back over to the river. Down on the bank, half hidden by a patch of weeds, is a bicycle wheel. A seagull stands on the rim of the wheel and picks at something between the spokes. A green and cream bus trundles across Newport Bridge.

My mother died when I was thirteen. She killed herself. My father hid the truth from me for over six years. For nine years afterwards I thought it was because she was a coward. Truth is, it was me who was afraid. Afraid to let her go, to let it all go.

'...we at Corona wanted to commemorate this important occasion, this melding of two world-class companies, two great countries, this coming together of the latest scientific and technological innovations...'

All of us have the capacity for infinity. Our spirits, our souls, are not limited to time and space. But in order to reach inside the wellspring of our being, we first have to embrace all our own imperfections and those of the people around us. First we have to accept ourselves, each other for who we are. First we have to forgive. Only then can we pursue fully rounded realities.

Only then can we delight in the ultimate reality.

Truth is in the story. Truth is in all the choices made.

This is all we have to trust in. This is all we can believe.

'...and what better way than with a beautiful and permanent representation of this miracle of evolution that has taken place so recently in your fine town, and which...'

Drizzle becoming scattered showers becoming rain. Crowd shuffling its feet. One of the minions unfurls a large black umbrella over Bob Koch's head.

'...And so I now ask Daryl herself to come and unveil her sculpture in celebration of an unusual and inspiring discovery, and in dedication to an unusual and inspiring man. Daryl? Would you step up, please?'

This is it then.

To a faint ripple of applause, the odd giggle, I climb the three short steps up onto the platform and walk across to the flag-draped stand, the large red button. Smiling at Bob Koch, Mr and Mrs Mayor, the two minions, the crowd, and with the TV camera lenses zooming in on my shoestring tie, sideburns, painted-on moustache, I press the large red button, then stand perfectly still and watch the steel arm of the crane behind me creak into action and slowly winch the wooden tent up and off the platform, up twenty feet into the air to reveal ...

not the sculpture set out in the plans and sketches faxed back and forth between Newport and New Jersey over the past few weeks.

not the complex glass and steel dragon structure with shimmering and moving air-filled wings.

But a solid, life-sized dragon shaped out of mud. Fine-grained alluvial mud scooped up and brought inside the wooden tent under cover of night.

A solid six-hundred pound, grey-green-brown dragon, shaped out of untreated river mud and supported underneath only by a crude wooden frame.

A lumpen, wholly imperfect, but still recognisable mud dragon which, under the increasingly heavy rain, is already beginning to slip off its internal supports and wash away, back into the river.

Back to the beginning. Back to the end.

Breath and heartbeat, heartbeat and breath.

I stand perfectly still and watch.

Watch Bob Koch bring his face right up to mine, screaming at me that I'll never get away with this, that we have a contract, that he will sue me for every penny I don't have, that he will ensure I never get another commission on the face of this planet.

Watch Mr Mayor usher Mrs Mayor on dainty tiptoe away from the mud, away from the mess.

Watch the minions scrabbling around, trying bizarrely to stop the mud from slipping away, trying to rebuild the dragon, but then finally giving up and letting go, letting it all go.

Breath and heartbeat. Heartbeat and breath.

I stand perfectly still and watch the rain wash everything away. All my work, breaking down the form, the time and space. Until all you can see is mud. Mud is all there is. Mud of the highest quality. Newport comes tops in the mud department. Rivulets of mud. Nature in abundance.

Running and rolling into a world of constant movement, change. A world without boundaries and borders, rules or controls. A world of pure energy where you are free to choose between independence and interaction, where you can create any choice, live out all possibilities, delight in the ultimate reality.

You just have to put your hand inside the Dream Box, say the magic words.

Are you ready?

I know you are afraid. We are all afraid. But it is just a question of belief.

Yet with the dragon gone, what on earth is there left to believe in?

Maybe the miracle isn't in the answer. Maybe the miracle isn't even in the question.

Maybe the miracle is in daring to believe there might, just possibly, maybe, be a question in the first place.

I believe in perfection.

I believe in change.

I believe in story.

I even believe in evolution.

Well, most of the time, anyway. Maybe.